MW01243400

HOTSHOT BOSS

SHANDI BOYES

SKYE HIGH PUBLISHING

COPYRIGHT

Betaread: Carolyn Wallace

Editing by: Swish Design and Editing

Proof read 1: Swish Design and Editing

Proof read 2: Chavonne Eklund (Master proofer).

Cover Image: Wander Aguiar

Model: Kyle M

Design: SSB Covers and Design

Publisher: Skye High Publishing.

❀ Created with Vellum

DEDICATION

To the people who have supported me nonstop during every mini meltdown that convinces me I should stop writing and find a new 'hobby.'

This one is for you!

Shandi xx

DEDICATION

ALSO BY SHANDI BOYES

Lady In Waiting (Regan & Alex #1)

Man in Queue (Regan & Alex #2)

Couple on Hold(Regan & Alex #3)

Enigma: The Wedding (Isaac and Isabelle)

Silent Vigilante (Brandon and Melody #1)

Hushed Guardian (Brandon & Melody #2)

Quiet Protector (Brandon & Melody #3)

Twisted Lies (Jae & CJ)

Enigma: An Isaac Retelling

Bound Series

Chains (Marcus & Cleo #1)

Links(Marcus & Cleo #2)

Bound(Marcus & Cleo #3)

Restrain(Marcus & Cleo #4)

The Misfits (Dexter & Megan).

Russian Mob Chronicles

Nikolai: A Mafia Prince Romance (Nikolai & Justine #1)

Nikolai: Taking Back What's Mine (Nikolai & Justine #2)

Nikolai: What's Left of Me(Nikolai & Justine #3)

Nikolai: Mine to Protect(Nikolai & Justine #4)

Asher: My Russian Revenge (Asher & Zariah)

Nikolai: Through the Devil's Eyes(Nikolai & Justine #5)

Trey (Trey & K)

The Italian Cartel

Dimitri

Roxanne

Reign

Mafia Ties (Novella)

Maddox

Demi

Rocco

Clover

Smith

RomCom Standalones

Just Playin' (Elvis & Willow)

Ain't Happenin' (Lorenzo & Skylar)

The Drop Zone (Colby & Jamie)

Very Unlikely (Brand New Couple)

One Night Only

Hotshot Boss (Mr. Carson & Octavia)

Hotshot Neighbor (Caleb & Jess)

Short Stories

Christmas Trio (Wesley, Andrew & Mallory -- short story)

Falling For A Stranger (Short Story)

WANT TO STAY IN TOUCH?

Facebook: facebook.com/authorshandi

Instagram: instagram.com/authorshandi

Email: authorshandi@gmail.com

Reader's Group: bit.ly/ShandiBookBabes

Website: authorshandi.com

Newsletter: https://www.subscribepage.com/AuthorShandi

FOREWORD

Reader warning: please note this book is fun, sexy, and full of heat, but it also deals with very serious issues that may be hard for some readers to experience. You can find a list of trigger warnings on my website.

If you are experiencing or have experienced anything that the characters in this book have faced, there are people willing to help you, so please reach out to someone. *Anyone.*

Also remember, you did **NOTHING** wrong.

Stay safe and please remember this is the work of fiction.

Shandi xx

CHAPTER 1
OCTAVIA

orse dung and blowflies the size of Texas are *not* my ideas of a fun time. Whoever convinced management that this would be a great way to spend a Saturday afternoon should be shot. My Vizzanos don't have the same red bottoms as shoes triple their price, but their sentimental value means they don't deserve the manure burial they're about to face if I don't get my heel free from the deluge.

This is my punishment for being short with my Uber driver. He wanted to take a west on Prichard. Everyone on this side of the country knows you *never* take a west on Prichard. You'll be in gridlock for hours—and then I would have been subjected to the driver's creepy gawk for longer than our forty-minute trip.

My request for him to lift the rearview mirror back to its original position when I slid into the back of his car already had me one step away from hitchhiking to Emerald Race Fields, so you can imagine how much more dire things became when I insulted his map-reading abilities.

He probably would have dropped me off at the front entrance as planned if I hadn't mumbled under my breath that maps went out of fashion around the same time people stopped using lamb intestines for protection. Alas, my mouth gets me in more trouble than the inappropriate length of the miniskirt Jess convinced me to wear.

It's been this way since I was a kid. My father said it would get me in shit, and it appears as if he was right for once. I'm heel-deep in a massive pile of poo, and despite the desperate wiggle of my foot, I can't get free.

The horse picked well when choosing a patch of grass to defecate. The ground underneath its droppings is extra soft, meaning its poo didn't simply absorb the heel of my favorite red stiletto when I was almost trampled by a sweaty horse and its even hairier guardian, but it swallowed my foot as well.

"Please," I beg to no one in particular. "If I miss this meet-up, I'll be benched for the rest of the year. You don't want that, do you?"

I stop stupidly waiting for the horse dropping to reply when a crack rips through my ears. It isn't solely the sound of my heel breaking away from my shoe. It is my heart breaking at the realization a piece of my Vizzanos is about to go to horse-poo heaven.

My heel is no longer attached to my shoe, and as much as I've loved and admired it over the years, there is no way I'm going to fish it out from a pile of brown goop that smells worse than Caleb's early morning rituals.

Caleb is my cousin. He's a six-foot brute of a man with a face many women have loved at one stage in their life but with the dreadful bathroom habits of a ninety-year-old geriatric who eats prunes every day to keep regular.

"I'm sorry, but you can't come with us," I whisper to a piece of my heart before attempting another tiptoe through the poop-riddled grass I once unwisely believed was a shortcut.

I make it halfway to freedom when my heel becomes lodged for the second time.

Thankfully, this time around, it's minus stinky horse dung.

I thought the rain last night was a godsend. Now, I'm cursing it to hell. Although my heel is stuck solely in muddy goop, my anger isn't any less notable. "Come on! It's thirty feet if that. You couldn't let me walk a measly thirty feet without forcing me to swim in horse poo?"

The one time I'm not anticipating an answer, I get one. "It could have…" The man's deep timbre is laced with unconcealed humor. "If you had used the footpath designed for such travels."

After rolling my eyes at his poor attempt of banter, I sling my head to my accoster. It's one of many poor choices I've made today. His inky dark hair, chiseled cheekbones, and a rigid jawline I'm sure Caleb would consider tracing with his tongue at least once shouldn't belong to a man whose tailored suit show-cases every impeccable inch of his body.

His hands are shoved into his trouser pockets, so why does the bulge in his crotch still appear so large?

Talking about crotches, stop staring, Tivy, before you find yourself on the wrong end of a lawsuit.

Mortified, I snap my eyes to the stranger's face in just enough time to witness a smirk that exposes he noticed my gawk at his crotch.

"Your zipper is undone," I lie, willing to say anything to get me out of this sticky situation unscathed.

"No, it isn't," he replies, his voice still laced with humor. "But I will tell my tailor that you appreciate the high thread count of my zipper's stitch the next time I see him." When I angle my head, certain there's a flirty edge to his reply, he drops his eyes to my stuck foot. "Do you need help?"

"Depends." My one word doesn't have quite the same level of insinuation his voice had, but there's definitely an edge of playfulness to it. "Are they pricy?"

When I jerk my head to his polished black shoes that gleam as brightly as my cheeks when he has to rock his hips back to take in his fancy footwear, he mutters, "Not particularly." He returns his eyes to my face. They're even more flirty now. "But even if they were, I have another half a dozen in my closet, so I'm sure I can face the injustice if they go to horse poo heaven."

His reply reveals that he's been watching me longer than a couple of seconds, but before I can drill him about his stalker ways, he pinches the crease in his trousers, then heads my way like the half-inch leverage he gave his pants will save them from being ruined by manure.

I'd hate to tell him he's wrong. I am wearing a miniskirt, but I'm still on the verge of checking it for splatters of mud and poo.

"When you next see your tailor, can you please keep my name out of your mouth?" I request when his slippery scoot across the sloshy terrain almost sees him landing butt first onto a steaming pile of poo. "The last thing a fashionable lass wants is her name muttered in disdain while discussing fabrics."

"I could." He skates another two sloshy steps before locking his eyes with mine. They're somewhat tormented but still gleaming like a kid at a toy store with an unlimited budget. "But I'd have to know your name to do that."

"Smooth," I murmur, smitten by the hope in his voice but also successfully concealing that fact. "Does that line often work for you?"

His shy grin—Kill. Me. Now.

It could only be hotter if it were flashed while his head was between my legs.

My highly inappropriate thoughts detour when he answers, "Not at all." He twists his kissable lips to lower the leverage of his smile. "But I've never given it a whirl while dodging horse secretions as if they are landmines."

"*Secretions?* In my part of the country, we just call them poo." I make sure my Jersey girl heritage rings true in my tone during the second half of my reply. It is weird of me to do, but alas, today seems to be a day of extraordinary weirdness. First, the miniskirt. Now, flirting with a stranger like I have nothing to lose.

After sidestepping a grassy landmine, the handsome stranger bands his arm around my waist then tugs me into his body. I knew he was fit from the way his tailored jacket couldn't hide the ridges in his dress shirt, but I had no idea it would be this impressive. "What makes you think your part of the country isn't also *my* part of the country?"

"Your Rolex," I blurt out before I can stop myself. It was either keep our conversation alight or dig my nose into his neck and take a long whiff of his expensive cologne. I went for the one that wouldn't have my wrists slapped with handcuffs. My family name has enough controversy staining it. I don't need to sling more mud at it. "You also don't have the accent for *my* side of the country."

"Ahh… I learned to flatten my tongue right around the time I hit puberty." I grin like a fool when his reply comes out with a twang I've stupidly missed the past three years. "Does this sound more authentic? Once I get you out of here, we should go for *cawfee*."

The Jerseyite delivery of his last word has me scanning the area, certain the goop coating the bottom of my shoes is from the muddy sands of Plemont Bay instead of a horse's bathroom.

When I fail to find another Jersey native in sight, I focus on the stranger wrangling my pump from a muddy grave. His slide, yank, and pull maneuver is loosening my shoe from its tight confines.

The same could be said for my legs.

I've never had a man as handsome as him fondle my thighs without an introduction, but instead of my body opposing the idea of strangers getting freaky, it relishes it.

I guess sometimes it's okay not walking in a straight line.
What?
Needing to divert this wreck from imminent disaster, I ask,

"Why do you hide your accent?" I have a good reason to keep my family lineage on the down-low, but he doesn't seem like the type to be drowning in controversy.

He grunts and groans before he eventually spits out, "For what I suspect is the same reason you went over instead of around." When he peers at me through a strand of black hair that has fallen in front of his almost as dark eyes, he mutters, "Sometimes it's easier to avoid an interrogation than welcome one." His final word comes out with a grunt. He isn't frustrated about the inquisitive bomb his tone set off in my eyes. Well, I don't think he is. I don't know him well enough to read his invisible 'fuck-off' prompts. He merely seems more appreciative of the removal of my stiletto from the sloshy ground than annoyed about my line of questioning.

"Woah. Okay." I cough to clear my voice of a need it shouldn't have before trying again to announce that I have legs so the stranger doesn't need to carry me like a husband ushering his bride into the honeymoon suite on their wedding night. "I can take it from here." When he strays his eyes across the measly ten feet I trekked without his help, I gulp before pushing out, "But what kind of damsel in distress would I be if I didn't let your feet get a little muddy?"

A helicopter's rotator gobbles up any reply he's planning to give. I'm not talking about one of those cute dome helicopters where the pilot and his passenger get chummy no matter their sexual preferences. I'm talking about a multiple-seat monstrosity with three blades and an engine powerful enough to whip up horse poo like it's confetti.

While wiping away a chunk of gunk from my cheek, I grumble, "You can put me down now. I'm more than happy to die here. It will be nicer than any burial I could face if I turned up at a work function reeking of horse *secretions*."

The stranger murmurs something under his breath as he continues skating across the no-longer-poo-riddled land, but he's too quiet for me to hear. Perhaps it is in appreciation that the giant landmines have been swept away, even with half of them entangled within my hair.

I've always wanted to know what I'd look like as a brunette. Now I know. I could totally pull it off—*if* my stomach would stop churning in protest about the smell.

"*Ahhh...*" I drift my eyes to the promotional tent I was racing for when the stranger takes a left upon exiting the livestock lavatory instead of a right. "I took a shortcut through Dung Valley for *that*." I point to the tent during the 'that' part of my comment. "I can't be late. We have a very special guest arriving today... *if he hasn't already arrived*."

My eyes roll skyward when the stranger mutters, "He can wait."

"You can say that because you look like you can afford to lose your 401K. I cannot."

If he grips my butt cheeks any firmer, I may have to reconsider my belief that pain is a no-go zone for me. "You have nothing to worry about. He hasn't even arrived yet."

I wait for him to enter the door a man in a pristine black suit is holding open for him before asking, "How do you know that? Do you have x-ray vision?"

With nothing but glossy tiles under our feet, he could place me down, but he keeps my body plastered to his like he appreciates my curves while strolling through the race club's suites as if he were the owner. "I was looking for him when I stumbled onto you. Why do you think I was in that area of the track in the middle of a race meet?"

"I thought you were as tardy as me, but clearly, that isn't the case."

His tone is as witty as mine when he mimics, "Clearly."

I shoot my eyes around an elegantly decorated office when he barges through a cracked-open door without knocking. Considering the less desirable conditions outside, the inside of the race suites is far more elaborate. The big desk the stranger is striding toward has the latest Mac sitting at the side, a leather-stitched planner open to today's date, and the window stretching from one wall to the next has a prime view of the finish line of the track.

Suites like this would be charged at a premium, but the stranger appears disinterested in the spectacle occurring outside. His strides don't falter when he pushes a button on the wall to draw the blinds closed, then he continues for the desk.

"Are we allowed in here?" I ask, suddenly put off by the eerie quietness.

The stranger answers me by dragging his forearm not curled around the not-as-generous-as-I'd-like curves of my backside to clear the desk of its wireless keyboard, tablet, and writing instruments that look like they belong in the historical era.

Once they're discarded on the floor along with the planner, my backside takes their place, and then he gets super handsy with me again.

I'm either too shocked about the sparks shooting through my body to respond to the gentle sweeps of his hands as he clears brown blobs from my skin or too horny to care. Since there are no butterflies fluttering in my stomach, I'd say it is most likely the latter. It's been a while—and by a while, I mean not since Pete Reynolds won the talent show at a state fair five years ago.

My breathing shallows when Mr. Dark and Dangerous's hands slide from my forearms to my thighs. The change-up isn't solely to blame for the sudden influx of restlessness bombarding me. It is the fact no man will ever spark more interest from me than one willing to walk around with poop-scented hands just to make sure my skin is *secretion* free.

It won't matter how hard he scrubs, shit sticks then lingers for years on end.

I learned that the hard way, but since my miniskirt is representing a belt, and I'm not the only one noticing, I'll have to save that story for a more appropriate time.

After tugging down my skirt to a more appropriate length, I switch my focus to my poo-dotted shirt. We work in silence for several long minutes, the tension as teeming as the heat of the stranger's hooded gaze raking my body.

The way he peers at me beneath lowered lashes sets my skin on fire, and it takes everything I have to remember we've only just met.

I don't even know his name for crying out loud, so none of the inappropriate thoughts streaming through my head should seem like a good idea, but for some inane reason, they're presented as ingenious.

When I can't hold back the desire to clench my thigh muscles together for a second longer, the stranger's eyes lift and lock with mine. They're even darker since we're in a square box with no natural light and brimming with lust.

I'm confident my expressions mirror his. The energy zapping between us is intense, and for once, it isn't bad friction.

After a reminder that we're perfect strangers, I ask, "Do you think we could get away with calling that a bronzer streak?"

Our eye contact holds strong until I chicken out first. His eyes eventually follow suit when I lower my hooded gaze to the brown streak smeared down my inner thigh. I only know this because instead of his heated gaze scorching my face, it does wickedly naughty things to my insides.

My body has never responded to a man like this before.

Not once.

"I am overdue for a spray tan, and the hipsters these days are all about natural products." I swallow to soothe my suddenly parched throat before muttering, "And *that* is about as organic as it gets."

It's only when he endeavors to clean up the mess I'm referencing do I realize I returned the focus to my microskirt instead of veering away from it. The tip of his index finger is a mere inch from my panties that grow damper the longer his girthy fingers mop up the goop.

After several womb-tingling seconds, he mutters, "It's a stubborn little thing, isn't it?"

The tension turns blistering when he pulls a tissue out of his pocket and spits into it. The stain is a determined smudge that will require some wetness to force it to move on, so a spit-covered tissue makes sense, but to my woozy head, its sweeps across my heated skin represent something far more sinister than a stranger aiding a stranger.

It's a man taking care of his woman in all meanings of the word, and it has me one step away from begging like I've never begged before.

Skip that.

I'm already there.

The tension is too much to bear.

"*Please.*"

My plea is barely a whisper but obviously loud enough for the stranger to hear. Hot air whizzes out of his nose as the tissue slips from beneath his hand. When his thumb treks over the flushed skin high on my thigh, it grips the skin more than it caresses it, proving his body temperature is as roasting as mine, his veins just as molten. "Did you say something?"

I shake my head, denying the pleas of my body, but my mouth has other ideas. "I said please…" Too pigheaded for my own good, I quickly add, "… let me do that."

He snatches up the tissue before I can and tosses it into a bin at the side of the desk like he's intimate with the floorplan. "It's done. You're clean." He steps even closer, forcing my legs to part like a big wedge of wood won't stop him from aligning our crotches. "*Almost.*"

I'm on fire. Everywhere. My skin is bubbling with blisters. That's how hot the liquid ecstasy rolling through my body is from him cupping my ankle and raising my leg into the air. I've read books when the dominant alpha male curls his woman's leg over his shoulder before going down on her in public, but I've never experienced it.

Before my five-year hiatus from sex, my scarce number of bed partners were adventurous but selfish. They loved receiving head, but reciprocating wasn't really their forte.

Feeding off the tension instead of the niggle of doubt in the back of my head, I tilt back to ensure the handsome stranger has room to explore. I'm seconds from my damp panties being exposed when a crack sounds through my ears. It could be my libido breaking through the wall I built around it years ago, but my intuition is warning me not to be so stupid. A travesty has occurred, but instead of it being my senseless wish to get freaky with a stranger, it is my second Vizzano pump's torturous crawl to shoe heaven.

The stranger snapped off the remaining heel, my mouth gaping to the point it would be fruitless to act as if I couldn't take a man of his size between my lips. "What the hell?" I snap back to a seated position, then snatch my poor, defenseless heel from his grasp. "Why did you do that? What did my shoe ever do to you?"

With my mind blinded by both grief and a rampant horniness I've never experienced, I hook my foot onto my lap, then endeavor to return the heel to its rightful spot.

When not even the goop coating it can save it from imminent death, I toss it into the bin housing the tissue, then fold my arms under my chest. "I would have hobbled. Any girl this side of Jersey would choose to hobble over wearing flats." I gag like the stranger's pricy aftershave hasn't overtaken the scent of horse poop. "But *nooo*... you had to ruin a perfectly good shoe just so it looked *exactly* like the other one..." My words trail off when the stranger doesn't respond to my rant.

He's so still, I'm not even sure he's breathing.

I've been told my death stare is killer, but I had no clue how potent it was until now.

"Sir..."

I stop talking for the second time when my eyes lock with his lidded gaze. His chest is as unmoving as mine, but he is very much alive because try as I may, I can't miss the bulge in his pants that requires a functioning heart to keep inflated. He's hard and staring at my damp panties—my unhidden lace panties since my ankle is hooked on my thigh and my skirt has disappeared into the abyss of an unflattering stomach roll.

Horrified, I tug on my skirt while muttering, "Sorry—"

He interrupts my apology with the same confidence he used when he caught me staring at his crotch. "No, you're not." As he licks his lips, his eyes slowly lift to my face. "But I am." Before I can ask what in the world he has to be sorry about, he relieves me of some of my confusion. "Because as much as my brain is screaming for me not to do this, I'm going to do it anyway."

An unladylike moan rolls up my chest when he grips my thighs, drags me forward until my damp panties are hidden by the massive rock beneath his zipper, then he spears his tongue into my gaped mouth.

Sweet lord. He tastes good—a hint of mint and a refined liquid you'd only find on the top shelf of a bar in New York. It's a scrumptious palette I lock away for future use before I mimic the hungry movements of his tongue and lips.

We kiss for several panty-wetting minutes, our embrace only ending when his wandering hands have my breathless lungs demanding an influx of air.

His fingers are no longer stroking the seam of my damp panties.

They've slipped beneath them.

When the stranger's eyes lock with mine under a curtain of dark hair fallen in front of them, I bob my chin, permitting him to do *all* the wicked things streaming through my deviant mind.

Mercifully, he answers the wordless screams of my body even quicker than my mouth can articulate its needs. He slides a thick digit inside me, groaning into my neck when it presents as slippery as my outer bits.

"Christ," he murmurs, his breath hot. "This could get me sued."

You wouldn't believe he was worried with how fast he pumps his finger in and out of me. He pushes my race to climax within an inch of the finish line admirably fast, and even quicker than that, our freight train of destruction derails the tracks.

Not because I climax, but because we're interrupted by a friendly yet highly suspicious voice. "Oh, goodness. I'm so sorry. I thought you were trackside."

As a pretty lady with short blonde curls and a tiny button nose darts her hand up to cover her eyes, the stranger yanks his finger out of my vagina, snaps my panties back into place, then tugs down my skirt as if he knew where it disappeared to all along.

The situation goes from bad to worse when the interrupter's sixth sense has her focus returning to us. She isn't drinking in my flushed cheeks, wide eyes, and sweat-dotted neck. She's staring at the brown dots splattered across the stranger's pricy suit, her brows pulling together more the longer she stares.

Oh God, I hope she doesn't think I have a scat fetish!

My panic has me on the verge of heaving, but despite the numerous churns of my stomach announcing that I'm about to barf, the stranger refuses to relinquish his grip on my wrist. He encircled it a second after a demand to run filtered through my brain, which was a nanosecond after we were interrupted.

Our interrupter jumps to the command in the stranger's voice like he's the Crowned Prince of Denmark when he snaps out, "Have Moses bring one of my suits." As she races for a cell phone on the large walnut desk I almost desecrated, he adds, "And a dress for Ms…"

I can't tell if it's humor tugging his lips or another emotion, but whatever it is, his smirk has me filling in his wordless request with only the slightest bit of hesitation. "Henslee. Octavia Henslee."

What? He had his finger in my vagina mere seconds ago. It is too late to play hard to get.

"*Ms.* Octavia Henslee?" Now I can't mistake the curl of his lips. It is ninety-nine percent possessive with the final one percent reserved for the panic that he almost finger-fucked a taken woman on a rando's desk.

"Yes, *Ms.*" I fight my smile for almost three seconds before it wins. "Although it may not be for much longer. A thirty-second feel-up borders on a committed relationship these days, so imagine the shackles that come with a three-minute..." I let the rake of my teeth over my lower lip finalize my reply. We still have an audience, and although shame is often associated with my family's name, it isn't an emotion I voluntarily force on others.

Like all men scared of the C-word, Mr. Dark and Daring frees my wrist from his firm yet arousing grip before shifting on his feet to face the woman hanging on his every word.

I'm doing the same, but dribble is pooling in the corner of my mouth, whereas hers only has wrinkles.

Our interrupter is attractive, but I don't think they're messing the sheets. Mr. Handsy During First Meets would be in his late twenties to early thirties maximum, whereas she appears to be mid to late sixties.

She bows her head like a servant when the mysterious stranger demands, "Have a dress couriered for Ms. Henslee. Size ten. If the bodice is fitted, perhaps a size larger."

I skirt around him before foiling his personal assistant's wish to jump to his command mid-dial. "A size ten is perfectly fine, thank you very much." Recognizing she doesn't deserve the wrath of my stink eye, I shift my attention back to the suit-clad man. "Adjustments aren't needed for certain regions of my body." If my tone doesn't hint at what I'm referencing, I drag my eyes down his still pricy-looking suit, even with it being dotted with horse dung. "I thought you'd know that better than anyone?"

With my sassiness too high for me to rein in, I peer at the middle-aged woman's frame that isn't blocked by his wide-girthed shoulders before asking her directions to the closest bathroom.

I don't sprint when she announces a bathroom is three doors down, but I am on the verge of power walking. If I don't scrub my face free of controversy, I'll shove it into Mr. Dark and Moody's crotch. Since that would have desperation entering the equation, an air stiletto wobble must do because there's no way in hell I'm walking away from a man as devastatingly hand-some as him without the sultry hip swing that comes from wearing a sexy pair of heels.

CHAPTER 2
JACK

E laine coughs, drawing my focus from the indecent length of Octavia's miniskirt that had me retracing my steps three times before I eventually announced my watch to her. "Mr. Carson…" She waits for our eyes to meet before asking, "Did you have any stipulation on price?"

"No." My reply is curt and to the point. It would send most people scuttling back a few places, but Elaine is accustomed to it. She's worked for me for the past several years. Her attention to detail is impeccable, and we get far more work done since she doesn't spend her day gawking at me with lusty eyes like the twelve assistants before her did.

They all had the same horny gleam Octavia's eyes had when her head slung my way for the first time. I should have approached her sooner, but the quickest twang of an accent I strive to keep hidden had my steps freezing as quickly as my heart.

Jerseyites span the globe, but it's rare to find one with an accent as thick and authentic as Octavia's this far across the country. It was even more distinct when she whispered farewell to a portion of her shoe she left to fend for itself.

The reminder of her devastation has my focus returning to the present. "I'll also need a pair of shoes. Size..." I stop, honestly lost. Determining Octavia's dress size was easy. Curvaceous enough to steal a man's devotion for days on end and so mouthwatering years of conflict suddenly seem nowhere near as heavy as they once did.

"Mr. Carson..." Elaine drawls out again, her accent as southern as it comes.

"I need to check what shoe size she wears." I stuff my hands into my pocket when my demand for Elaine to enter the bathroom on my behalf sits on the tip of my tongue but refuses to be relinquished from my mouth. "Which I will get for you now."

"Mr. Carson... uh... that's the *ladies'* bathroom," Elaine stammers out when I make a beeline for the door Octavia whizzed through only moments ago.

The unease in Elaine's tone should slow me down. I should be backing away in an instant, but before either Elaine or my shrewdness can talk me out of it, I barrel into the women's bathroom like my mother never taught me any manners.

My plan is simple. Ask Octavia her shoe size, then leave. I wouldn't have faced an issue if her lust-crammed eyes didn't align with mine in the mirror the instant I entered. Something about her dazzling eyes has me wanting to throw caution to the wind. And that is precisely what I do for the second time today when I mutter, "Come with me."

"With you where, exactly?" There's no hesitation in her voice. No unease. She isn't even looking at me like I'm a man of such substantial wealth I could gift her everything her heart desires ten times over. She sees the adrenaline junkie I must keep hidden from board members and the playboy undeserving of the title.

She sees a Jerseyite in the wild who doesn't have a grip on reality any better than her.

"Anywhere."

The confused crinkle between her faultless blonde brows is cute, but I'd rather witness it without the words delivered shortly after its arrival. "I can't. If I skip this meet-up, that's strike three for me. I'll be out on my ass first thing Monday." Her eyes drag down the front of her body while mine peruse the back. "And I'm far too disheveled for any indoor activities."

"Then we'll keep things outdoors." Not giving her the chance to deny me for the second time, I band my arm around her tiny waist and then guide her out of the bathroom as quickly as I entered it.

"Mr. C—"

I cut Elaine off with a rueful sideways glare before saying, "Your services will not be required for the rest of the day."

She attempts to argue, but my determination is unbendable. In general, it is as stiff as my overly laundered ties, but today, it is even more aloof than the personality that comes out during dreary functions like the one I was about to attend.

Elaine bows her head in defeat. "Very well. I shall see you first thing tomorrow morning."

As I race Octavia to the door, Elaine gathers her jacket and cell phone from behind one of the many desks I have dotted on this side of the coast before following us out.

She veers for a bank of town cars at the front of the race club, but since Octavia's earlier worry is still in the forefront of my mind, I steer us in the opposite direction.

Octavia breathes out a relieved sigh when she notices the direction we're traveling. It isn't in respite that she won't end up homeless like Elaine would have if she had disclosed my identity. She's sighing in relief on behalf of my crotch. "Jersey girls don't take kindly to being manhandled. I thought you—"

"I know. Believe me, I know," I interrupt as a long berate by my sister pops into my head. She turned forty-five last month, but the maturity that should come with her age wouldn't have stopped her from kneeing a guy in the balls if he burst in on her in the bathroom and then ordered her around like she's a member of his staff.

Although if Octavia's attendance today is as believed, that could very well be the case. She could be an employee of mine.

Once again, you'd think my confession would halve the length of my strides.

It doesn't.

Not in the slightest.

It doubles them.

"Tivy," a petite brunette with massive hazel eyes shouts when we enter the promotional tent at the side of the track. Since horses are galloping by, most gamblers' eyes are glued to the race instead of two tardy attendees.

I see their distraction as good fortune.

It isn't often a billionaire enters a room unnoticed.

When the brunette throws her arms around Octavia's neck, she dislodges mine from her back. "I thought you were going to be a no-show again, then I would have been left to fend off Mr. Kell's sick comments alone." She hugs Octavia tighter. "Thank God you arrived when you did because they're more perverted since he's drunk."

I take a mental snapshot of the man who sinks to the back of the group when the unknown woman's eyes stray in his direction. He has the seedy, demoralizing watch down-pat, and although it frustrates me when I notice he's glaring at Octavia's colleague's bottom, it downright infuriates me when it switches to Octavia's shirt. He's not scanning the flecks of manure my pilot will pay dearly for when I visit him this evening, he is gawking at Octavia's cleavage.

I have enough details to take down Octavia's unwanted admirer in a sea of millions within seconds, but just in case, I inconspicuously point him out to Fitz, my head of security. While he moves to evict my no-longer-welcomed guest from the festivities, I wordlessly gesture for Trent to bring one of the town cars to the side of the pavilion so I won't need to risk a second stomp through a horse-poo riddled swamp to leave.

I was late to the proceedings as Octavia suggested, but since my helicopter was responsible for coating her silky mane with manure, I'll keep that confession on the down-low for a little longer.

This event was organized months ago. It is meant to announce the merger of two companies in a fun, non-threatening manner. Often when companies amalgamate, the less established of the two feels threatened. Workers commence seeking new placements, and management lets them go instead of fighting to keep the staff we acquired their company for to begin with.

I shift my eyes from Fitz's infamous neck pinch that subdues assailants quicker than my surly attitude when the brunette's nostrils flare in response to Octavia's new scent. "Is that—"

"Poop? Yep. That's what you're smelling," Octavia interrupts, horrified.

The brunette's glossy locks fall off her shoulders when she slants her head to the side and arches a brow. "I was going to say…" She freezes when it finally dawns on her that Octavia hasn't arrived alone. "Oh… hello." She gives Octavia an opened-mouthed commendation before locking her eyes with mine. She's dressed similar to Octavia, but her captivating frame and beautiful face only stop men in their tracks instead of altering their personalities altogether. "And *you* are?"

"Ah… Jess, this is…" Octavia curses under her breath before voicelessly requesting my assistance like she did earlier when she wanted me to fix more than the obscurity coating her sweltering skin.

Appreciative of the return of the groove between her brows, I leave her hanging for a couple of seconds before introducing, "Jack. Nice to meet you, Jess."

When I offer her my hand to shake, she accepts it, albeit hesitantly. "Have I seen you around?" She tightens her grip before yanking me in close, which should be no easy feat considering I'm six-three, and she's the size of a fairy. "You're not from HR, are you? Those guys give me the heebie-jeebies."

"No." I step back before straightening my suit jacket like it isn't sullied with manure. "I'm not from HR." *Well, not exactly. I'm technically their boss.*

Missing the deceit in my tone, Jess wipes at the invisible sweat on her brow. I can't say the same for Octavia. She's eyeing me more curiously now than when I suggested she play hooky with the stranger who skipped an introduction to go straight to third base. "Phew, because from what I heard, they won't be around that long either." Her bottom lip quivers as she drops it into a pout. "None of us will be." I shoot my eyes to my newest business partner when she adds, "We've been bought out. Some hotshot billionaire with a corn kernel for a dick offered Mr. Potts a few million too many."

I told Mr. Potts to keep news of a merger under wraps until I arrived. The fact he can't follow a simple order reveals I'll be looking for new management long before I replace the creeps in human resources.

"Potts Holdings has been sold?" Octavia asks at the same time I mutter, "Are you basing your corn kernel assumption on facts or hearsay?"

Jess smiles in a way that exposes you couldn't torture an answer out of her before she curls her arm around Octavia's back and guides her deeper into the tent.

I let her go so I can simply have a word with Mr. Potts before the opening of trade Monday morning.

"Jack... ah, Mr. Carson. Welcome." Mr. Potts fumbles for a glass of wine on a waiter's tray as clumsily as he stumbles out a greeting. "Festivities turned out nice, yes?"

"Yes." My reply is purely based on my unexpected meeting with Ms. Octavia Henslee, not an event that cost almost a million dollars to orchestrate. "But I was of the belief you were not to mention the merger of our companies until I had arrived."

"Oh… yes… umm. That would be correct. I… just… ah… wasn't sure if you were still planning to attend today when you didn't arrive before the first race." For his slow start, he certainly finishes quickly. "I know how much you love a punt on race day, so something quite spectacular must have kept you occupied for you to miss the opener."

"It was spectacular," I agree while watching Octavia accept the glass of bubbly I declined. "However, that doesn't give you free-for-all to say what you want. We had an agreement. You didn't keep your end of the agreement."

"Jack… ah, Mr. Carson—"

"Which means you will no longer be sheltered under Global Ten's umbrella."

"Mr. Carson—"

"Good day, Mr. Potts."

"But—"

"I said… *good day*." I've been walked over, spat on, and ridiculed while building my company into a global sensation, but you can sure as hell be confident that I will not be spoken down to by a man as weak as Mr. Potts. If it isn't already frustrating that he disobeyed a direct order, it is infuriating that he watches staff members be harassed and not do anything about it.

Workplace harassment laws were brought in for a reason, and I uphold them at every available opportunity.

"Except perhaps when it comes to *her*," I murmur to myself when Mr. Potts's storm for the closest exit sees Octavia's curious gaze locking with mine.

Just like when she peered at me when I slid my finger inside her, I've got her on the hook.

Now I just need to reel her in.

"If his stares get any hotter, I will have to check you for burns."

I bump Jess with my hip before swiveling away from Jack. He's been liaising with the who's who of media for the past thirty minutes, but he's barely taken his eyes off me for a second —not even while scaring Mr. Potts away from festivities with hushed words. "He's remorseful for the mess he made of my outfit."

"Ah… but wasn't it you who took a shortcut through Dung Valley?"

I grin to hide my gag. "Yeah, but I'm not talking about *that* mess." Jess giggles like a schoolgirl when I lean in close and mutter, "It's the travesty he caused my panties that I'm referencing."

I love Jess like a sister. She took me under her wing when I arrived in Seattle with barely a penny to my name and an attitude in desperate need of an overhaul, but I want to stab her with a blunt instrument when she murmurs, "I can understand why. He sure is pretty."

"Maybe you should let Caleb hear that, then he might stop playing the friend card."

That snaps her back from her Jack dreamscape. For months, she and Caleb have been tiptoeing around their feelings, and the tension is thick enough to cut.

Almost like it was between Jack and me in what I suspect was his office.

It gives credit to him being where he was at the time of our meeting. Only staff and crew are allowed back there, and although his suit is designer, it isn't pompous like many of the uber-rich Seattleites wear. It is suave and cool—even when dotted with horse poo.

I drift my eyes back to Jess when she mutters with a groan, "I tried the whole jealousy thing when we went out drinking last month. All it got me was a guy's number I didn't want and a severely bruised ego."

My second hip bump almost knocks her over. I'm not tall compared to men like Jack, but I'm not tiny like Jess either. I'm average height for a girl, standing a little over five-eight. "I've seen the haunts you frequent, Jess. That wouldn't be close to the response you'd get if you took Mr. Devastating home for the night. More than Caleb's ego would get bruised." I snap my mouth shut when determination fortifies in Jess's enormous hazel eyes, then I try to act as if Jack's face is as ugly as a gorilla's rear end. "But then you'd need Jack to slum it with the rest of the South Park gang. I don't like your chances, especially since he mentioned his tailor twice during our brief conversation. Once is a purposeful slip, but two times exposes an affluent edge we South Park girls aren't seeking."

"Who says we don't want affluent? I want affluent." Her nostrils flare when she leans in close. "It is effluent you want to avoid."

After a frisky wink that has me two seconds away from yanking off her wig, she thrusts out her moderately sized breasts, then moseys over to Jack and his bevy of suit-clad companions for a last-minute punt.

Her three-to-one odds tumble to triple digits when Jack side-steps her partway across the catering tent. He shuts down one man's attempt to speak to him with a stern finger point before deflecting JJ from Accounting by directing him to a man with a belittling one-finger summons before he eventually stops to stand in front of me. "Are you ready?"

"For?" A one-word sentence should be nowhere near as breathy as mine just came out. You'd swear his finger was back inside my vagina for how needy it is.

"For..." He pauses to build the suspense. I don't know what industry he works in, but he should consider moving to Hollywood. He'd win an Oscar in no time. "Our adventurous day." Before I can tell him I'm not dressed for a day out nor known to venture into the wilderness with strangers, he squashes his dismissing finger to my lip. It is the same finger he stuffed into my vagina only an hour ago. "Elaine has a selection of clothes for you in the car. Fitz activated the tracking feature on your phone, so your family and friends can find you if you go missing, and if you're still worried about spending time alone with me, you can always invite Jess to come with us."

Elaine? Fitz? Why is he speaking as if I know who they are?

"Ah..." He appears more grateful for my daftness than concerned about it. "Morris was wrong. You truly are in the dark."

If he's asking a question, he doesn't wait for me to reply. He simply gestures for Jess to join us before invisibly handing the baton to me.

"What?" I mutter under my breath when Jess stares at me with a pointed brow. "Jack was..." I take a good three to four seconds to think of something, "... wondering if you'd..." Jack looks on the verge of coronary failure right alongside Jess, but I yank him off the ledge with a couple of words. "If you'd like to take his bets because we're about to head out for the afternoon."

Jess appears devastated.

Jack is on the other end of the scale.

He looks like a man who just spotted a pot of gold under the rainbow.

"Oh… sure. That will be great."

Jess's disappointment races toward the silver lining when I sling my arms around her shoulders and mutter in her ear, "Caleb forgets to lock the front door every afternoon before showering after his workout. The earrings you want to borrow for your night out are on the vanity sink."

I'm torn between sending Caleb a warning message about an unexpected visitor and throwing him into the deep end when Jess's eyes drop to her watch so fast, I'm afraid she may have burst a blood vessel. I'd do the former if I weren't confident Caleb wouldn't appreciate an afternoon visit. They've denied their attraction for months, so perhaps an X-rated run-in will help them sort out their shit.

After locking her massively dilated eyes with Jack, Jess says, "Thank you for the offer, but I must decline. I have somewhere very important to be." With the wave of a psychopath, she makes a beeline for the closest exit, uncaring that today's fiasco was supposed to be about meeting the new owner of *Seattle Socialites*, a fashionista magazine that was raved about across the globe but is no longer relevant with upcoming trends.

It's been a Titanic for years now, but it grew worse when an elite member of Mr. Potts's upper management got slapped with a sexual harassment claim from a client. The allegation cleared out about half of the riffraff. I'm hopeful the new owner will handle the rest.

Sexual assault isn't kosher no matter the heir, but instead of avoiding the ramifications by moving twenty-eight hundred miles away from my hometown, I found myself smack bang back in the middle of a lawsuit my first year after accepting an intern position even with a graduate diploma in Business under my belt.

"Octavia?"

I gravitate toward the nurturing voice long before the briefest brush of Jack's fingers down my white cheek has me leaning in even closer. "Yes."

"Are you okay?"

Before all his question leaves his mouth, I nod. "Yes. I was just reminiscing."

"About?"

He seems genuinely interested in my reply. Like nothing I could tell him would see him backing down now, but just in case, I murmur, "About whose office we left in shambles." His half-concealed smile has my usually vibrant self striving to emerge from a dark pit I tossed it in, so I throw some extra glitter into the mix to light up the path even more. "And if there was any chance of a rerun."

Jack's grin gains him the eye of every lady in the room and even a handful of men. "There's a chance. A *very* good chance." He curls his arm around my waist like we didn't meet only an hour ago before leading me toward the closest exit. "Although we may need to take it somewhere more private. Elaine has never been as muted as she was earlier."

"I'll have to issue her my apologies."

After a farewell head bob to one of the creeps I mentioned earlier and a wave to another well-dressed man, Jack guides me out of the tent Mr. Potts had a coronary about when he learned how much they cost to hire. "You can do that tomorrow..." I can't tell you which feature I like more. His panty-wetting face or the lust darting through his eyes when he mutters, "... when she issues me my wake-up call."

"That's a little bit presumptuous, isn't it, Mr. ..." I leave my reply hanging open for him to fill in as I did earlier, but when he fails to take the bait, I finalize, "Sleepovers are on the top of the commitment scale."

Someone call in an emergency. I combust when he presses his meaty lips to the shell of my ear and whispers, "Not if you don't get any sleep."

With a breathy exhale that reveals I am swimming in waters way out of my depth, he pulls back, assists me into the back of a car that looks more sporty than all-terrain, then jogs around to the other side. I can't hear what he mutters to the man holding open his door for him, but whatever he says, it must be unusual because not only does the African American man's brows lift, but his eyes also almost pop out of his head.

"What did you tell him?" I ask Jack when he slips into the plush leather seat next to me.

Before he can answer me, another gentleman joins us in the dark SUV. He's attractive with burnt orange hair, a trimmed beard that's more blond than ginger, and a twinkle in his eyes that exposes he's nowhere near as stuffy as the suit he's forced to wear day in and day out.

There's no doubt he's a security detail. His hand signal when he advises the driver to go announces this, much less his disclosure that the eagle is on the move into his suit's cuff. He's so on-point with preventive measures, I check the front of Jack's car for foreign dignitary flags because aren't they the only ones who get around with an entourage these days?

When I fail to find any, I lean into Jack's side and ask, "You're not the Crown Prince of Denmark, are you?"

Jack laughs before shaking his head. "No. Frederik is many years older than me." He stops, swallows, then locks his eyes with mine. "Now, I'm curious to discover how old you think I am."

"Not old enough to halt the constant wicked thoughts steam-rolling through my head, so there's no need to panic."

Jack isn't the only one who laughs this time around. His

security detail gets in on the act as well. I'm glad he has a sense of humor—I doubt his day-to-day takings are welcoming of an upbeat demeanor—but it changes the dynamic between Jack and me in an instant. Instead of brimming with sexual chemistry and undeniable attraction, it is suffocating and dire. It reminds me of the last time I stood on the stoop of my family's local church, breathing through what I was certain would be a debilitating panic attack, and it seems as if I am not the only one noticing.

A second after demanding the driver to pull over, Jack curls his hand over the door latch. I assume he's going to toss his security detail out of the car in the middle of a bustling freeway, so you can picture my shock when he flashes me a flirty grin before he throws open his door, slips out of his now stationary vehicle, then bobs down to offer me a hand out of the car.

"We're getting out here?" Shock is evident in my tone.

"Yep." I can barely hear him over the cars roaring past him, but there's no doubting his next set of words is a command, not a suggestion. "And they're staying here."

"Jack..." his bodyguard murmurs at the same time an exciting patter restarts my sluggish heart.

Ignoring the warning tone of the man with furrowed brows, Jack locks his eyes with mine. "Unless you want them to stay? The ball is in your court, Octavia."

No offense to the handsome gent, but I shake my head before all of Jack's question leaves his mouth. Then, even quicker than that, I slip out of the pricy vehicle the best I can without flashing his muted guest my panties to join Jack on the side of the freeway.

Giddiness hits me from all sides when Jack unbuttons his suit jacket and tie. I'm not just excited about his impromptu strip. I'm squirming like a pig eyeing a spit from the sparkle that ignites in his eyes when he encloses his hand over mine a second after dumping his restrictive clothes onto the seat we vacated.

With the sleeves of his dress shirt rolled up to the elbows, his tie ditched, and his hair rumpled, he has the playful, mischievous bad-boy vibe down pat. He looks hot, so much so, I check I haven't left a puddle in my wake when he races us toward the closest off-ramp like a five-star suite is hidden under the concrete pillars.

After silencing Morris's fifth call in the past fifteen minutes, I tug two one-hundred-dollar bills out of my wallet, then lock my eyes with the salesperson of a thrift shop half a mile from the off-ramp Octavia and I navigated like my bank balance is nowhere near as impressive as it is.

"She will need somewhere to shower and change once she's made her selections." I place down one of the bills. "This should cover the inconvenience of using your loft apartment above the shop." I give him an intense stare while sitting the final bill on top of the first one. "And this shall ensure your discretion." When his eyes drop to the credit card only a handful of Americans have access to, I close my leather wallet and stuff it into the back pocket of my trousers. "Do we have an agreement?"

The assertiveness my question is delivered with warns I will only accept one answer.

It isn't 'no.'

"Yes." He almost stammers, but he regains some of the pigheadedness he bombarded Octavia with when she asked him where the dressing room was located. "We have an agreement."

"Good." I lock my eyes with a television mounted behind the

salesman when the broadcaster announces my earlier-than-expected arrival to Seattle before returning them to the unnamed gent.

He'd be mid to late thirties, but his gangster swagger conceals the wrinkles in the corner of his eyes. Although his pants are so baggy, his boxer shorts are exposed, and his wifebeater hasn't been white in an incredibly long time, he knows a good thing when he sees it. Instead of negotiating for a better rate when it dawns on him that I'm the man in the news broadcast, he accepts the bills I set down with an appreciative head bob before switching off the dated television.

I stop believing I got out of negotiation lightly when he murmurs, "Although I could get in a lot of trouble if I take an hour lunch break." When he stuffs his reimbursement into the front pocket of his jeans, his belt is the only thing stopping him from exposing himself. "I usually just eat behind the counter." He rubs his hands together while shifting on his feet to face the changing room. It is a curtain hung in the middle of the shop that is several feet too short and nowhere near wide enough to hide Octavia's enticing frame as she squeezes into a designer number she found on the clearance rack within ten minutes of us entering. "And do you really need an hour? Her lips..." His pause to grab his crotch has steam attempting to billow from my ears. "They could suck the marrow from any man's bones in not even two minutes. She has a mouth that doesn't need consent—"

I grip his greasy shirt in my fist and drag him to within an inch of my face. "If you finish that sentence, I will *finish* you." There's no playfulness to my tone. No friendliness. Nothing but a voiced threat and a silent assurance that I am a man of my word. "And if you even glance her way during your agreed *hour* lunch break, I'll bury this business and *everything* in it." I stare straight at him so he knows exactly who I'm referencing. "Do I make myself clear?"

For the first time in the past fifteen minutes, he stops bouncing foot to foot like he's on more than a high for weekend pay. With a chin dip, he pulls himself out of my hold, straightens his wifebeater, then instructs me to lock up before leaving the keys he dumps onto the counter wedged between us with the dry cleaner next door.

Halfway to the door, he mutters, "It probably would have been cheaper to launder your stuff than replace it."

"Probably," I mimic, my voice not as stern as it was moments ago. "But nowhere near as much fun." My last sentence is solely for my ears.

He didn't see how Octavia's eyes lit up when we walked past the shop window brimming with shoes with their heels still attached. She looked like a kid on Christmas morning, and since it was an expression I haven't experienced since my twelfth birthday, I'll do everything in my power to see it again.

When the salesperson stops at the door to flip the open sign to closed, he seems tempted to sneak a peek at the 'changing room,' but he must think better of it because with a murmured swear word and his chin balancing on his chest, he exits without so much as a backward glance.

I lock the door to ensure we don't have any unwanted customers before joining Octavia near the changing room. "How are you doing?"

"Great!" She huffs, grunts, then sighs. "*Real* great."

Recognizing the same dejected tone she used while leaving the heel of her shoe in a steaming pile of poo, I ask, "You're not stuck again, are you?"

It takes her almost half a minute to reply. "What makes you ask that?" Her tone is more exposing than her reply. She has the same dismal mannerisms my cousin, Elliot, used when he got stuck in the slide at a McDonald's on his eighth birthday. He's always been 'big boned,' so he shouldn't have tempted fate any day, much less after eating three double-stacked Quarter Pounders.

After ensuring not an ounce of humor can be heard in my voice, I ask, "Do you need help?"

I imagine Octavia's face holding the same drooped lip, twinkled-eye expression she had when I snapped the heel on her good shoe when she murmurs, "Please." After another handful of grunts, she mutters, "I think the latch is stuck. *That or I need breast augmentation.*" Her last sentence is choked with embarrassment.

Neither wanting nor needing a lawsuit, I ask, "Is it safe for me to enter?"

I learn the reason for the shame in Octavia's tone when she permits me to join her in the 'changing room.' Her arms are raised above her head, a designer dress that should have gone out of fashion two decades ago has flattened her chest to the point it doesn't seem anywhere near as mesmerizing as it once did, and her panties that caught me in a trance almost two hours ago are even more exposed since not an article of clothing covers the lower half of her body from my avid gaze.

She should look ridiculous, but the stiffening of my cock announces my body and head are of opposing opinions again. Her 'restraints' have me imagining her tied to a Saint Andrew's Cross in a playroom, blindfolded and gagged, and they're even more confronting than her screams for me to put down the scissors when I snatch them off a makeshift counter at the side of the changing room.

"This is a vintage couture dress. You can't destroy vintage couture."

After taking a moment to relish how her accent is more pronounced when she is being sassy, I ask, "Then how am I meant to get you out of it?"

When she peers at me from beneath a mountain load of silky

ruffles, her eye roll is cuter than her flushed expression. "You need to find the zipper. I swear it's here somewhere."

She stops spinning in a circle when I place my hands on her hips to keep her still. She was circling so fast she was making me dizzy. "Give me a minute or two to explore."

Octavia mumbles something under her breath. If given a bible and asked to swear on it, I'm confident enough in my assessment of the situation to place my hand on top and pledge that she muttered, 'Oh God.'

After a handful of feather-like brushes of her skin and a heap of inappropriate gawks, I ask, "Do you remember if it was a side zipper? Or did it fasten at the back?"

"I don't know," she replies with a whine. "I wasn't paying that much attention. I saw a couture dress with a fourteen-dollar price tag. You don't willy-nilly when it comes to a fourteen-dollar couture."

I grin about her eagerness to sniff out a bargain before continuing my hunt. I won't lie. Just like when I was removing the blobs of mud from her silky-smooth skin, I take my time searching for the dress's fastener. Octavia has beautiful, flawless skin that blooms with heat after only the slightest brush of my fingertips. Her provocative scent had me refusing to put her down even after we were clear from the carnage. And her face... don't get me started on the uniqueness of her bluish-green eyes, plump bottom lip, and how her tiny nostrils flare along with the generous swells on her chest when she's riled up, or I'll never leave this changing room with my respect intact.

I almost threw it away when Fitz laughed in the town car. I was so overwhelmed by my swiftness of reeling Octavia in that I forgot we were with company—company who knows all my dirty secrets.

That's why I fled. Secrets are hard to contain in general, but they're almost impossible to keep under wraps when everything you are and have become is solely based on them.

With my mood nowhere near as playful, I find the latch under Octavia's underarm, slide it down to her waist, then tell Octavia I'll wait for her outside.

I'm out of the changing room faster than Octavia can breathe out my name in a breathless whisper and even faster than my lusty head can work out why a bra was dangling from the hanger I rushed by instead of on Octavia's sweltering body.

J ack is playful, handsome, and good company, but so damn hard for me to read. I've felt a little lost more than a handful of times in the past few hours. We switched out our smelly clothes at a trendy thrift store I'm dying to tell Jess about, ate at a cute little hole-in-the-wall joint half a mile from the race track that almost ruined my day, and have spent the last hour walking the backstreets of an eclectic suburb I didn't know existed, yet I'm still none the wiser to what caused Jack to vacate the changing room like my miniskirt didn't announce to him that I was gifted the dreaded flat-bottom genes from my mother.

His sudden departure had me worried he did more than scare away the salesman when I went to try on some outfits. I'm beginning to wonder if he researched me, and although I am confident in my family's lawyer's ability to keep our dirty secrets hidden, I'm just as worried Jack could have access to someone capable of digging up years of hidden shame in a matter of minutes. The generous tip he left the bubbly server at our last stop alludes to this, not to mention his super pricy watch.

Incapable of harnessing my curiosity for a second longer, I mutter, "Did I say something wrong back there?"

I nudge my head in the direction of the thrift shop, but since it is also in the direction of the Mexican restaurant, Jack sounds as lost as I feel when he replies, "I don't speak fluent Spanish, but the waitress seemed to have no trouble understanding you."

"Not at the restaurant." I pause, unsure if you can call a couple of park benches down an alleyway a restaurant before starting again, "At the thrift store." I bump him with my hip like we're lifelong friends. It weakens the groove between his brows by shunting his unease onto me. "I figured your earlier grope would have announced I lack the booty gene." I shake my ample chest. "My mom said I must have gone back for boobs twice." That gets a smile out of him, but it isn't as big as it was before we went to the thrift store. "I was fine hanging with your friends if that's your jam. You didn't have to go outside your comfort zone to keep me happy."

Jack spins around and walks backward. "What makes you say this isn't my comfort zone?" Before the words can leave my mouth, he quickly adds, "Other than my watch."

I'd rib him with my elbow if he weren't two steps in front of me. "It just doesn't seem like your jam."

He slants his head, which only just conceals his smirk. "It?"

When I wave my hand toward the alleyway we've taken a detour down, his dark eyes drink in the bland palette before he confesses, "This was pretty much all I did in my early teens." The twinkle I've been dying to ignite for the past three hours resurfaces more vigorously than ever. "Although there were a few more shopping carts and empty beer cans back then." His laugh echoes in the silence of the alley. It buds my nipples and has me paying careful attention to his mouth when he speaks, "We couldn't afford skateboards, so we used what we could."

"It was probably for the best. The stone edging at the museum was the equivalent of a grater if you landed on it wrong." I pull up the sleeve of the fitted shirt I purchased from the thrift shop to show him the scar on my elbow. "This baby saw Caleb's vomit landing on my shoes. He hates blood."

"Caleb?" Back is the jealous, possessive man I've missed the past three hours. It isn't Jack's obvious wealth that's kept my heart pumping excessively the past several hours. It is the look in his eye whenever I catch him watching me—how he stares at me like I'm some sort of gift. Like not a million dollars could compare to watching me eat sloppy tacos and grimace when half of the toppings land on my plate instead of in my mouth.

I wait a beat to make sure he doesn't mistake the flirtiness in my tone as the wrong type of affection for my cousin before replying, "Caleb is my cousin slash almost brother. Our mothers are best friends as well as sisters-in-law, and since we were born on the same dark, demented night, we class ourselves as siblings."

Jack's smile could light up the darkest night and call me cocky, but I'm reasonably sure he's blinding me with it so I can't see the relief gleaming in his eyes. "And where is Caleb now?"

"Most likely dodging Jess's eagerness," I huff out with a laugh.

His dark brow quirks. "Jess from the meeting, Jess?"

I nod. "One and the same. She has a thing for unattainable men."

I'm envious of his tongue when he delves it out to lick his top lip before he asks with a wry grin, "And you don't?"

My lips twist to hide my smile. It doesn't lessen Jack's interest in staring at my mouth, but it makes it hard to articulate my reply with the edgy playfulness I'm aiming for. "I don't know yet. I guess it depends on how you answer my question."

A move to Hollywood is still in his cards when he mutters, "Question?"

"Nice try, buddy, but I have the memory of an elephant. I

forget *nothing*." My voice is super dramatic, and it echoes down the isolated alleyway.

After spinning back around and standing so close our hands almost touch, Jack mutters, "It was nothing you said or did. I just..." The briefest connection of our pinkies makes his next words seem nowhere near as alarming as they should be. "Let my past get away from me."

I have enough baggage to ban me from flying for the next century, so I don't have room for more, but something about Jack has me throwing caution to the wind. "I wish it hadn't... because I wasn't really stuck. I just wanted an excuse for you to join me in the changing room."

He slants his head, arches a brow, then stares at me for several long seconds to gauge the authenticity of my reply. When he gets a lot of truth with only the slightest smear of dishonesty, he asks, "And why did you want that?"

I shrug. "I don't know. I thought maybe we could have finished what we started in your office." Now it's my turn to walk backward. "That is why you sent away the salesperson, wasn't it?"

"Not entirely." I search his face for dishonesty as aggressively as he did mine when he murmurs, "But I'd be a liar if I said the thought hadn't crossed my mind. One taste of your lips wasn't enough, and I'm more than ready for a second helping."

"But?" I query when I hear one hanging in the air.

Walking backward has both advantages and disadvantages. A disadvantage is that you're a little bit disorientated so you can unknowingly be backed into a corner, but the advantage is the exact same thing.

Scrap that.

I'm crowded against the brickwork in an isolated alleyway, and a handsome man with a panty-wetting face is honing in on me.

There are no disadvantages here.

None whatsoever.

"No buts…" Jack murmurs as he weaves his fingers through my hair that doesn't smell anywhere near as dreadful as it should. "Just a ton of apologies—"

I cut him off with my tongue this time around. It is bold of me, but most of today has been an out-of-body experience for me, so I run with it.

Our kiss is gentle but assertive at the same time. It has the perfect amount of tongue, and since I have to tilt my head to align our lips, my moans roll up my throat without hindrance. They sound desperate but also hot. Like one kiss will never be enough.

After banding his arms around my back, Jack tugs me in closer. This level of spark shouldn't be the case with strangers. It's intense, breathless, and desperate, and no matter how hard I fight not to get caught up in the hype of a life-altering kiss, I can't help but be swept away by it.

Goosebumps prickle my skin as the fire low in my belly grows wild. My legs shake, and my mind races as I struggle to settle the intense pulse between my thighs. I never knew kissing could be so all-consuming and mind-blurring, but this kiss goes above and beyond. It will stay with me forever.

By the time Jack pulls back to catch his breath, I'm desperate. "Jack…"

"Shh. You need to be quiet. We can't have anyone see us." His voice is as hoarse as mine, the need in his eyes just as rampant.

After leaning into me deeper, he then steals more than the air from my lungs when he wraps my legs around his waist. My sanity goes right along with it.

Over the next several minutes, we make out like horny teens with no repercussions for our actions.

Our make-out session only ends when I need more than the rock behind his zipper to get me off. It takes all my willpower to pull away from Jack's sinful mouth. His lips are scrumptious—the yummiest I've ever tasted—but if we don't take this somewhere private, his wish for our romp to remain a secret will falter. I'm not loud, but I've never been with someone who kisses as good as Jack, so who knows what is to come?

"We need to take this somewhere else. Somewhere clean." I don't know if his tugs on my hair are responsible for my last two words or the stench down the alleyway, but whatever it is, it is honest. "My foot was lodged in poo only hours ago, so I'm not kneeling on filth tonight."

"Kneeling?" Jack murmurs against my neck before he peppers it with kisses.

"Yeah... kneeling." I inch back, then drop my eyes to his face since his lips have fallen to my collarbone. "When I..." I make the most unladylike gesture with my tongue and the inside of my cheek, then die of embarrassment two seconds later. "I'm sorry. I suck at flirting."

"No, you don't," Jack denies, his voice a mix of hilarity and horniness. "But I'm sure you *suck* a lot when giving head."

I sock him in the stomach like the need in his voice doesn't have me on the cusp of climax before muttering, "You'll never know if we stay here." My teeth rake my bottom lip before I confess, "I'm not usually a one-night-stand type of girl... but I could be for you."

"No," he denies again before shaking his head. "This isn't a one-night thing. I'll need more than a night."

His reply excites me more than I care to admit, but I play it cool. "How do you know that? We've barely skidded past first base."

He rocks his hips forward, stealing the nerves from my head and clustering them much lower. "This tells me everything I need to know."

I burrow my head into his neck when his second grind has me grunting like a wild animal. I'm so close to detonation I'm not even sure I need more than his zipper anymore. It could get the job done. Hell, even just the scent of Jack's aftershave lingering in the wake of his touch could push me over the edge of hysteria.

"Jack…"

"Shh," he murmurs for a second time before doing the quickest glance down the alleyway.

Once he's sure the coast is clear, he sets me back on my feet, slips my panties to the side without a fraction of hesitation, then locks his eyes with mine. I nod to the silent questions in his eyes, confident I will die if he doesn't touch me as they are begging him to do. That's how intense our connection is—how fire-sparking.

"This should tie you over until we can find somewhere better to take this."

The brickwork scratches my back when my knees buckle out from beneath me. It isn't solely Jack stuffing a girthy finger into my vagina causing my collapsing response. It is the fact a man with a one-hundred-thousand-dollar watch circling his wrist is willing to fall to his knees and eat me for dessert that has me incapable of staying upright.

My unstable legs are a thing of the past when Jack spears his tongue into my vagina. He slithers it along his index finger before he slowly drags it toward my clit.

It takes everything I have not to come when the vibrations of his deep voice tremble on my clit when he asks, "Tell me what you like?"

"*That.*" I snake my fingers through his almost black hair before gently swaying my hips in rhythm to the grinds of his finger. "I like… *that.*"

For what should mimic a quick and nasty romp in an alleyway, our get-together is on the opposing end of the equation. Jack's licks on my clit are fast and frantic, but the pumps of his finger are slow and leisured.

The odd combination is arousing as hell, and within seconds, I'm tugging on his hair in warning of an impending climax instead of encouraging a faster speed.

"Jack. Oh, God… oh."

I yank on his hair harder as my eyes dart up and down the alleyway. I then let go of a sensation so overwhelming there's no doubt I'd crumple to the ground in a sticky, sweaty heap if Jack weren't groping my ass with as much eagerness as he did earlier today.

My orgasm rips through me at the same time my moans ripple down the still isolated alleyway. It's long, frantic, and so overwhelming, if Jack wasn't a stranger only hours ago, a girl might be tempted to scream three little words she's never said to a man before—not even her father.

Once my surging pulse returns to a normal level, Jack lessens the severity of his licks. He sucks my overstimulated clit into his mouth, kisses the nervy bud like he didn't just torment it into hysteria, slowly withdraws his finger, then stands until we meet almost eye to eye. "We need a room, and we need one now."

Incapable of denying the absolute honesty of his statement, I nod.

W rangling a cab in New York on a Saturday night is a tricky feat, but it has nothing on a suburban community on the outskirts of Seattle. With the knees of my trousers scuffed and cut up from my eagerness to learn if Octavia's pussy tastes as delicious as her mouth and almost exact replicas of my watch being sold by every street vendor at a flea market, the first three cabs drove by without stopping. The fourth demanded both cash and that we share a fare with someone he had already agreed to collect, and the fifth cab driver's car reeked of alcohol.

I was desperate to take my date with Octavia somewhere more private, but I wasn't so desperate to put her in harm's way.

That's what led us to this. A twenty-minute Uber drive with a man who smells of garlic and tomatoes and has two seconds to lift his rearview mirror back to its original setting before I add an assault charge to the long list of felonies I've undertaken thus far today.

When the driver catches my wrath stare in the rearview

mirror, he coughs to clear his throat, adjusts the mirror back to its rightful spot, then signals to turn down Prichard Street.

My lips move in preparation to speak, but Octavia curls her hand over my balled one before they can. "Don't bother. He's taking Prichard no matter what you say." Her voice is still husky from the scream of ecstasy she released in the alleyway, and her eyes are wide and dilated. She looks like a woman who's been thoroughly fucked even with our adventurous night only just beginning.

I like that.

I like that very much.

The thickness of my cock hasn't deflated an inch in the past thirty minutes. I'm so hard, I continually grab myself to make sure I haven't busted through my zipper. That's how hearty he's knocking at the metal teeth, begging to be freed. It has *never* pumped as much blood through it as it has tonight.

"Was that your first?"

My heart whacks my ribs as I swing my eyes in the direction of my questioner.

Octavia peers at me with flushed cheeks and slightly parted lips before she murmurs, "Was that your first time doing *that* in an alleyway?"

After a slight delay to compose myself, I jerk up my chin before insensitively inquiring, "You?"

"If I say no, will it get me in trouble?" She takes a moment to drink in my slitted eyes, fisted hands, and still-extended crotch before confessing, "It was my first time *not* in a bedroom." She pauses again. This one is more for personal reflection than to stir me. "Actually, it was the first time not in a bed." She locks her eyes with mine, the lust in them stiffening my cock even more. "I've never been overly adventurous, but for some reason, I feel as if that is set to change."

"Very much so," I murmur before taking in how much

longer we have left to travel on the Uber app the driver refuses to use along with the GPS mounted on his dashboard.

I scarcely hold back a curse word when the app announces we still have fifteen minutes to travel, but the torture seems nowhere near as bad when Octavia mutters, "My place is five minutes from here. If you're willing to slum it with the lesser half, we could always go there." When my brows crinkle at her underhanded comment that she's financially struggling, she waves her hand across the front of her body. "We're not having that conversation now." She twists her lips. "Perhaps not ever."

After scooting forward so inches upon inches of her thighs become exposed in a miniskirt oddly similar to the one she was wearing earlier, she advises the driver of a change in route. Once she's back in her original position, she slings her eyes to me. Ever so slowly, she rakes her hooded gaze down my body before muttering, *"That* better be as impressive outside of its tight restraints as it is in them because we're about to do another first." She looks more ashamed than teasing when she mutters, "This is the first time I've taken a guy home."

With her eyes locked back on the traffic and my words more a hushed whisper than a verbal confirmation, I mutter, "It will be one of many firsts tonight."

Apartment buildings without elevators should be illegal. Octavia and I barely make it up two flights of stairs before we're clawing at one another. Buttons pop and threads are shredded before I pin her to her apartment door on the third level to ravish her mouth. The damp smell in the corridor assures me there are no cameras watching my every move, not to mention the lack of a doorman.

After peppering Octavia's neck with kisses long enough to make up for the ten minutes of no contact we had during our commute, I aid in her endeavor to find her keys in her clutch purse. For its small size, it is amazing what it carries—lip gloss, credit card, driver's license, enough coins to pay our Uber fare in small change, a foil packet I'm desperate to discover if it is still in date, and finally, a set of house keys.

"I knew they were there somewhere." Octavia breathes out with a relieved sigh before she jabs a silver key into a lock and swings open her door. Before I can enter hot on her heel, she spins back around and fans her hand across my chest. "This isn't the Rit—"

Uncaring about our difference in wealth and hungry for another taste of her lip gloss, I weave my fingers through her hair, then drag my tongue across her delicious mouth. We moan in sync when the commanding licks of my tongue have her legs wrapping around my waist and her damp panties grinding against my lowered zipper.

I pull back from Octavia's delicious mouth when she murmurs against my lips, "Just jimmy the lock. The deadbolt hasn't worked in weeks, and the lock only works from the outside."

Although appreciative of our quick entrance into her apartment—my shirt is half undone, and the lowered zipper in my trousers is exposing my briefs—my back molars still grind together when I realize there's nothing between Octavia and the shady-looking men outside her apartment building but a flimsy door with an even flimsier lock.

"You need to get that fixed."

"Uh-huh. On the list," she murmurs with a grin when I hook a chair from a writing desk near the door and jam it under the lock. No one will get close to hurting her while I'm around, but since I don't want any interruptions, I'll take precautionary measures to ensure that doesn't occur.

I barely glance at the compact yet tidy living room for three seconds before my perusal is interrupted by a far more impressive visual. Octavia's ruddy lips are even more swollen from the kisses we shared while navigating three flights of stairs, but they become plumper when she drags her teeth over them. Her eyes are hungry and wanton, and when I notice the direction of her gaze, the lust in them deepens.

She's staring at my crotch.

"*Now* my fly is undone," I murmur, incapable of not reminding her I didn't miss her gawk at my crotch earlier today.

"Uh-huh," she half murmurs and half whimpers before she answers the numerous pleas beaming from her hooded gaze. She races my way, reaching me in barely a second, then she slings her arms around my neck and reacquaints our lips. As she kisses me to the point my dick is aching, her hand slithers down the bumps in my midsection. "And I very much look forward to hearing how you explain the buckles in its metal teeth to your tailor the next time you see him," she whispers into my ear a second before she slips her hand under my briefs and curls it around my rock-hard shaft.

Her brazenness turns me on even more, and before I realize we're walking, I'm carrying her through her apartment like I'm intimate with the floorplan. We kiss and tear at each other's clothing along the way, leaving a trail of destruction in our wake.

"Left," Octavia murmurs breathlessly when our short walk down a tight corridor ends with two doors on each side.

By the time we enter her room, my wallet is flopped open on the floor, my pants are huddled around my shoes, and Octavia's long-sleeve shirt is over her head and halfway up her arms.

When we fall onto her bed with a breathy moan, I wedge a knee between her legs to stop them from closing before using her stuck shirt to my advantage.

"Oh, God," Octavia murmurs under her breath when I

double her clothes' restrictiveness by tying her shirt's sleeves together and knotting them at her wrists. "You *were* having the same dirty thoughts as me in the dressing room."

With a smirk that exposes my answer, I scoot her up the bed until I can restrain her hands to the metal fittings at the end, and her long legs are straight and without encumbrance.

"Are you okay?" I ask after admiring my handiwork.

She nods without hindrance. "I'm more than okay." She rakes her teeth over her lower lip before shifting her eyes to her bedside table. "I have condoms in there if you don't have any."

I almost say the one in my wallet would have expired years ago, but I keep my mouth shut. She's tied and at my mercy, so the last thing she needs is concern that I don't know what I'm doing. I'm also not sure I could speak even if I wanted to. Octavia is a beautiful woman, and this should be ludicrous for me to say, but she is even more beautiful without clothing. There are no flaws or imperfections. Her body is perfect, and the lust beaming from her eyes is even more impeccable.

Her moan is as audible as my pulse in my words when I mutter, "I'll get to them... *eventually*. But first..." I drop my eyes to her damp panties before licking my lips, "... I think I have another matter to take care of first."

When Jack drags the back of his hand down my damp panties, my mouth gapes, but no words leave my lips. I can't speak. The sexual chemistry firing between us makes it hard for me to breathe, much less talk. It's been crackling and hissing all night, and now, it is as if someone lit the fireworks box on fire instead of a select few.

My ass lifts off the mattress when he skims a finger along the seam of the cotton material. He edges it away from the area aching as if it hasn't been touched in years before he locks his eyes with mine.

"Please," I beg, certain there are more questions in his lusty gaze than demands.

His smile sets me on fire. It is as molten as the image of him toeing off his shoes so he can fully remove his pants.

Once he's standing before me in nothing but a pair of briefs that have no chance in hell of hiding the impressive bulge between his legs, he returns his eyes to my face before hooking his index fingers into the waistband of my panties and once again wordlessly seeking permission to remove them.

I nod. My head bob is frantic, but it barely touches my chin before he drags my panties down my quaking thighs and raises them to his nose.

"Oh God." Yes, a more intellectual response is above me right now. That was insanely hot, and the way the material looks fragile and weak in his large hand makes the lust burning me alive even more potent. "If you don't touch me soon, I'm going to need you to untie me so I can take care of business myself."

I regret my choice of words when Jack murmurs, "And *exactly* how would you do that, Octavia?"

Involuntarily, my eyes stray to the drawer I mentioned earlier. There are more than just condoms in there. A whole arsenal of sex apparatuses is at our disposal.

With a grin that would have the devil agreeing to an intervention, he murmurs, "Can I?"

My head is screaming no, but before my mouth can articulate that, I dip my chin, granting him access to a drawer not even Jess knows about.

Fortunately, my brain's sluggish reboot occurs before Jack can shuffle off the bed. After hooking my legs around his waist, holding him in place, I mutter, "But it's only fair if you get to see my equipment that I get to see yours."

I hate the words leaving my mouth. They're immature and borderline creepy, but mercifully, Jack sees through the shame of my words. With no hesitation firing in his eyes, and nothing but a playful smirk on his lips, he jerks up his chin before slipping off the edge of the bed and lowering his briefs down his slim yet still muscular thighs.

"Sweet lord," I murmur when the rising of his cock to his belly button leaves no barrier between my greedy eyes and his impressive manhood. "Does that thing come with a warning label?" Horrified I spoke my thoughts out loud, I snap my eyes to Jack's face. "I'm sorry."

My earlier assumption about his smile only being hotter if it was delivered while his head is in between my legs is one hundred percent accurate when he murmurs, "No, you're not," a second after wedging himself back between my legs. The drawer of sex toys has been forgotten, and once again, only my pussy is on the dessert menu. "But I'm more than happy to pretend you are if it has you begging like you were in the alleyway earlier."

"I wasn't begging."

Scrap that.

Yes, I was.

Just like I will now when his heated breaths are the only thing that bombard my aching sex over the next several long seconds.

"Jack..." That's not exactly a beg, but if you heard how it was delivered, you wouldn't doubt its authenticity. And let's not mention the bucks of my hips as I try to mash my pussy with his mouth. "I need..." I swallow the desperate pleas ringing through my head on repeat when my measly beg gets me over the line.

Jack's mouth is on my pussy, and it feels fantastic.

After dragging his tongue up my slit, he circles it around my clit before giving it a gentle graze with his teeth. The pressure of his tongue on the nervy bud isn't enough to set me off, but it does have pleas for him to take me hard and faster spilling from my mouth.

The curving of his mouth's corners exposes he likes the begs seeping from my lips, not to mention the way he eats me faster and more expertly with every one that leaves my mouth.

He either loves giving head or hearing me beg.

Whatever it is, I'm enjoying the hell out of it.

My screams ramp up along with the bucks of my hips. I'm on fire. Both inside and out, and only one man is holding the extinguisher.

"Jack—"

The sting of his fingers when he grips my ass to raise it off the bed cuts off my plea. I'm practically screaming a roaring review about the exemplary expertise of the man with his head between my legs.

"Please…"

As I lose all cognitive thoughts, I grind down on Jack's mouth before arching my spine and throwing my head back with a long, husky moan.

And still, Jack doesn't stop.

He licks me, eats me, and fucks me with his tongue, and all I can do is surrender to the madness, his movements fast and steady. Wave after wave crashes through me until eventually, the stars detonate, and a desperate urge to return the favor swamps me.

"Please…" I wiggle and shake my arms, endeavoring to get free. "I want to touch you. I *need* to touch you." Nothing but pure unbridled lust rings in my tone when I mutter, "I want your dick between my lips."

Evidence of my multiple arousals drips off Jack's rigid chin when he climbs up my body to release my hands from their tight restraints, but before they get close to touching his sweat-slicked skin, he pins them above my head, and the crown of his fat cock knocks at the entrance of my drenched pussy.

"Condom," I pant between frantic breaths. "We need a condom."

Just like my toys left his mind only minutes ago, a wish to suck his dick also vacates mine when I wiggle a hand free before leaning over to grab a condom out of a box in my drawer. They're in date but untouched.

"Are you sure?" Jack double-checks after accepting the condom from my grasp.

Even with his tearing open the condom and sliding it down his mouth-wateringly thick cock, a glint in his eyes exposes this will end the instant I want it to. He won't take it any further than I feel comfortable with.

"I'm sure." I hook my legs around his waist until my feet are dangling above his glorious ass, doubling my assurance.

Although I'm confident he could rock my world in any position, Jack ups the ante by flipping us over. With my thighs straddling his hips and his dark hair extra inky against my white pillowcases, Jack circles his hand around the base of his sheathed cock like it needs assistance staying hard before he uses his other hand to guide me onto my knees until I'm perched above him.

The first inch burns.

The second inch stretches.

And the third inch rips.

When a grimace I can't hide crosses my face, Jack mutters, "Stop—"

"No," I interrupt, determined to take him. "It's been a while, so I just need time to adjust."

Jack looks torn, but mercifully, he loosens his grip on my hip and lets me sink another two or three inches. I'm not close to taking him all, but the sensation of being so full already makes the pain so much more bearable.

"See... it just needs... a little bit... of patience." My words are spaced by big, needy breaths. It hurts, but I'd be a liar if I said it wasn't an enjoyable experience. Pete Reynolds had stamina by the bucketloads during oral activities. When it came to sex, it was generally over before it began.

That isn't the case with Jack. He rocks in and out of me several times in a row before he weakens his stranglehold on the base of his cock and shifts his hand's focus to my clit.

I purr like a kitty when he strokes the nervy bud with the back of his fingers before he slowly raises his eyes to my face. "Shall I touch you there while you fuck me?"

"Yes." I nod like an insane woman. "Please."

His comment that I'm fucking him already has me on the

verge of climax, not to mention his mumbled, "Show me what to do, and I'll do it. Teach me what you like."

"I like you, Jack."

Kill. Me. Now.

I can't be stuffed to the brim by his fat cock and look at his gorgeous face while he's smiling a shy grin. That's above my caliber of expertise. A woman with years of sexual encounters couldn't do that, much less one who's only had three bed companions.

"Please, Jack." His name comes out with a garble from his thumb gently stimulating my clit. He circles, strokes, and rubs the area near where our bodies are intimately joined all the while watching my face cross through various stages of ecstasy.

Tension rapidly builds inside me for the hundredth time today when I lean forward to grasp the bed's metal frame in my slippery hands. My breasts are now thrust into Jack's face, and the stability my sturdy grip gives my legs has me rising and falling onto his cock at a steady yet somewhat desperate pace.

Hungry, needy pressure forms low in my core when Jack takes my pert nipple between his lips before swiveling it with his tongue. He grazes it with his teeth, bringing it to the point of being sharp, then shifts his focus to my other breast.

I bite my lip to muffle my scream when the sensation burning through me becomes too much. I'm already swollen and aching from countless orgasms. My body can't be subjected to more, can it?

Pleasure sears through me when my body proves my heart and head are liars. I come with a hoarse cry while whispering Jack's name into the humid night air. It is a beautiful, chaotic time that makes me utterly boneless and unresponsive to orders. I can barely lift my head, much less move my Jell-O legs.

Thankfully, Jack is strong enough for us both. After rolling us over so I'm once again splayed beneath him, he curls my tired legs around his waist, pins my arms above my head, then drives home.

The brushing of his pecs as he rocks in and out of me is detrimental to my sanity. My nipples harden as a new fire ignites in my core. Within seconds, I'm rolling my hips in rhythm to his while also squirming to get free from his hold.

He seems more reluctant this time around, and I understand why when he mutters the quickest, "No touching," requirement under his breath before he releases my wrists from his firm yet painless grip.

Too caught up in the moment to realize his request isn't normal, I mutter, "Okay," before weaving my fingers through his hair like he allowed earlier then angling my mouth so it aligns better with his. "Is this okay?"

He barely breathes out, "Yes," before he spears his tongue between my lips and drags it along the roof of my mouth.

His body pinning mine to the mattress, the fullness of him being almost fully seated inside me, and his kiss are too much. My chest tightens as every muscle in my body pulls taut.

Then I fall, and I fall hard.

"God, Octavia," Jack grunts against my lips when the walls of my pussy clench around him.

Once every tremor has been exhausted, I open my thighs wider for him, let more of him in, then fully surrender to his brilliance.

He never relents.

Not once.

He pumps and pumps and pumps into me until I'm on the cusp of exhaustion and screaming his name once more. Sweat dots his top lip, and his chest heaves with frantic breaths as the throbs of his cock get faster and more urgent.

"Please, Jack," I beg, certain I'll never experience anything more sensational than his face during climax. "Please. Please. *Please.*"

"Oh. Fuck. Christ." His teeth sink into his lower lip as the thrusts of his hips turn frantic. He fucks me like a maniac, the banging of my bed frame against the wall a sure-fire sign of this, not to mention my relentless moans.

He gets thicker and harder with every grind of our pelvises, and I watch him like a hawk. I categorize every expression that crosses his face and every flare that darts through his eyes before the vision is stripped away from me by an orgasm more blinding than I've ever had.

As I shimmy and shake through the energy-zapping spasms rocketing through my body, Jack sinks me deeper and deeper into the mattress. He slams into me, bottoming out at my cervix before the most beautiful noise in the world fills my ears.

He doesn't scream my name. His grunt is barely a whisper, but his expression while his cock throbs inside me with untamed wildness as he finds his release speaks volumes.

We achieved greatness, but the immensity of the situation was lost on me until I recall the words Jack whispered in our Uber.

"It will be one of many firsts tonight."

I thought he meant going home with someone you've just met. But after drinking in his bewildered expression as his condom fills with cum, and his numerous requests for guidance tonight, I'm beginning to have doubts.

He rocked my world, but did I take more from him than a night of passion?

O ctavia's breaths come out heavy and fast on my chest when I roll off her, taking her with me. My body tingles as shockwaves dart through every inch of me. That was phenomenal, unlike anything I've ever had. The blistering connection between us grew tenfold when I positioned myself between her legs. I would have been happy to consume her for dessert for the second time and call it a night. That's generally as far as my 'dates' go, but I wanted more for Octavia.

I needed more.

An arrogant grin tugs on my lips when Octavia breathes out a breathless, "Wow," several long seconds later. Her body is covered with a dense layer of sweat, and her breathing is sharp and laborious. She is as exhausted as me. "That was amazing."

After concealing my toothy grin with my lips, I press them to her sticky temple before dropping my eyes to her disheveled head. Her plump lips, flushed cheeks, and mussed hair have me primed and ready for round two, but a loud grumble rumbling from her mid-section deviates my thoughts for the hundredth time today.

"We should eat."

Octavia pops her head up and balances it on her palm with the help of a cranked elbow. "Are you hungry again?" Her tone is more sexually suggestive than teasing.

"Not particularly." I drag my index finger down her slim nose, halving the deep groove between her brows before confessing, "But it seems as if you are."

She shakes her head, which only just conceals her smile. "Not for food anyway."

"Your stomach just grumbled."

She tickles the fine hairs splayed across my pelvis with the hand not being used to hold up her head. "My stomach just *settled* itself… but if it were hungry, it would have *nothing* to do with food." When she peers up at me, the confident, eat-men-alive woman I've been wrangling these past several hours has been replaced with someone a little unsure. "You… *went down on me* twice, so it's only fair that I return the favor, isn't it?"

Although appreciative of her wish to even the score between us, her worries are unnecessary. "I didn't go *down on you* to force reciprocation. I did it because I enjoy it."

My reply stumps her for half a minute. "You like giving head?"

"No," I answer, my tone as on point as the ones I used earlier to deflect her fibs. "I enjoy giving *you* head." When she shivers, my exhaustion is a forgotten memory. "So much so, perhaps I should have another sample."

"Oh, God, no, Jack. I'm-I'm tired, and exhausted, an-and sticky. You really don't need to do that again." She's telling me no, but her body is already on the other side of the fence. When she rolls onto her back, her thighs naturally sweep open to accommodate my shoulders.

After snapping off my condom, knotting it, and dumping it on the bedside table, I once again position myself between Octavia's legs. This time, I take my time exploring and examining her. Her pussy lips are swollen, and her labia is a little more red than pink, but other than that, it is the most gloriously satisfying visual. She smells delicious, and the way her breasts rise and fall as she peers down at me between her legs is an image I could savor time and time again.

"Are you sore?" When she shakes her head, I test the sensitivity of her clit by rubbing my thumb over it. My briefest touch sweeps her legs open more and adds to the shimmer on her pussy lips. "What about here?" While watching her face, I dip my thumb inside her before slowly dragging it back out. "Are you sore here?"

"No." Her one word sounds like a sentence since it is delivered with a husky moan that's quickly followed by my name. "Jack..."

"Shh. I've got you."

Only an hour ago, I wouldn't have had the confidence to say that. I've built an empire of impeccable wealth, won *People* magazine's Bachelor of the Year contest twice, and am toted as one of the most successful men of modern times, but my personal accomplishments are far less stellar.

I thought parts of me were broken beyond repair.

Then I spotted Octavia.

Now the world is my oyster.

When I scoot down the bed, a spark of electricity jolts up my legs and surges toward my balls. I'm hard again in an instant, and the revelation is shocking.

As I bring my mouth down close to Octavia's fragrant-smelling pussy, I rock against the mattress to make sure I'm not misreading the prompts of my body. The springs I'm certain my back will complain about in the morning feel good when they dig into my stiffened shaft. It's a painful encounter that ensures my focus will remain on pleasing Octavia instead of taking advantage of a second hard-on in a matter of minutes.

"Watch me, Tivy." I don't know why I use her nickname. I

guess it feels too casual for stuffy salutations. It is why I introduced myself as Jack. Tonight, I'm not a media mogul of a billionaire entity. I am Jack, a once New Jersey teen who wanted to play minor league baseball and participate in a hot dog eating contest until he hurled.

When Octavia's lust-crammed eyes drop to mine, mine silently plead for permission to ravish her. To take her to the brink. To force her to scream my name over and over again until I can no longer hear the whimpers of my past that usually surface right around now.

I want her to come on my face.

"Please, Jack... *please.*"

Her last plea barely leaves her mouth when I probe my tongue between the slick flesh at the top of her thighs. I push it deep inside her, growling when I recognize the reason for the different texture of her slickness. It's mixed with the powder on the latex condom we used.

"Are you on the pill, Octavia?" I ask after my tongue flicks her swollen clit.

Her pussy grinds against my mouth before the briefest, "Yes," falls from her lips.

Her hip bucks turn relentless when I murmur against her heated skin, "Good, because the next time I do this, I want to feel my cum inside you, between my fingers, and against my lips. I want to watch it flowing out of you before pushing it back deep inside you."

"Oh..." Anything she says next is garbled by long, heated screams. She moans nonstop while her limbs shake through a ferocious orgasm. "I'm... I'm... I'm..."

As she violently convulses, I push two fingers inside her and curl them upward before hitting her clit with back-to-back rapid-fire hits with my tongue. It lengthens her orgasm, pushing her moans to a point I have no doubt the shady men outside her apartment building can hear.

The knowledge should have me lessening the furling movements of my fingers and swivels of my tongue but try as I may, I need Octavia's screams more than my lungs need their next breath.

"Again," I murmur against her hot, slicked skin when her thrashes simmer from a full-blown body quake to a soft shake.

"No." Shiny blonde locks stick to her temples when she shakes her head. "I can't. No more. I'm done."

"One more, then we'll shower together and get some shut-eye before doing it all again tomorrow."

"*Ohh...*" I don't know what gets me over the line. The quickening of my pumps or my confession that I'm not planning to leave any time soon. Whatever it is, my hips rock into the mattress in rhythm to the slow, steady pace Octavia uses as she fucks my face. "One more. Then we shower, sleep, I'll cook for you, then we'll go for round two." Heat rolls through me, thickening my cock even more when she locks her lust-crammed eyes with mine, then murmurs, "Deal?"

"Deal."

Her legs shake relentlessly when she raises her ass off the mattress to give me unlimited access to her sweet pussy. I take advantage of her leverage by replacing my fingers with my thumb and sliding the remaining fingers on my hand between the crevice of her backside. I expect her to flinch or dig the pad of her feet into my shoulder to push me away, so you can picture my shock when the grunts leaving her mouth turn wild.

"Do you want me to touch you here?" I ask while placing the smallest bit of pressure on her back entrance.

Her reply is choked by a moan, but even a deaf man wouldn't miss it. It is a resounding "Yes!"

"Has anyone ever touched you here?"

When Octavia answers me with a head shake, I yank my hand away so fast, my thumb slips from her vagina with an edge of cruelty.

"Jack..."

"Shh." I scan her bedroom, seeking something to keep her moaning my name the way she is without risking the chance of hurting her. "I need something to lube you up to lessen the friction. Your cum isn't enough. Trust me, it fucking hurts if you're not prepped right."

Fuck!

I freeze along with Octavia.

I hadn't meant to articulate my comment at all, much less out loud.

"I... ah... I thought you—"

I cut her off for the second time today, and once again, it is my mouth saving the day. I kiss her pussy as I did her mouth on my desk, suffocating the worries bubbling in her chest as effectively as it lightens the crippling weight on mine.

In a matter of seconds, her nails claw my head as she shakes through her fifth or so orgasm for the night. Growling, I lick up the remnants of her climax at a much slower and more leisured pace compared to how I brought her to orgasm.

Once her shudders have dulled to a quiver, I gather Octavia's spent body in my arms then head for the bathroom I spotted during our travels down the hallway. Since there are no other doors in Octavia's room bar the one I kicked closed upon entering, I assume a shared bathroom is the only one she has access to.

When a giggle sounds from below, I drop my eyes to Octavia. The last thing I was anticipating so soon after that shitshow was laughter.

Upon spotting my shock, Octavia mutters, "I was going to remind you that I have legs, so I am more than capable of walking." She licks her lips before cracking them into a smile. "But I held back when I realized how boneless you've made me feel. I don't think I could stand, let alone take steps."

My chest puffs out like a rooster.

Regretfully, it doesn't stay inflated for long. Calling Octavia's bathroom 'compact' is an understatement. It is the size of a broom closet, but instead of the vanity mirror keeping with the theme, it's stretched across one wall, making it almost impossible for me to enter the shower on the other side without exposing the marks on my back.

From how hard Octavia clawed at my head, I'm sure she could make the scars on my back seem less sinister after only one night, but since that would open a can of worms I'm not willing to dredge through right now, I keep the bathroom light switch off and my back angled away from the mirror.

"If you're hoping the dark will have me forgetting that I've yet to return the favor, you're shit out of luck, Mister. This…" as I switch on the shower faucet, Octavia stuffs her hand between us to grip my cock, "… is too impressive to let it deflate."

As my bewilderment grows, my eyes bounce between hers. I shouldn't be stiff. My cock should be deflating like someone letting the air out of a balloon. That's what usually happens, especially when memories of my past get away from me, but that isn't what occurs this time around. I'm hard—*still*—and the thought of Octavia on her knees, taking me between her plump lips has me throwing caution to the wind for the third time tonight.

"We should turn on the light," I mutter to myself when Octavia wiggles out of my hold and commences lowering herself onto her knees. "I want to see."

I blink to adjust my eyes to the blinding light in the bathroom when Octavia claps her hands together two times.

"Clap lights in this era?"

After raking her teeth over her lower lip, Octavia eventually locks her eyes with mine. It's a slow process because she stops to admire my washboard abs, smooth pecs, and the vein in my neck that won't quit thudding no matter how much my head promises my body that this will be a pleasurable experience instead of a painful one. "Dated apartments have their advantages… especially when you're too lazy to get out of bed to switch off a damn light."

When I throw my head back and laugh, the tension weighing heavily on my shoulders slackens, and a new, friskier want takes its place.

Steam is billowing around us, but the water feels icy cold when Octavia circles her hand around the base of my shaft to give it a gentle squeeze. "My mom always said my mouth would get me in trouble." Her smile has pre-cum pooling at the tip of my cock. "I think she was right."

My hands shoot out to balance on the tiles mere feet from me when she finalizes her sentence by drawing her lips over her teeth and guiding her mouth over the crown of my cock. She doesn't suck down hard or try to impress me by taking me to the very back of her throat. She merely swivels her tongue around my throbbing head before enticing more pre-cum by dragging her vibrating tongue along the underside of my cock.

"Do you like that?" she murmurs after bringing her lips back to the tip several long, teasing sucks later.

As my nails scratch at the tiles, desperate to grip something, I nod.

Speaking is above my abilities right now.

When she takes me into her mouth for the second time, her suck is a little firmer this time around, a sound I've never heard before leaves my throat. It is gruff and unhinged but also exposes both my therapist and urologist are full of shit.

At one stage, they had me questioning more than my sanity. My sexuality was right on the line with it. I couldn't maintain an erection no matter what method I tried. Super models and silver-screen starlets made my cock throb, but it never reached the thickness it is maintaining now.

I was diagnosed as impotent not long after my eighteenth birthday. I hadn't had a complete erection for years before that, and despite undertaking test after test after test to determine the cause of my malfunctioning manhood, every report returned the same result. Inconclusive.

I was convinced I'd die a virgin, so can you understand my somewhat manic desire to interact with Octavia even after hearing her accent that usually gives me the hives? My cock wasn't just twitching while roaming her gorgeous body. It was headbutting the zipper in my trousers, begging for the chance to live up to the playboy title I was undeserving of.

That's how I know whatever is happening between Octavia and me will be more than a one-night affair. I have years of missed opportunities to make up for and a beautiful woman capable of fixing the injustice. I'd be insane to throw away this opportunity.

It could be the head between my legs talking or an insatiable need I never thought I'd quench, but even if our connection costs me my livelihood, I'm willing to risk it.

Everything I've built was founded on a lie, so as long as it is stripped from me honorably, I can rebuild. The thickness of my cock as Octavia swivels her tongue around the rim is proof of this.

"Lick it again," I demand, my voice rough from the ecstasy clutching my throat.

"Like this?" Octavia stares straight at me while dragging her tongue from the crown of my cock to the base. When she reaches my balls sitting heavy against my thighs, she rubs her cheek over them, marking them with her scent before returning her lips to the tip.

"Again."

When she does as asked more urgently this time around, I drop one of my hands from the tiles and dig it through her glossy locks. She doesn't need any pointers. I'm on the verge of blowing my load down her throat, but the intensity of her sucks grows tenfold when I weave my fingers through her hair, so I keep my hand exactly where it is.

While jacking me off with one hand, she hollows her cheeks then draws me in deep. Arousal burns through me as I award her efforts with a spurt of pre-cum. She moans against my knob before her tongue flicks over the slit to gather up any leftovers.

"God," I grunt again, incapable of a better response. "Your mouth... your lips..." I pull on her hair harder as the tightening sensation low in my balls reaches fruition again. "I don't think I'll ever get enough."

As my hips rock forward and back, Octavia's pleasurable moans increase another decibel. She seems to get off on pleasing me, and the thought has cum racing to the crown of my cock, begging to be released.

"In or out?" When she doesn't answer me, I ask more roughly, "In or out? I can't fucking hold back a second longer."

Her nails digging into my ass to hold me in place should have me pulling back. It should have the contents in my stomach evacuating and my cock returning to hibernation, but the instant Octavia locks her eyes with mine to wordlessly grant me permission to come in her mouth, the nightmares of my past stay where they belong, and I release more than pent-up frustrations into her mouth.

I'm not usually a person who wakes up smiling, especially when it is Sunday and my body is aching, but today is different. My muscles aren't screaming because they were exhausted from running miles at Ravenna Park. They're sexually depleted and stupidly craving for a second round.

Last night was wild.

Actually, scrap that.

Yesterday as a whole was the equivalent of a dream.

Jack is a little hard for me to read—you don't need more proof of that than me stupidly believing he was a virgin even after he rocked my core to the next galaxy—but if you look past his sheltered eyes and somewhat concealed personality, we gel together like peanut butter and jelly.

He fucks, and he fucks well, yet he is still an attentive and nurturing lover. He made sure my needs were met long before his, and even when he exhausted them to the point of me passing out, he didn't become selfish.

I had barely finished swallowing the thick streams of cum pumping out of his cock when he returned the favor on the bathroom sink. Until the wee hours of this morning, we tested out almost every solid piece of furniture in my apartment, but instead of being grossed out like I was when Caleb did the same thing, I'm grinning like a loon.

You won't believe how good it feels to have years of sexual frustrations taken care of in one night. I feel like I could float to the bathroom. That's how lightweight I feel, and the airiness doubles when my stretch ends with my hand landing on the curves of a scrumptious ass.

Jack didn't sneak out while I was sleeping. His leg is peeking out the side of my sheets, and although his back is covered by the long sleeve olive shirt he purchased at the thrift store yesterday, the two dimples in his lower back are exposed along with a tiny portion of his glorious brief-covered backside.

If my bladder weren't screaming at me, I'd see if Jack was planning to hold true to his promise of this being more than a one-night affair, but since it won't hold for another marathon romp, I slip out of the bed and pad toward the closed door.

Caleb must have come home at some stage last night because he's the only one who closes my door.

I discover that to be the case a second after I flush the toilet. His shoulder is propped against the doorframe of his room, and his bare feet are crossed in front of him. After drinking in my flushed cheeks, wide eyes, and mussed hair, he angles his head to the side and cocks a mousy brown brow. "I thought the bathroom was a no-go?"

"It is," I answer while pushing off my feet.

"Then why did it reek of raunchy sex this morning?"

I take a moment to ponder. I don't keep anything from Caleb, so that's not the cause of my delay. It is the fact he's admitting he didn't come home until this morning that has me needing a moment.

"You first," he gabbers out when he spots the inquisitiveness brewing in my eyes. "From what Jess told me last night, you had some pompous event to attend with stiffs in suits yesterday, yet here you are, looking like you hit the jackpot only hours later."

I can't hide my smile, so I set it free. "I did have a pompous event to attend... but not everyone there was a stiff in a suit."

"It wasn't Roach from advertising, was it?"

I gag. "No. He's called Roach for a reason." I poke him in the midsection with my index finger. "And when have your dates with Jess been an overnight affair? You usually have her tucked in bed by ten o'clock."

My hope that they've sorted their shit out sails into abyss when Caleb's back molars grind together. "Don't even go there, Tivy. That's *not* a conversation we're going to have this week much less after realizing there's a partially naked man in your room."

My eyes rocket in the direction he's looking so fast I make myself dizzy. More than a tiny portion of Jack's backside is now peeking out of the sheets, and it sets my pulse racing.

Caleb chuckles under his breath when he spots my bug-eyed expression before he saunters back to his bed for a little more shut-eye. "Keep your theatrics out of the bathroom. Every other piece of furniture is up for negotiation, but not the one place we're meant to get clean of controversy."

"If it helps you sleep any better, we didn't have sex in there," I murmur, my voice only just loud enough for him to hear.

"Not helping me have a restful slumber, Tivy."

I smile so brightly, the sun beaming through the curtains in Caleb's room bounces off my teeth when I close his door and enter the one across from it. I grimace more than I smile when my entrance to my room reminds me of how messy it is. I got in somewhat of a tizzy when I realized I didn't have anything suitable to wear to yesterday's event. My work clothes aren't appropriate for private parties, and the dresses and shoes I usually wear out clubbing seemed a little too risqué.

When you're meeting your new boss outside of work for the

first time, the last thing you want to do is leave a bad taste in his mouth.

The same can be said for bringing home a date for the first time, Tivy.

Confident I can clean up the mess before Jack wakes, I set to work on returning my unworn clothes to the freestanding closet and set of drawers.

I have most items packed away when I spot Jack's trousers on the foot of my bed. They're the same trousers he wore when poo whipped around us like confetti, and when I gather them in my arms, it dawns on me why he didn't switch them out. Not only is a reputable designer's name woven in the stitchwork, but they're also free of 'secretions.'

Not a single brown dot can be found.

Just as I hang Jack's pants over the chair of the vanity desk, where I apply my makeup in front of each morning, a vibration darts up my arm. The ringtone is barely audible since it's muffled by two layers of expensive material but loud enough for Jack to stir.

Happy for him to continue sleeping until I've finished tidying up, I snatch his cell phone out of his pocket, then search for the silent switch. His phone is a little different than I'm used to. It is a flip phone, but it isn't outdated and old like the ones my parents used when they started dating. It has a sleek compressed glass appearance, and when it's folded out, it is larger than the most current iPhone.

When I fail to locate the silence button, I hit the mute button on the screen before snapping his phone in half. I almost place it back into his pocket, but two messages popping up on the main screen stop me in my tracks. One states he missed a call from Elaine, but it is the second one I pay the most attention to. It is advising Jack of a scheduled meeting Monday afternoon.

Usually, confirmation of a business meeting wouldn't make my skin clammy and my pulse dull. I handle them numerous times throughout the day in my position as Mr. Pott's assistant. However, this is different. The name of the attendee is extremely familiar, and it has my chipper mood circling the drain even faster than my race into Caleb's room.

"Where are those documents? The ones I begged you to place into storage."

Caleb peers up at me with wide, sleepy eyes. "What?"

"The documents! The ones you should have destroyed. Where are they?"

He scrubs the sleep from his drooping eyes while asking, "The depositions?"

I nod so fast, a salty blob trickles down my cheek. "Yes. Where are they?"

"In the broom closet next to the bathroom. Why?"

I'm out the door before the concern in his voice registers.

Half of the contents in the box that exposes every single one of my family's secrets fall to the floor when I yank out the water-damaged box with more force than required. After pulling a shirt over his heaving frame, Caleb gathers the hundreds of sheets of paper from the floor while I sort through the remaining stack still in some sort of order.

I don't know what I'm looking for. I just know it could be in this box.

Caleb dumps a stack of papers next to the ones I'm rummaging through before asking, "What are you looking for? No good will come from looking at this shit—" He eats his words when I thrust the screen of Jack's phone into his face. After cursing under his breath, he mutters, "Do we have a name to work off or…"

He sounds as dirty as I feel when I answer, "Jack. He intro-duced himself as Jack." My breaths rattle my ribcage when I confess, "I don't know his last name. I don't even know if that's his real name. God, Caleb, what if—"

"Calm down," he suggests when a near panic attack steals

my words. "It could mean anything. It doesn't necessarily mean what you think it does."

"He has phobias about touch, Caleb." Tears fling off my cheeks when I mutter, "He didn't want me to touch him."

With his curse word hidden by a grunt, he pulls out a chair from under our four-seater dining table, spins it, then straddles it backward. Only three years ago, we promised to never peruse the documents again. They caused a ton of pain without a solution to lessen the hurt, so we figured it was best to act as if they didn't exist.

We can't do that today.

Only a heartless person could do that today.

Several painful minutes later, Caleb mutters, "I'm not seeing anything. I can't see anything that resembles a Jack. I don't think he's in here." As the confidence in his deep voice falters, his index finger stops gliding down the printed court transcripts to snatch up a slip of tattered paper to its left. "Shit..."

"What?" I yank the paper out from beneath him so fast it rips. Tears burn my eyes when they roam over a name scribbled on a piece of paper that could correspond with anything. Jackson. His surname only shows the first initial, a 'C,' but the rest has been doctored from the evidence. It appears to be a short name, only half the size of his first name.

"It might not be him," Caleb suggests, drawing me from my dark thoughts. "And that could mean anything. It's a scrap of paper, not actual evidence."

"But it also *could* be him. I often introduce myself as Tivy, so who's to say Jackson wouldn't do the same."

He grips my arms when my sways reach a point of being unsafe. "Stop. Breathe. And evaluate. You know the steps, Tivy. Use them."

While staring into his eyes that are almost identical to mine, I suck in a deep breath before slowly exhaling it. My panic could be for nothing. I could be searching for the negatives since I'm more a pessimist than an optimist, but before my heart can convince my brain of this, I lose the ability to maintain rational thoughts when it dawns on me that Caleb and I aren't the only two people in our kitchen.

Jack is awake.

"Jack... ah... good morning."

I move to stand in front of the stacks of paperwork I don't want any man to see much less one I had an immediate fascination for.

When Jack looks set to swoop down and kiss my temple in greeting, I yank Caleb to my side then blurt out. "Jack, this is my husband... Stefon." Caleb glares at me with the same disgruntled expression Jack is hitting me with. "I was just telling him how you had a little bit too much to drink at our work function yesterday and that no one would give you a ride home so I offered for you to sleep in our spare room."

Caleb's squinted eyes snap to mine. "Spare room? What spare room?"

I stomp on his foot, switching his whisper to a whimper before his words can reach Jack's ears, then say, "Stefon was away on business. He... ah... left early to surprise me. Didn't you, Stefon?"

Caleb looks sick when I cozy up to his side, but he plays the role of a devoted spouse well. "Of course. Anything for my little snookums."

After clearing the devastation from my face, I devote my focus back to Jack. I shouldn't have bothered settling my emotions because they surge to a never before reached level when I spot the anger projecting from him, but I play it cool as I've been taught. "So, I guess now that you're feeling better, you'll probably want to get going."

Not giving him the chance to recant my statement, I shove his cell phone into his chest then pivot him to face the door.

"I—"

"No thanks necessary, Jack. What are friends for if not to sleep off a drunken haze?"

He shrugs me off him. It hurts even more than the pain in his eyes when he spins back around to face me. "I wasn't offering you my thanks. I was going to ask if you could collect my wallet from the bedside table."

When an interrogative bomb detonates in his eyes as he peers at Caleb over my shoulder, I suggest, "Why don't you go grab it since you know where you placed it." I shove him toward the hallway. "It will be safer this way."

My comment is more for Caleb than Jack. Jack looks ready to tear him a new asshole, and I'm about ready to join him when Caleb pins me in place with a rueful glare a second after Jack storms down the corridor.

"You're an idiot, Tivy."

I snatch up the paperwork from the dining room table and stuff it into the moldy box while replying, "Says the guy treating the love of his life as if she's nothing more than a friend."

That gets his back up. "Don't bring Jess into this."

"How do you know I was talking about Jess? I could have been referring to anyone."

He rams a bundle of paperwork into the box with so much force, there's no chance in hell it will make the trip from the dining table to the broom closet intact before he pulls it in close to his chest. "Fix this, Tivy."

My big exhale blows my sex-rumpled hair out of my face when I reply, "And how am I meant to do that?"

"I don't know," Caleb confesses, shocking me. He never admits he doesn't know anything, even when he's swimming in waters way out of his depth. "But I do know that this isn't right."

He nudges his head to Jack, who's walking down the corridor, looking indecisive. I don't know whether he's torn on leaving or calling me out as the liar I am, but mercifully, he saves me from discovering the truth by dipping his chin and exiting without so much of a backward glance.

After taking a moment to breathe through the pain crippling me, I shift on my feet to face Caleb. He takes a second jab at my ego when I attempt to remove the box from his grasp. "Nu-uh. This is going in the dumpster where it belongs."

Although that is what I wanted him to do with it all along, I can't help but reply, "You can't leave *that* in a dumpster. What if someone finds it?"

"Oh, don't worry," Caleb mutters under his breath as he stomps back to his room. "It will be well lit before *and* after I've seconded it to hell along with our grandfather."

He slams his bedroom door shut so forcefully my feet jump into action before my head knows I'm moving. I naturally gravitate toward my room. It is my sanction, my private abode, the one place I've always felt safe, and it is the sole reason I don't usually invite anyone back to my place.

Jack was different, though. He was unique, and if I need any more proof of that, I get it when I notice a note propped against the lamp on my bedside table.

It's from Jack, and it reads:

*You have until 9 AM tomorrow to
come up with an excuse as to why you lied to me today.
If I believe your intentions were good, I'll let
this go. But if I don't, we're not over.*

Jack C.

His note excites me... until I spot the C at the end of his signature.

E laine's eyes pop up from her MacBook when I enter the hotel suite she initially booked for a three-night stay. She looks well presented. I, on the other hand, appear as if I slept in the gutter. My outfit is from a thrift store, and my trousers reek of the exhaust fumes of the cab I took back to my hotel. Even though it's Sunday afternoon, traffic is gridlocked.

"Mr.—"

I cut Elaine off by slicing my hand through the air. I need a shower and a second to wrap my head around Octavia's lie before I can face whatever battle Elaine is about to present.

Running multiple million-dollar entities isn't a walk in the park. I'm on call twenty-four-seven, and usually, I don't take a day off unless it is for something dire.

Yesterday was dire.

Octavia… *God*. She had me acting as if I'm not juggling a dozen balls at once, so if I don't take a moment to evaluate, I'll be sure to drop one.

"Have Morris attend the meeting tomorrow on my behalf. He knows the figures and upcoming projects. If he has any issues, he can contact me here." Elaine nods before snatching up her digital notepad to jot down the rest of my demands. They rarely stop at one. "Also, have our stay extended." I pause to consider how fast I'm jumping into things with Octavia. My assessment is nowhere long enough for me to believe the lie she told this morning. "Stretch it until the end of the month. If it goes longer than that, we will re-evaluate. I'll also need a town car here tomorrow morning no later than seven."

Hotel prices in Seattle are high, so purchasing a property may be more economical. I have money to burn, but I'd rather use it more resourcefully.

I freeze partway to the bathroom when a final demand pops into my head. My pivot is too quick for Elaine to wipe the shock from her face, but I act ignorant. "See if Dr. Avery is available for a phone consultation. I'd prefer for it to be today, but if she can't fit me in until tomorrow, that will suffice."

Dr. Avery is a shrink, and although I've never been a fan of them, she was the first woman in a long time I could talk to without clamming up.

Octavia was the second.

As Elaine gathers her cell phone to call a number she's not dialed in months, I enter the master suite before veering for the attached bathroom. I shred my clothes as I go, my disappointment growing when I notice the thickness still throbbing between my legs. I don't know why I'm frustrated. This is exactly what I've wanted for years. I think it is more to do with the fact the woman I planned to exert years of pent-up frustrations out on wants to play chase instead, not the thought of my dick never deflating.

Under normal circumstances, the grenade Octavia threw out first would have had me immediately backtracking. I have no interest in mowing another man's lawn, but her deflect won't work this time around. I know the man she introduced as her husband isn't her husband. For one, he had far too many similarities to Octavia for anyone to feel comfortable about their pairing. And two, they had no spark whatsoever.

Don't get me wrong. They had an undeniable connection, but it wasn't the same spark that fed the connection between Octavia and me the past twenty-four hours.

Ours took hours of sex to smother, and even then, it only lowered the flame to a simmer instead of completely extinguishing it.

Lucky, because when I catch sight of the scars on my back in the bathroom mirror, my cock finally gets the memo that it isn't meant to maintain an erection twenty-four-seven. Visual reminders of a fucked-up childhood are enough to bring any man down from a high.

Dr. Avery has claimed for years that my 'issues' downstairs don't stem from a medical misdiagnosis. Now, I'm starting to believe her. But it has nothing to do with missed opportunities or clashing schedules. It's solely based on the woman who stopped me in my tracks more than once.

That's why I won't give up.

Come hell or highwater, Octavia *will* be mine.

I'm aware of the steps to ensure that happens. I just got one matter to take care of first.

The thickness between my legs with memories of my night with Octavia reinflated faster than my past tried to snuff it out.

"D on't." I give more oomph to my clipped command by pinning Caleb in place with a stern finger point. "I don't have time for a lecture. I'm already late."

"You wouldn't be late if you didn't spend half your night tossing and turning." When my rummage through the entryway table doesn't locate my keys, he grabs them out of the junk bowl on the dining room table and tosses them into my chest. "Unless being late is the point?"

After stuffing my house key into my pocket and snatching up my purse from the dining table, I spin to face him. "Why would I want to be purposely late? I'm already on my last legs, and newsflash, I'm the only one paying our rent at the moment."

"Hey, that's not fair. You told me to quit." He's right. I did tell him to quit. No one deserves to be abused twelve hours of the day by a man who thinks the title of 'manager' gives him the right to belittle his staff, but I had no clue that it would take him more than a couple of days to find another job. Caleb can do pretty much anything, but ever since COVID-19 hit, there's been thousands of applicants for every employment opportunity.

"I'm sorry. I am being a…"

"Bitch?" Caleb fills in when words allude me. There's no malice in his tone. No anger. Because he isn't being mean. He is simply being honest. "It's okay to have a bad day. Hell, it's okay to have a few bad weeks, but I still think there's more to your sleep-in than you're letting on. The last time you slept past your alarm was the day you asked me to move to Seattle with you."

Once again, he's right. There is more to my dillydallying than I'm letting on. I convinced myself multiple times last night that I don't want Jack to make true on his threat, but I'd be a liar if I said I didn't watch the clock for every second that passed when it hit nine o'clock.

"Did you want a ride to work?" Caleb asks when I tug on my running shoes so my daily walk will be cut in half.

I shake my head. "No, that's fine. I've got plenty of energy to exert before a nine-hour stint at snooze-palooza." I give him a small smile, both remorseful for my words and desperate to know he isn't mad at me before we spend the day apart.

When he returns my grin with a cheeky wink, I practically skip to the door. "Good luck with your interview today," I singsong as I gallop through the front door of our apartment. "I'm sure you'll ace it."

His reply is gobbled up by the door slamming shut and my runners hitting the concrete stairs at the speed of a freight train. Usually, I leisurely walk to work while taking in the scenery. Today, it will seem as if I am competing in a mini-marathon. At this time of the year, the footpaths are forever overloaded with tourists, so I'd hate to think how bad the ferry will be.

The walk from my apartment building to the ferry terminal usually takes around thirty-five minutes, but today, I shave ten minutes off the time.

"Good morning, Merrick."

Merrick tugs a raincoat over his WSDOT uniform as untrusting of the clouds on the horizon as me before he spins to greet me with a smile. "Good morning, Tivy. You're late this morning."

"I know. I had a rather *interesting* weekend."

What? Merrick is older than my grandfather. I can't give him all the juicy details like Jess demanded yesterday afternoon. Furthermore, wouldn't that be the equivalent of rubbing salt into my wounds? I kicked Jack out, but I wasn't spared from the carnage. My ego was as severely wounded as his.

When thunder claps above our heads, Merrick raises his to the sky. "Looks a little nasty this morning."

"Is it ever not nasty?" I thought New York's weather was bipolar, but it has nothing on Seattle. Their idea of a heatwave is seventy-five. I find that a little chilly. "Lucky I remembered my umbrella." I wiggle the flimsy four-dollar thrift shop purchase I gathered from the foyer of my building before waving my pass across the terminal and entering the platoon area. "See you tomorrow, Merrick."

He mutters a goodbye under his breath before closing the gate separating us and giving the captain the all-clear to go. The ferry is mostly covered, but with my mind on an obvious blink, I move to the bow of the boat to take in a sight I'll never grow weary of witnessing.

The Seattle skyline is mesmerizing. I only saw it in photographs before moving here. I wouldn't say shifting to the other side of the country on a whim was the best decision I've ever made, but it certainly has its advantages.

A handful of children eager to race to the Seattle Great Wheel dart past me when the ferry arrives downtown. The glee on their faces has me envious they're on holiday, and I'm not. Not even the rain has dampened their eagerness. It isn't surprising. When you're on vacation, nothing matters.

I can't recall the last time I went on vacation. It was before my family's entire existence was upended, and we didn't have to count pennies to pay for luxuries.

I want to say I miss those days, but in all honesty, I don't. Greed is a terrible thing, and it truly does prove that money cannot buy happiness.

With my mind focused on my past, I lower my umbrella, then push through the revolving doors of a downtown office building without registering that someone is partway through their rotation.

"I'm so sorry," I blubber out when my shove slingshots the traveler out the other side. "I was deep in my thoughts." My words quiver at the end when the man lifts his head a second after correcting his slanted tie. "Jack..."

I've got no more words.

Not a single one.

Except perhaps...

"What are you doing here? You can't come here. This is my place of employment. I could be terminated if you cause a ruckus." Although remorseful for the way I kicked him out, I wasn't lying this morning when I said I'm paying both Caleb's and my share of the rent. I can't lose my job. We will be homeless in a week if that happens.

Jack's shy grin doubles the already brisk speed of my heart. "There's no chance of that happening," he mutters more to himself than me before he places his hand on my elbow and guides me to a bank of elevators. "And I also don't believe you're sorry." He peers at me through a dark strand of wet hair flopped in front of his right eye. "Well, not for the shove anyway. Last night, though—"

"Floor! What... ah... floor are you visiting today?" I bark out, needing to veer our conversation away from an incident I may never be ready to discuss.

Jack pushes the button for level seventeen before he cages me between him and the glass elevator wall.

"Jack..." I murmur, familiar with the gleam in his eyes even after only witnessing it a handful of times in an embarrassingly quick fifteen hours.

"Shh…" His reply makes me sticky, and it has nothing to do with the humidity of a rainy summer morning. "These elevators are monitored, and I want to keep this between us."

I nod. Don't ask me why. I just do.

He appears pleased by my agreeing gesture, but his stamp of approval gets smudged only seconds later.

"Why did you lie?"

"I didn't—"

He pushes his index finger to my lips, making not just our conversation extra stuffy but the elevator car as well. "Why did you lie?" he repeats, slower this time.

"I… ah…" I stop, certain we can't have this conversation while others are listening in. "Umm…"

Jack frees me from making a fool of myself by snatching the baton out of my hand. "Is it because I was… did I not…" As my eyes bounce between his, confused by the embarrassment choking his muttered words, he asks, "Did I not please you properly?" My deviant mind begs for him to start proceedings now when he presses his lips to the shell of my ear and murmurs, "I can learn. You can teach me what you like."

He inches back to peer into my eyes when I reply, "You don't need classes, Jack. You exceeded all my expectations and then some. I've never been more satisfied."

Relief passes through his dark eyes a mere second before confusion returns. "Then why did you lie?"

"Because—"

Jack doesn't interrupt me this time around. The ding of the elevator arriving at my floor does.

When I glance out at the bustling hive of activity waiting for me, I say, "We can't talk about this now."

"This afternoon then."

"Jack—"

He squashes his finger to my lips once more before moving

in so close if anyone is lingering outside the elevator, waiting to enter, they wouldn't realize there are two people inside. "This afternoon. I'll drive you home so you won't get wet in another downpour."

I look at him like he's bonkers. "What downpour? The rain has already burned off."

I curse karma to hell when fat droplets roll down the exposed wall of the elevator. It's tinted so no one outside the building can see me pushed up against the wall by a man in an impeccably tailored suit, but the glass does little to douse the heat that roars through me when Jack mutters, "Or perhaps I should say, then I won't get saturated following you home." He runs his fingers through his drenched hair, making mine green with envy. "Not all of us were smart enough to collect an umbrella this morning."

With a smirk that exposes he loves my gaped mouth and wide eyes, he drops his arms from the wall, then steps to the side, exposing me to the frenzied hub of my office.

Jess spots me first. "Tivy! Thank God."

In a flurry, she whizzes me out of the elevator and into the thick of it. Upper management is darting in all directions, their assistants are following them like lost puppies, and the thick stench of awkwardness is depriving the air of oxygen.

"What's going on?" I dump my purse onto my desk, then pivot to drink in the circus. "It isn't another lawsuit, is it?" My eyes stray to the idling elevator during my last sentence. It's as empty as my chest cavity feels since my heart is sitting in my stomach. My body shouldn't crave Jack as much as it does, but no matter how hard my head warns me to tread cautiously, all I want to do is race back into the elevator so he can squash me against the glass once more.

When my eyes return to Jess, she shakes her head. "Mr. Potts and everyone in human resources were fired this morning."

"What?" My eyes bulge, shell-shocked.

"Yep." The 'p' pops from her mouth. "And that isn't the half of it. Rumors are the new owner has scheduled meetings with upper management. No one is safe."

"Especially me." As I look at the door my boss once sat behind, my stomach gurgles. "I can't be Mr. Potts's assistant if there's no Mr. Potts."

Before Jess can reassure me my head isn't on the chopping block, my name is called by a familiar yet still unrecognizable voice.

"Elaine?" I murmur more to myself than her when her sprouts of blonde locks register as familiar. We only met for the quickest second, but her face is hard to forget. It is too cute to belong to a lady in her mid-sixties. "What are you doing here?"

She smiles at the unease in my voice before gesturing for me to enter Mr. Potts's office before her. "Being downgraded, from what I can tell."

My head rockets to the side when a scrumptious voice says, "You're not being downgraded." Jack smirks at my wide-eyed expression before he sinks low in Mr. Potts's big leather chair and shifts his amused gaze to Elaine. "You are merely being put to better use until we get everything in order." His eyes are back on me, and there's something more burning inside them than humor. "Elaine is the new HR Manager, and you are Head of Recruitment."

"What?" Words are above my caliber today. I can't get over the image of Jack sitting behind Mr. Potts's desk, let alone speak. "I know *nothing* about recruitment." I shift on my feet to face Elaine. "I can't do this job. I'm not qualified."

"I disagree." Jack stands from his chair then moseys around his desk. *His* desk. That should sound foreign coming out of my mouth, but for some reason, it doesn't. "You understand people. You have a knack for reading them, so I think you are perfect for this position."

"You're insane. I'm an assistant if that. And not a very good one." I snap my mouth shut, mortified I spoke my thoughts out loud. I need this job, and despite the excited patter of my heart that he thinks more highly of me than my last boss, I must keep a rational head. Caleb is more qualified than me, yet he hasn't had a job in months. "I can't do this, Jack. I appreciate the opportunity, but this *isn't* the position for me."

Jack joins Elaine and me on the other side of his desk. "If I prove otherwise, will you at least consider it?" Before I can answer him, he clicks his fingers two times, summoning Mr. Simone, Marketing Manager, into his office. "Elaine cleared out most of the riffraff this morning, but I still have a handful of employees for us to go through." He gestures his hand to Mr. Potts's big leather chair, silently gesturing for me to take a seat. "So how about we get proceedings under way?"

Either too stunned to think straight or secretly loving the chance to watch Jack in his element, I walk around the desk and slap my backside into Mr. Potts's chair. Rafael hides his shock well when he spots me sitting behind Mr. Potts's monstrosity of a desk. That may have more to do with the fact Jack introduces me as the Head of Recruitment than believing I've filled Mr. Potts's shoes.

"Thank you for agreeing to meet with me so soon. I understand it was short notice, but I'm sure you are aware that if we're going to save this sinking ship, we need to move quickly."

A buzz of electricity darts through me when Jack joins me on the other side of the desk. He pulls over a chair at the side, plonks his backside into it, then balances his elbows on the desk. He is a good two to three inches away from me, but from the way my body reacts, you'd swear I was sitting on his lap.

Our connection is staggering, and it seems to have grown tenfold since we spent the night together.

I expect Jack to jump into questions regarding the excessive marketing budget for a magazine that hasn't seen a readership close to target range in the past three years, so you can imagine my shock when he commences the interview in a direction I never anticipated. "I've heard a number of stories the past few days regarding the annual Christmas party held each year. Would you care to elaborate on them?"

"The Christmas party?" Rafael asks with his pointy nose screwed up in confusion. "Why would you want to know about the Christmas party?"

"I'm just curious, that's all." Jack slouches back in his chair. When his arm balances on the chair's sidearm, it brushes mine. His briefest touch ignites fireworks in the lower half of my stomach, but you'd swear he was clueless to the zap firing between us when he continues talking without the slightest bit of jitter to his words. "That and perhaps the fact half of the marketing budget this year was seconded to event planning." He makes a teepee with his index finger and thumb. "Considering the only event held the past twelve months was the annual Christmas party, I'm a little lost as to why so much of the marketing budget was filtered to an event that won't increase readership."

"Staff morale—"

"Is at an all-time low," Jack interrupts, his voice stern yet still controlled. "I guess that's understandable when you see the hobnobs at the top receiving excessive bonuses without doing any of the work entailed for said bonus."

"If you're implying—"

"I'm not implying anything. I am merely advising you what has happened." After tossing a manila folder to his side of the desk, Jack says, "One point five million for an event not even half the attendees bothered to turn up for. I can assure you if I were invited to an event that was billed at $10,000 a plate, you can guarantee I'd be there with bells on."

I choke on my spit. "Ten thousand dollars a plate?" Although I'm technically asking a question, I continue talking as if I am not. "I organized last year's event. My budget wasn't even close to $100 per guest, so whatever you're referencing can't be right."

When I snatch up the document from the desk, my temples pound against my skull. Everything Jack said is true. Tax records show they claimed $10,000 a head for a staff Christmas party each year. And what's even more concerning is the fact that my signature is on the bottom of the documents.

"This is forged. I never signed this document." When the guilt marring Rafael's expression barely overtakes his smugness, I realize I've been played for a fool. After shifting my eyes to Jack, gulping when I notice his inconspicuous watch, I ask, "Does my new position come with full perks, such as hiring and firing?" When he nods, I shift my gaze back to Rafael. "You're fired."

He scoffs and harps on before he dismisses my words as if they have no substance. "I've worked for this company for years."

"And now you will work somewhere else." The power exuding from Jack spurs on a wild and frantic desire deep inside me. It has me hungry for skin-on-skin friction, and my desires grow even more potent when he adds, "*If* Octavia gives you a favorable reference." When Rafael scoffs again, Jack holds his finger in the air. "Think wisely before you speak. Because from where I'm standing, you have no power whatsoever at the moment. The ball isn't even in your court, and Octavia is the only person wielding a racket."

Rafael considers his options for several painstaking seconds before he marches out of the office in defeat, grumbling under his breath on the way. As several eyes lock with mine, I shift mine to Jack. He looks very much the part of a powerful magnate with impeccably styled hair and a designer suit out of most men's range. He is in his element, and it is in this moment that I realize who he is.

"You're Jack Carson, a media mogul worth tens of millions of dollars." I shake my head in shock before I continue quoting something I heard a radio host announce this morning, "Seattle's newest Hotshot Boss."

I didn't put two and two together until now. When all the pieces of the puzzle are slotted together, the disclosure of his identity makes sense, but when he introduces himself as Jack and instigates a fun, carefree day, I was missing more than a handful of pieces to his complex jigsaw.

"Why are you here? What interest do you have in this little old magazine?"

A gleam in his eyes answers my questions on his behalf.

He isn't here for the magazine.

He is here for me.

Although flattered, I'm still shocked. "What were your intentions before we met?" The Jack Carson I've read about in the media doesn't buy sinking ships to keep them afloat. He prefers admiring them from the ocean floor. The reason his companies do so well is because he wipes out the competition, then he offers the readers and viewers left floundering something better, newer, and fresher. "Jess was right. You were planning to close us down."

"Not necessarily—"

I press my finger to his lip, stopping his lies before he can spill them. I'm meant to be mad or at the very least upset at my potential unemployment, but within a second of my skin touching Jack's, I've forgotten the reason I'm meant to be mad.

With every second that ticks by, our connection grows, deepens, and becomes so overwhelming I not only forget that he's my boss, but I also overlook all the horrible reasons we most likely can't be together.

"Why?" I murmur more to myself than Jack.

Why me?

Why him?

Why us?

And last but not at all least, *why does this have to be so fucking hard?*

Before Jack can answer the stream of questions pumping out of me, we're interrupted. "Are we ready for candidate number two?" Elaine asks with a soft note of amusement in her tone.

I understand her amusement. Jack and I are staring at each other, and the connection our locked gazes hold is intensively searing, even a nun couldn't miss it.

"Yes," Jack replies after briefly dragging the tip of his pinky across the inflamed skin on my wrist. It is the briefest touch, but it is detrimental to my sanity.

Mercifully, Mr. Kell's arrival in Jack's office takes care of any leftover buzz from his touch. He may not be skimming funds from the magazine, but his crimes are far worse.

I've never taken sexual harassment lightly, and it will become more perverse if it has any chance of negatively impacting the man sitting beside me.

"You like him." I choke on the ghastly thick coffee supplied in the office break room before spinning around to face Jess, my interrogator. "You said it was a one-night stand, but that isn't what I'm seeing." She wiggles her finger in front of my face, acting oblivious to my expression from the scalding hot coffee scorching my throat on the way to my stomach. "It's a good look for you. You should wear it more often."

"I don't *like him* like him. I'm just in awe at the way he reads people. He read through Thomas's bullshit within thirty seconds of meeting him. It took you even longer than that." I bump her with my hip, smiling when my little knock sends her crashing into the kitchen cabinets. "I also appreciate that he's not going to shut us down. You know how badly I need this job."

"Oh... this is your I'm-so-grateful-to-be-employed face. My bad... I thought it was your please-fuck-me-until-my-legs-give-out face."

I put more oomph into my hip bump this time around. "Shut up. I don't have neither the I'm-so-grateful-to-be-employed nor please-fuck-me-until-my-legs-give-out face. Eat-me-until-your-hunger-is-sexually-sated, on the other hand, I'm reasonably sure I have one of them."

Jess giggles like a schoolgirl. It's a nice thing to hear after what she was subjected to in Jack's office. He didn't go hard on her, but with our ratio leaning more toward letting people go than keeping them on, even the most confident person would have been nervous.

Once Jess has rinsed her coffee cup in the sink and placed it on the drying rack, she shifts on her feet to face Jack. "I don't know how you can't feel it. There's a huge sturdy wall between us and multiple cubicles, yet I can still feel the heat radiating between you two. It's explosive."

I know what she's talking about. The bristling of energy between us has been intense for the past several hours, but you'd swear I'm the only one feeling it. The man I was wrestling with in the elevator this morning is not the man I've been sitting next to for the past three hours. It could be that Jack has his work hat on, but it feels more than that.

Perhaps I read too much into his pledge that whatever we were stepping toward would be more than a one-night thing. Maybe he wakes up in every one of his dates' beds the following morning because he isn't a runner. Or perhaps he's just being nice because he doesn't want a workplace harassment claim slapped on him the instant he takes over ownership of a new company.

I truly don't know. I am the most bewildered I've ever been.

"He's different," I eventually settle on. "And I like that about him. You don't often find a guy you feel comfortable around within a minute of meeting them." I sigh. "But this isn't something I should be doing. He's my boss..." *not to mention possibly many other things.*

"Who is insanely hot and hasn't been anything but a gentleman the entire day. I can't remember the last time I wasn't propositioned before lunch. The only reason that hasn't happened today is because of Jack." The smile she directs at Jack makes me a little jealous. "I think I'm going to like having him around." She locks her eyes with mine. "And I think you will too if you'd give him half a chance."

Stealing my chance to retort, she returns my hip bump before sauntering to her cubicle.

I've barely had the chance to summarize why her suggestion is bad for so many reasons when I'm joined in the break room by a man who exudes such power and wealth, I can't believe I didn't realize who he was earlier. I wasn't seeing Mr. Carson, media extraordinaire. I was seeing Jack, a Jerseyite expat who had a gleam in his eyes that revealed his heart was made out of gold despite the cruelties it may have faced in its short thirty years.

"Octavia..." The back of Jack's fingers brush my cheek before I register him calling my name. "Are you okay?"

"Uh-huh," I reply, a better response above me. I can't have his hands on me and maintain normal brain function. "I was just wondering how many more performance reviews we have left for today."

I peer at Jack in shock when he replies, "None. We're done for the day. The rest can wait." He scoops up the leftover lunch I was sharing with Jess from the break room table, pops on the lid, then places it back into the refrigerator. "But there is some-where I need us to be."

"Us?" My voice is way too high for my liking.

He jerks up his chin. "Yes, us." I like it just as much out of his mouth as I did mine. "Grab your coat. It is cool outside."

"Ah... I don't have a coat with me."

I eye him curiously when a jacket magically appears in his hand two seconds later. It is oddly similar-looking to the one I was eyeing at the thrift shop on Saturday, only this one is the right size. I wouldn't have left a merino wool coat on the hanger if it weren't two sizes too small.

"Where did you purchase this?"

He suggests I turn around before replying, "Elaine secured it from a supplier in Los Angeles. It was shipped this morning."

I freeze, shocked as hell. "You bought me a coat?"

"No," he corrects. "A supplier gifted it to you with the hope you'll be photographed wearing it."

"Then they're shit out of luck, aren't they? I haven't been to the movies in months, much less an event that will have me photographed by someone of any importance."

Jack's plump lips tug into a smirk. "Then perhaps you can wear it to the gala this weekend?"

I bounce my eyes between his. "Gala? What gala?"

He finishes assisting me into my coat before disclosing, "The gala you are attending with me this weekend."

"That's a little presumptuous, wouldn't you say, Mr. Carson?" His surname tastes bitter in my mouth, but I pretend it doesn't. "You're meant to ask someone to attend the event with you. Not assume they'll be your plus one."

"Not when it is for charity." He fixes the collar on my jacket before lowering his eyes to mine. "This event raises funds for victims of abuse. The more people in attendance, the higher the reserve of each auction. It's a worthwhile cause I don't see anyone refusing an invitation to attend." He pulls a gilded invitation out of the breast pocket of his jacket and hands it to me. My name is etched across it in elaborate gold foil. "Unless you have something else in mind for this weekend"

I shake my head, my emotions too askew to pay attention to the crumbling of the wall around my heart. "I don't have any plans." *Nor a dress,* but I keep that snippet of information to myself. If he purchased a coat for me after only one appreciative glance, imagine what he will do if I inform him I don't own a single ballgown. "But to stave off rumors, perhaps I should meet you there?"

"No," Jack immediately disagrees. "My private life and my

business life are two completely separate entities. I'd like to keep it that way." A grin involuntarily tugs on my lips when he adds with a murmur, "Except perhaps when it comes to you."

With that, he places his hand on the curve of my back and guides me toward a waiting elevator. Either aware of his plans or knowledgeable about his indecisiveness, Elaine arrives in just enough time to hand me my purse and sunglasses from my desk.

I thank her with a smile. Jack uses words. "We shall meet with you later."

She bobs her chin with barely a second to spare. It only balanced on her chest once when the elevator door snaps shut, and I'm plastered against the wall by a suit-covered body and a man who smells divine. "You still haven't answered me." Jack peers down at me with stormy, temperamental eyes. "And the wondering has left me barely functional." He breathes in heavily, pushing his chest deeper into mine. "I've never had urges like this, Octavia. You've got my head in a spin. I've been hard all day." His words set my body on fire. I'm hot all over, almost feverish. "Tell me you feel the same way? Tell me I'm not going insane?"

"You're not going insane," I answer before my brain can talk me out of it. It's mush from his closeness. Nothing but goop. "But I may very well be if you don't touch me."

His eyes stray to the camera in the corner of the elevator before they rocket back to mine. "Not here. I can't touch you here. Why do you think I've been restraining myself all day?"

"Because you decided one night was all you needed?"

The mad throb in the lower half of my body doubles when Jack throws his head back and laughs. He thinks I am being funny. I'm not. I am too horny to think up skits on the go. The carnal urges roaring through me right now are unlike anything I've experienced before. They're desperate and needy. Overwhelming. They have me on the verge of dropping to my knees and begging, and it appears as if I'm not the only one who's noticed that.

"Tivy..." Jack grumbles on a moan, his voice hardened by lust.

When he wedges his hand between my legs, my awareness of his closeness turns excruciatingly painful. His pupils are massively dilated, and his handsome face is mere inches from mine. He's a devastatingly attractive man, almost too beautiful to be so manly.

"This should tie you over until we get to the boutique." He squashes one of his palms to the glass wall behind me, caging me in further before his other hand skims over my panties.

The sharp breath he releases when he discovers how wet I am almost buckles my knees out from beneath me.

"Look at me, Octavia." His voice is hot and heavy on my neck, adding to the beads of sweat forming on my nape.

Arousal surges through me when our eyes lock and hold. There is so much want in his eyes. So much need. "Now keep them there," he demands before he slips my panties to the side and teasingly braces one of his fingers at my entrance. When I nod, too blinded by horniness to care about where we are, he inserts one finger inside me. "Christ," he bites out when the walls of my vagina clench around him. "You're so damn snug." The groan that delivers his words is the most erotic thing I've ever heard. "You need to be quick, Octavia. The ride from the seventeenth floor is never long."

If he delivers every word he speaks like he did the past two sentences, I will forever be on the cusp of orgasm. The way he growls my name already has me teetering, much less his urgency to have me anywhere he can get me.

"Yes." Jack moans into my neck when the rock of my hips matches the grinds of his finger.

He pumps in and out of me in a rhythm that steals my sanity even quicker than it fails to remind me that we're in an enclosed box with monitored surveillance, then his thumb gets in on the action. It circles my clit while his finger drives me to the edge of hysteria.

"Now, Tivy. You need to give it to me now."

As fireworks explode low in my stomach, I clench around him and moan his name. My orgasm is short yet captivating—a mesmerizing few seconds that have me wishing for a dozen more.

"Fuck," Jack curses when the endorphins wear off, and he realizes where we are.

He looks at the emergency stop button on the dashboard then back at me several times before the decision is taken out of his hands. Even if he wanted to force the elevator into an emergency stop, he can't. We've reached the lobby, and riders flood the elevator like it is the only one.

Jack's fingers feel damp when he curls them around my hand and guides me out of the elevator before we're forced to ride in the wrong direction. He weaves us past a group of bumbling security guards, through an even more people-dotted sidewalk, and into an awaiting car idling at the curb.

"Crystal Boutique on Pyke," Jack demands a second after assisting me into the back seat of an SUV with two security details inside and a driver.

I barely get the chance to cool the heat on my cheeks when the car comes to a stop outside a retail building on a leafy yet busy street. We're only a few blocks from headquarters. "You took a car to travel a few hundred feet?"

As he flings open his door, Jack replies, "It's chilly out. I don't want you catching a cold."

"In the wool coat you *gifted* me." I air quote gifted like I don't truly believe his recollection of events. He purchased me this coat, whether with money or a guarantee I'd be photographed in it, but he purchased it, nonetheless.

Jack smirks, his expression smug before he slides out of his town car and bobs down to offer me a hand. I won't lie. I am in love with his chivalry.

After handing our coats to the doorman, we enter a gold-embossed door being held open by a man in a crisp black suit before we're greeted by a woman whose voice is as pointy as her nose. "Good afternoon, Mr. Carson. What a pleasure to see you today." I roll my eyes when she swoops in to plant a kiss on the edge of his mouth before she drifts her eyes to me. They're nowhere near as friendly now, filled with bitterness. "And you must be Octavia. Pleasure." Her puckered lips barely touch my cheek before she whips around, slapping me in the face with the fake hair hanging from the top of her head to her tiny waist. "We've pulled a range of garments off the racks for your approval, but you're more than welcome to peruse them yourself."

"What about the special order I requested?" Jack asks while shadowing the saleswoman into a boutique that looks more empty than full. The dresses and garments are gorgeous but sparce, and I'll be surprised to discover if any of them come close to fitting my chest. Even eating nothing but celery sticks for a week won't help. You can't squeeze double Ds into outfits not designed with voluptuous women in mind. "Marsha also stated any alterations will be finalized by Friday. Is that correct?"

The light bulb in my head finally switches on. He's not attempting to buy me a new wardrobe that I'd decline even with their designer tags making me giddy with excitement. He's purchasing a dress for the gala he wants me to attend with him.

"A last-minute fitting isn't necessary. I have dresses at home."

When Jack pivots to face me, my heart patters. He looks content and peaceful, like spoiling me will make me as happy as I was in the elevator. "I know." He squeezes my hand, reminding me he's not once let go of it in the past several minutes. "But none of the colors match the tie I'm being forced to wear."

"Then we'll find you a new tie." I slant closer to him, loving the way my nearness flares his nostrils before muttering, "And exactly when did you snoop through my closet? Between fuck session one, two, or three?"

He drags his index finger down my screwed-up nose before replying, "It was after session four while I was struggling not to instigate exchange number five." He articulates his words without a hint of shame and loud enough for both the sales-woman to hear and the men shadowing his every move. "And although I'm not a fan of the peacock-blue coloring Elaine picked, the last time I went against her selection, I landed on the worst-dressed list at the Oscars. I'd rather avoid another misde-meanor than encourage it."

The man with the burnt orange hair chuckles under his breath before he spins away from us with a cough. His response makes it obvious Jack isn't lying, but it also has me curious as to their dynamic. He seems more influential to Jack than purely a security detail.

I'm about to tell Jack I'm not comfortable with him spending money on me, but his next lot of whispered words steal my thoughts as effectively as they speed my pulse. "And this way, I get the chance to correct the error I made on Saturday when I fled the changing room." His hand feels extra clammy from the heat that roars through our conjoined bodies when he whispers, "I look very much forward to undressing you, Ms. Henslee."

"Jack…"

I don't know if that's a needy please-fuck-me moan or we're-stepping-over-a-fine-line groan but whatever it is, it doubles the zap of electricity roaring through me when Jack winks about the husky deliverance of his name before he requests the sales-woman to take us to the private changing room.

"Holy moly," I mutter under my breath when my eyes are

inundated with silky gowns, glistening chandeliers, and a wall of mirrors that expose the shock on my face from every angle. "This changing room is bigger than my apartment."

Either miffed by my assumption or too snooty to hide her disdain, the saleslady scoffs before jiggling a bottle of champagne in her hand. "Krug, anyone?" Not waiting for an answer and oblivious to the excitement prickling my skin, she fills two glasses before attempting to hand one to me.

"Perhaps later," Jack mutters before veering me away from her. "We only have an hour until my next appointment. I plan to use the time wisely."

My drooped lips lift to a smile when he slowly walks us past the selection of dresses the saleswoman selected for me. They're gorgeous, and I'd be smitten to own any of them, but it's the way Jack drinks them in for merely a second before he stares at me long enough to imagine me in it that has my excitement growing.

"This one," he murmurs half a minute later while nudging his head at the exact dress I couldn't take my eyes off the instant we entered the elaborate space. "It's sexy and risqué but still tastefully refined." When his thumb rubs the vein throbbing overtime in my wrist, I realize he is matching the dress's persona to the woman standing next to him. "It is perfect."

After squeezing my hand for the second time, he releases it from his grip so he can move the dress from the rack to a hanger in front of the wall of mirrors. The way he strides across the room with such animalistic characteristics has the hunger inside me growing rampant.

My fascination with him didn't grow because I learned of his wealth and impeccable reputation. It is how he adapts himself to any situation. On Saturday, he was a carefree, laidback man who drank wine from a box and laughed when I told him he had lettuce stuck in his teeth.

Today, he is a refined media mogul with so much grace and

sophistication you'd swear he'd never use the word 'fuck' let alone during sheet-clenching sex in a rundown apartment with no working elevator.

He truly fascinates me. So much so, when he clears the room with an arrogant wave of his hand, I don't attempt to flee along with his security detail or the sales lady. I keep my feet rooted in place and my concerns in the back of my mind until there's no one in the rapidly-shrinking room but my hotshot boss and me.

The heat blooming on Octavia's milky white cheeks inflames even more when Fitz closes the door a second after he walks through it, leaving her defenseless to my charm. Although she looks impartial to staying, she won't flee because she knows I'm not a man who backs down without a fight. We tussled with men who thought their shit didn't stink the first half of today, and without fail, I came out on top.

I will with Octavia as well.

"Let me," I mutter when Octavia's hands move for the zipper in the skirt I've fantasized about shredding to pieces on more than one occasion today.

For how she attempted to end things at the beginning of the proceedings, today has been remarkably good. I had an early-morning counseling session with Dr. Avery, took advantage of the numerous mental snapshots I took of Octavia while she was sleeping to calm the throb between my legs this morning in the shower, and I've learned that although beautiful beyond comprehension, Octavia is also smart.

I only had to step in once during our meetings this morning, and that was more driven by my desire to protect Octavia than her needing my help, but she handled the rest of the arrogant, pompous men I tackle day in and day out without so much as a bead of sweat dotting her brow.

I won't lie. I fought temptation multiple times today. My hands itched to touch and fondle her during the brief interludes of our meetings, but the premise of our encounters kept my hands at my sides—for the most part.

The men Octavia fired today won't work again once I pass on their errant practices to fellow businessmen of my caliber, but neither will I if I don't practice what I preach.

Inside the walls of headquarters, Octavia is my employee.

All bets are off the instant we leave, though.

"Do you normally wear your hair down?" I ask while pulling away the glossy locks I'm disappointed no longer smell like me from her neck.

The faintest pink coloring hits her neck, and I'm hard in an instant. I love the way her body responds to my meekest touch as much as I love how uncontrollable mine is around her. Usually, I'd stand to greet my peers when they enter the room, but just the slightest scent of Octavia's perfume lingering from her skin had me too hard to do that.

I wasn't lying when I said she had my head in a tailspin.

I've barely had a cognitive thought all day.

"Not usually," Octavia eventually replies, her delayed response reminding me I asked a question. "I was running a little late this morning, so I didn't have time to pull it up."

Goosebumps follow the trek my finger makes when I glide it down her silky skin while lowering the zipper in her fitted shirt. "Was there something on your mind that made you late?" I lean close enough for my breath to bound off her skin before asking, "Or *someone*."

"Jack, we—"

"Shh," I interrupt. There aren't enough hours in the day to answer both the need in her voice and the concern, so I have to settle on one. "I've got you."

After pushing the stiff material off her shoulders, I lock my eyes on one of the many mirrors in front of her, desperate to view perfection for the second time this week.

When Octavia spots my hot and needy gaze, her shoulders naturally roll back and her chest thrusts forward. I breathe out of my nose to cool my skyrocketing body temperature when the buds of her nipples harden under my ardent watching. It is a stare I admire as much as I want to triumph.

"Now your skirt," I mutter more to myself than Octavia. "Do you remember if it is a side zipper or one at the back?"

I know her answer. I saw which direction her hand went when she commenced getting undressed. I am merely making sure she has no objection to me undressing her.

"It fastens at the side."

When her hand shoots to the zipper, I curl my hand over the top of hers, then lock eyes with her in the mirror. The intensity of the zap that roars through us is ridiculous, considering the only part of our bodies that is touching are our hands, but I'd be a two-faced liar if I tried to downplay it as merely the buzz of lust. It is something much more than that.

The rise and fall of Octavia's chest doubles when her skirt puddles at her feet. After carefully stepping out of the bunched material, she moves for the dress that's rich coloring starkly contrasts with her flawless skin. The tension is so great, her thighs wobble more from lust than her float-like strides.

She curses under her breath after taking in the price tag Ana promised would be removed from each garment before she unhooks it from its hanger and lowers the back zipper. Dr. Avery urged me to give Octavia space to grow within our fledging relationship, but I toss caution to the wind when the beading on the dress makes it difficult for Octavia to slip into it without stumbling.

After helping her guide the weighted garment up her curvy thighs and over her spectacular backside, we slide it past her midsection. When our eyes lock and hold for the quickest second as we both hold our breath on if it will mold to the generous curves on her chest or flatten them, she mutters, "I can't afford this dress. If it gets stuck, I can't afford to pay for it."

"I can—"

"No, Jack..." she forces out with a pained breath before correcting, "Mr. Carson. You cannot *legally* or *morally* purchase this dress for me."

Although I want to take her over my knee for formalizing a moment that shouldn't be formalized, I keep a calm, cool head—almost. "I wasn't offering to purchase it for you. I was going to offer you a staff discount. I own this boutique along with many other businesses along this stretch of the coastline."

"You own a clothing boutique?" Her tone is pitched with both shock and disbelief.

I'd love to wipe the riled expression off her face with my tongue, but I choose words instead. It is a hard feat. "Yes. Many of them." I fail to mention I only purchased this one yesterday purely with the hope of a retake of the scene I stumbled onto Saturday at the thrift shop. "Markup is ridiculous. Hence, couture dresses are being offered for fourteen dollars in thrift shops."

After taking a second to gauge the authenticity of my reply, Octavia exhales the breath she was holding in, lowering the swell of her chest by barely a smidge before saying, "You're a horrendous liar, Jack."

"No, I'm not," I deny before helping her slide the dress over her ample chest, grinning when the measurements I supplied Marsha last night showcase perfection. Octavia's dress fits her like a glove as will every other dress on the rack at our side because I had them all altered specifically for her. "But I'm considering giving it a whirl if it will have you willing to leave this dress dumped on the floor of your bedroom. You look hideous, Tivy. Completely and utterly disgusting."

Snippets of my mother's Hawaiian heritage ring true in my tone when I struggle to lie through the lust clutching my throat. Octavia looks so divine in the peacock-inspired dress, I'm suddenly envious of every man who may see her in it.

Only this morning, I considered attending the gala alone. Back then, my decision had nothing to do with jealousy and everything to do with exposing too much of myself too quickly to Octavia. I usually give space in abundance, especially when it comes to my personal life, but it took everything I had this morning not to step in and whiz Octavia away when the first droplet of rain falling from the sky landed on her cheek instead of her umbrella. I probably wouldn't have hesitated if Dr. Avery's cautions weren't still ringing in my ear.

She's afraid I'll scare Octavia off, and in all honesty, I'm worried the same.

I'm a difficult man to understand. However, this is the first time I want someone to see me instead of the man behind the title.

"Oh... my... God," Octavia slowly breathes out when she catches sight of her reflection in the mirror. "Is this a trick mirror? That can't be me, surely." The dress floats over the polished floorboards of the changing room when she steps closer to the bank of mirrors. "I feel..." she takes a moment to configure a response, and I approve of the delay when she mutters, "... worthy."

That's why I've worked sunup to sundown since the age of nineteen. Until Saturday, I hadn't had a single day off in all that time because I wanted to prove I was more than the man people saw when they looked at me.

I am more than a man forged from carnage.

I am worthy.

After taking a couple of moments to settle the flutter of her pulse, Octavia shifts on her feet to face me.

"Don't," I warn in a gravelly tone when numerous reasons as to why she can't accept my gift sit on the tip of her tongue. "Just like your coat, the benefits of you being seen in this dress will far outweigh production costs."

"Jack—"

"Octavia," I interrupt, my voice sterner than intended. "This isn't up for discussion. You work for a fashionista magazine. A clothing allowance should be a requirement not a stipulation." I whisper my next set of words, but Octavia's shocked expression announces she heard them. "Besides, it is too late. Payment for all these garments was transferred this morning."

Octavia whacks me in the stomach with her tiny fist before storming for the clothes left dumped on the floor as if they were worthless. "You can't do that. You can't spend thousands of dollars on someone you hardly know."

I almost correct her. The total was over one hundred thousand, but her beet-red cheeks stop me.

Once she's peeled out of the dress I plan to fuck her in, she slings her eyes to me. "I appreciate the offer, but I can't accept it."

"As I just said, it is too late."

"I don't care." She throws her hands in the air, wafting up more of her alluring scent. "Give them away, auction them at the gala, but I am *not* taking them home with me."

She gets dressed quicker than I undressed her before she hooks her purse under her arm, plops on her sunglasses like it will hide the amount of moisture brimming in her eyes, then attempts to storm out of the dressing room.

I say attempt because Fitz is standing in the way, blocking her exit with his wide frame.

I jerk up my chin, permitting him to move when he angles his head my way. I wish for not all my astuteness to vanish in Octavia's presence when she bypasses the doorman with her coat and my idling town car before she sprints down the hectic sidewalk.

CHAPTER 14
OCTAVIA

"Since when?" I interrupt when I overhear Gracie from Editorials telling Jess a generous clothing allowance is being added to our employment contracts.

Gracie purses her red-painted lips before she shrugs. "I just know it's more than enough to purchase that raunchy little number I've been eyeing at Maison's the past six months." Her eyes flare with lust. "Brayden will have a coronary." Brayden isn't her boyfriend, merely an uber rich Seattleite every single woman in Seattle wants to sink their claws into. "Anyway, spread the word. Mr. Carson wants to ensure all his team members are aware of the new benefits under his command, and he personally bequeathed that task to me."

I get both green with jealousy and red. "This is a directive from Ja... ah, Mr. Carson?"

"Uh-huh," Gracie murmurs with a head bob. "We had a lovely get-together shortly after lunch."

After straying my eyes from Mr. Pott's office that's sat empty since I fled Jack three hours ago, I bark out, "Where?"

Gracie stares at me in shock, but she hides her surprise in her tone while replying, "In my office. It was a very informal meeting—"

"Where he just happened to mention an extremely generous clothing allowance so you can purchase a *raunchy little number*." I air quote my last three words, my anger picking up. "Did he have any suggestions on what you could spend your allowance on while chatting in your office?"

"We weren't chatting—"

I continue talking as if she never spoke. "Or perhaps he planned that for a later date? Say at another location, such as one of the many boutiques he *supposedly* owns."

I have no clue why I'm angry. None whatsoever. But there's no denying it. My cheeks are red, my hands are balled, and I'm two seconds from marching to Elaine and telling her to shove my new position where the sun doesn't shine.

The only reason I don't is Jess's not-so-kind reminder that Jack isn't in the wrong here. "You fled from him, Tivy, so he's merely giving you the space you expressed you desperately wanted."

"I didn't run. I... I..."

I've got nothing.

I ran because I was scared.

I don't want to be bought. Tossing money at someone won't smooth volatile waters. Most of the time it makes matters worse. It most certainly did for my family.

Gracie attempts to suffocate my mood back to a manageable level with a ton of attitude. "I don't know what has your panties in a twist, Tivy, but you need to get over yourself. Mr. Carson has great concepts for this sinking disaster, and I, for one, am ready to follow him into the masses to achieve his vision."

Don't let her tone fool you. She means Jack's bedroom, not to the bible belt to beat the nonsense out of Seattle Socialites.

When Gracie storms off in a huff, Jess reminds me that anger is not a required emotion. "She would have been lining up for unemployment at nine this morning if you hadn't met Jack. He's only endeavoring to keep us afloat because of you, Tivy. Remember that before you chew him a new asshole for trying to be the nice guy." She rubs my arm, more to dig her nails into my skin than in comfort, but it is an arm rub, nonetheless. "The nice guy doesn't always have to come last... *except* in the bedroom." After a smile that's more pleading than menacing, she exits the break room and returns to her cubicle.

I nurse my half-empty coffee mug for a few more minutes before rinsing it and placing it on the drying rack. Although I'd love to call it a day, my tardiness this morning won't allow it, much less a position I'm not qualified to hold. I have dozens of employee contracts to go over and a bucketload of guilt for the way I reacted to Gracie's news she had a private one-on-one meeting with Jack.

In a way, my annoyance is understandable. Every meeting Jack and I held this morning was done together, then I went and screwed it up by acting like a lunatic with a nice-guy complex.

Ugh. Why is this so damn hard?

Almost four hours later, my attitude has somewhat improved, and I've gotten a ton of work done. I shouldn't have reacted to Jack the way I did at the boutique, but if you understood my family dynamic, you'd have a better understanding about my adversity of being bought, but since I'm being eyeballed by the very man I wrongly took my anger out on, I'll have to save that story for another day.

Jack is standing in the doorway of the conference room. His suit jacket has been removed, his tie is unknotted, and the top button of his dress shirt is undone. He looks delicious but as exhausted as me.

It has me wondering if the past couple of hours were as hard on him as they were me, but before I can ask, he says, "Are you ready?" His voice is not as rich and commanding as it was earlier.

I drop my pen onto a stack of papers. "For?"

He peers at me, puzzled for a couple of seconds before replying, "For me to drive you home. We organized it in the elevator this morning."

My heart whacks my ribs, but I play it cool. "I don't need—"

"Please let me do this, Octavia. Let me know you at least got home safe." He lowers his volume so dramatically I barely hear what he says next, "It may be the only way I'll get any sleep tonight."

The gut-wrenching torment in his voice has me rushing for the coat he gifted me before a single objection can fire through my head.

"Thank you," I murmur when he pulls the collar out from underneath the thick wool and tugs it up around my neck to keep me warm. The rain this morning brought on a cold front, and any Jersey girl would struggle to act nonchalantly to the brisk winds whipping off the coastline.

Our walk to the elevator is solemn, void of the electricity that usually zaps between us. After entering on the heels of Roach and Felicity, I move to the glass wall Jack had me pinned to earlier.

The slow descent of the elevator to the lobby is tortuous.

It felt super-fast only hours ago.

I offer Jack's security detail a tight grin when he meets us at the entry door with an umbrella. "Thank you, Fitz," Jack mutters when Fitz's dedication sees us entering the back of his town car without a drop of rain frizzing my hair. "We'll take it from here."

Not speaking another word, Jack closes the door with us on one side and Fitz on the other side, gestures for the driver to go, then raises the privacy partition between us and the back of the driver's head.

The silence is excruciating. It twists my chest with pain. I hardly know the man seated next to me, but I know him well enough to know when he's hurting.

"Is everything okay?" I query, no longer capable of ignoring the tension ridding the air of oxygen. "I didn't mean to upset you today. I just—"

"It wasn't anything you did, Octavia. It was presumptuous for me to assume you'd want anything from me." Since his tone is honest yet heartbreaking, I don't argue. I just wait patiently for the Mr. Carson shield he's been wearing most of the day to disappear and for Jack to arrive.

When that happens, his solemn mood makes sense. "I had a meeting this afternoon. An associate was meant to attend on my behalf, but his wife fell ill."

I suck in a sharp breath when it dawns on me that the reminder I saw on his phone Sunday morning was for this afternoon. If his meeting was with who I suspect, they're never pleasant.

My theory is proven when Jack stammers out, "They... ah... never go as planned." He scrubs at the back of his neck before a rare smile for this evening pops onto his face. It eases the turmoil but has me desperate to find a way to keep it on his face forever when he murmurs, "And since I wasn't in the right mind frame to discuss business, they tried to take advantage." Remorse floods his eyes when he locks them with mine. "I'm sorry if you were forced out of your comfort zone today. That was *not* my intention. I will *never* force you to do anything against your wishes—" He stops talking when I toss off my seat belt and bridge the small gap between us. "Tivy..."

"Shh," I murmur against his lips before dragging my tongue

across them. I can't take away his pain. I can't change it, but I sure as hell can help him forget it for an hour or two. "I've got you."

My worry that some of our spark dulled due to my theatrics today is tossed out the window when my kiss causes Jack to swell beneath me. He wasn't hard when I crawled onto his lap, but within a nanosecond of our lips locking, he's thick enough for me to grind against him without any hindrance.

Our kiss is hard and bruising, filled with both need and want. Jack's hand is in my hair, holding my mouth to his as the other fondles and explores the extra hot inches of my body.

"God, Octavia," he murmurs against my mouth, his breaths hot against my lips. "When you ran today, I thought I'd lost you... that I had lost this."

"No," I deny, my head shaking, almost causing tears to trickle down my cheeks. "I ran because I was scared." I brush his thumbs with my cheeks like they're as wet as mine before confessing, "I don't want to be bought. No one wants to be bought." I kiss him again to ensure he can't misunderstand my reply. I'm not blaming his actions today. I am blaming my grandfather. "But I shouldn't have run. Running doesn't fix anything."

My move to Seattle is proof of this.

As we kiss, the tension hanging thickly in the air dissipates, and a hungry, wanton need takes over. When I drag my tongue along the roof of his mouth, Jack growls before deepening our kiss. He strokes his tongue along mine before tasting every inch of my mouth.

I kiss him back just as hungrily, my skin dampening along with the crevice between my legs.

"Jack..."

He can't shush me this time since he's too busy peppering my neck with teasing kisses, but I don't need words to know he will fulfill my every want. The creeping of his hand between my legs is a sure-fire sign of this, not to mention the heaviness behind the zipper of his trousers.

The friction as I rock against him is amazing, and within seconds, the cab of his car is roasting, and I'm on the verge of begging.

Mercifully, Jack hears my pleas without them needing to leave my mouth. After dragging his sinful lips away from mine, he pushes a button on the console next to his seat. "Keep driving until I say otherwise."

If the driver responds, I don't hear a word he says. I'm too busy striving to lower the ringing of my pulse in my ears from Jack slipping his hand under my skirt to authenticate the dampness of my panties.

"Christ, Octavia. You're drenched."

His confession causes a second inundation of grinds, kisses, and moans. We make out like teens under the bleachers, rocking, licking, and moaning until I'm about to combust.

As I stroke his impressive cock through his trousers, he leans over to snag a condom out of a console wedged under the privacy partition. If the sorrow in his eyes that is swiftly being replaced with lust wasn't substantial, I'd excuse his surly attitude as a ruse for us to fool around in his town car. But since it is very much authentic, I yank my skirt to my waist, pull my panties to the side, then balance on my knees so he can tug his cock out of his trousers and roll down the latex protection.

The image of him prepping to get naughty stirs something deep inside me. It catapults my hunger to a new high and has me so desperate for skin-to-skin contact, I lower down on him before he has the chance to coat his crown with any of the slickness between my legs.

"Christ, Octavia. Slow down. I don't want to tear you."

The sting of his fingers when he attempts to hold me in place has me so desperate to be filled by him, I slip my knees out from beneath him and take him to the root.

"Fuck!" Jack roars before the blistering desire to fuck over-rides all sense of normality.

After raising his ass off the seat, he weaves one of his hands through my hair while the other grips the door handle. "God, Octavia," he mutters as his thigh muscles burn along with mine and sweat dots his brow. "If only I took us to be tested today instead of that stupid boutique, then a flimsy bit of latex wouldn't be between us, and I could feel how wet you are firsthand."

He drives into me deeper, making me moan with how exquisitely full I am.

"I'm clean," I confess between frantic thrusts. "I haven't been tested in months, but I haven't been with anyone either." Either shock or worry darts through his eyes when I ask, "Have you been with anyone since you were last tested?"

Strands of dark hair fall into his eyes when he eventually shakes his head. "I'm clean too. I just don't want you to take my word for it. Sometimes people need proof."

"Some may, but I don't." The air cracks and hisses with exquisite electricity when I rise far enough off his fat cock for it to be braced at the entrance of my pussy instead of ramming into my uterus. "Take it off."

"Are you sure, Tivy?" His revert to the shortening of my name assures me I am not being bedded by a media mogul. It's just Jack from Jersey.

"I'm sure."

He snaps off his condom so quickly, I have no clue how he doesn't soften when the rubber rim cracks against the angrily stretched skin before he parts the folds of my pussy with his cock's head and slowly notches back inside.

"Christ. Fuck. Shit," he bites out in a slow, tormented groan when my heat wraps around him for the first time with nothing between us. "You're so tight but so goddamn wet." He pushes in a little further before sinking his backside low into his seat.

"You're going to need to guide me, Octavia. I don't want to hurt you."

The absolute assuredness in his tone makes me wetter, and I slide down his girth without too much hindrance. "That's it," he mutters once he releases his back molars from grinding against each other. "Nice and slow."

Euphoria pumps through me when I take him almost to the root. He sheathed me like this only moments ago, but it's different now because he's even thicker than he was seconds ago.

Lust roars through me when I realize that he's the only man I've allowed inside me without protection. Even being on the pill since I was fourteen, I choose caution over lust every time. I just can't seem to do that with Jack. What started as a means to ease his turmoil has turned into something much more than that. Something much greater than I can control.

"Jack..."

"Shhh," he murmurs against my sticky skin before he licks up a droplet of sweat rolling down my neck. "I've got you."

After scooting his glorious backside to the edge of the seat, taking me with him, he tugs his crinkled dress shirt out of his trousers so roughly buttons pop and inches upon inches of his rock-hard abs are exposed before he drags his trousers over his ass.

I'm too busy drinking in his delectable V muscle to assist in his undressing. Luckily for me, he manages fine without me. Within seconds, his pants are huddled around his knees, his dress shirt is open, and the honed muscles I can't take my eyes off move with such grace, I'm overcome by their brilliance in seconds.

I climax with a shameless cry, uncaring of who may hear me. Jack's white-knuckled hold of the grip handle above his head doubles as my expression switches from uptight to relaxed.

When the shivers wreaking havoc with my body slowly

dissipate, he drops his hand to the area where our bodies are intimately joined before he rolls my aching clit with his thumb. How he ever thought he needed teaching is beyond me. Right now, he owns me. He could do anything, and I wouldn't protest.

After fisting my hair, he drives into me deeper, faster. The rhythmic slaps of our bodies boom throughout the cab of his car. We fuck like wild animals, hungry and craving another helping even with the first course not being fully consumed.

Jack's balls slam against my ass as he drives me to the brink while I moan his name on repeat, loving that he isn't a one-hit-wonder. He could have given in to his needs the instant I succumbed to mine, but he didn't because my desires will always come before his.

"Tivy," he grunts against my sweat-dotted skin as he powers into me.

I hold on for the ride, clawing at his chest as viciously as I struggle to keep a grip on my sanity.

It is a fruitless effort. His pounds are too relentless, his power over my body exhausting.

"I… I…"

"Give it to me," Jack demands while doubling the thrusts of his hips.

His fuck should be rough. It should be painful, but instead of being either of those things, it is nothing but brilliant.

I cry out, my body igniting from the roots of my hair to the tips of my toes. "Oh… please…"

My begs send Jack freefalling over the edge. With his hand curled around my sweaty neck and his cock fully sheathed inside me, he comes with a roar.

I follow right along with him.

As his V muscle grinds against my pulsating clit, hot cum erupts from his cock. He fills me to the brim before the throbs of his fleshy member stretch my orgasm from a slight shudder to a full-body shake.

I'm so spent and exhausted that when Jack sinks back, I balance my cheek on his thrusting chest for several long minutes. That was amazing, beyond anything I could have possibly imagined.

Many prolonged minutes later, my lips rise against his damp chest. Even with a stream of traffic on each side of us, the intimacy of our closeness hasn't been lost on Jack. He's still inside me, and even with exhaustion rendering us silent, his cock understands our intimacy well. It's primed and ready to go like it didn't achieve release only minutes ago.

"We're going to kill each other, you know? We're going to die of sexual exhaustion."

Jack's chuckles rumble in his chest before they escape his lips. "It has a mind of its own." After brushing back strands of hair stuck to my temples, he treks his finger down my inflamed cheek. "Especially when it comes to you." I study his gorgeous face for any regrets when he asks, "Let me feed you. Please."

After grazing my lower lip with my teeth, I nod. My head is screaming for me to step back and assess the situation with more diligence, but with my heart working for the opposition, I can't hear its protests over my heart's frantic thumps. "Although I don't like your chances of finding anywhere with a free table at this hour."

His smile—kill. Me. Now. It is a mixture of shy and cocky, the perfect combination.

"I think I have a few tricks up my sleeve."

After carefully lifting me off his lap, he cleans me with a tissue from the middle console, slips his trousers back over his backside, then instructs the driver to take us to Dick's Drive-In.

Jack drinks in my gaped mouth and wide eyes before muttering, "Jess invited me to movie night on one condition. I—"

"Pick up greasy burgers on the way," I interrupt, well-rehearsed on Jess's requirement for gatecrashers of Monday

Movie Marathon. Caleb and I were duped out of twenty burgers our first week in Seattle because we thought she was catering for a house full of guests. It turns out she's merely a fan of reheated garbage. She eats the greasy lumps of carbs throughout the week, not that you can tell by her svelte frame.

"So even if I hadn't forgiven you, our paths still would have crossed tonight?"

"Yes," Jack confesses, his smile uncontained. "Although I doubt it would have started quite as thrillingly."

I shrug. "Oh… I don't know. You seem to have a knack for sweet-talking my vagina every time we're in the same room, so I'm sure it would have eventually ended up in a sticky, twisted mess."

"Twisted?"

Jack puffs out a big breath when I sock him in the stomach. "Our night. Not my… *vagina*." Don't ask why my vagina comment this time around sounded like it was spoken by a prepubescent boy. It was high and nasally and not at all sexy, but you wouldn't know that by Jack's grin. He looks like a kid who won a race even after giving all the other contestants a head start.

"I've corrupted you," he murmurs under his breath before the back of his fingers trickle down my inflamed cheeks.

I scoff. "It will take more than a vag comment to corrupt me. You'd need an arsenal of controversy to dint my sullied reputation more than it already is. I doubt you have one of them."

"I bet I do," Jack mutters more to himself than me because our connection is stolen by the gridlocked traffic surrounding us.

Caleb eyes me over a spoonful of cereal when I enter the kitchen a little after seven the following morning. "You look like hell," he mutters around a mouthful of Frosted Flakes.

"Shut up," I snap back before moving toward the refrigerator.

I went to bed at a decent time, exhausted from multiple orgasms in the limousine, but I barely slept a wink. I couldn't stop tossing and turning while recalling my day and evening with Jack.

He is still so hard for me to read, my loss apparent when I seek assistance from the last man I should. "Did Jack seem different to you last night?"

"Different how?" Caleb accepted Jack's handshake when I offered a proper introduction last night, and he ate the burgers Jack supplied but gave him the cold shoulder most of the night. It isn't that he doesn't like him. He just thinks I'm playing with fire.

I'm beginning to have the same doubts.

"Like reserved? A little stand-offish?" I pull the orange juice out of the refrigerator before snagging a glass from the open cupboards above the burner. "Kinda like how you are with Jess?"

Caleb's spoon drops into his cereal like a bomb, sending splashes of milk over the dining table. "Don't bring her into this. She has *nothing* to do with your fucked-up idea of a fun time."

"Hey—"

"No, Tivy. I'm not *ever* going to be okay with this."

Aware of where his concerns lie, I say, "He may not be who you think he is." When he stands with a huff, I push out faster, "Who would call their kid Jackson Carson? That's just cruel. And you only met him for a second before last night, so you could be reading him wrong."

He pins me in place with a cruel glare before muttering, "You said he had an issue with touch."

I shrug before blurting out, "Maybe I was wrong. He didn't have a-any issues last night." I don't mention the fact most of Jack's body was plastered to the leather seats of the limousine or my body, so I couldn't technically touch him because that's just asking for trouble.

"You stuttered because you lied."

"N-no." I grind my teeth together before trying again. "I stuttered because I'm confused. He confuses me. You confuse me." I throw my hands into the air. "The whole fucking world confuses me."

My time in the limousine with Jack was mesmerizing. It was the highest of highs until I mentioned needing an arsenal of controversy to sully me, then it nosedived like the Chargers last season. He stayed throughout the two movies Jess selected and giggled at Jess's infamous impersonation of James Franco, but he wasn't the same attentive lover he was in the limousine.

Don't misconstrue. My heart melted when he carried me to my apartment after I fell asleep during *Zeroville*, but when I suggested he stay instead of dragging his driver out of bed to take him home, he said he couldn't. He brushed off my drooped lip with an excuse that he had an early meeting today, but I could tell he was lying. He was seeking an out, but since running mid-movie would be classed as rude, he held on until the end of Monday Movie Marathon, then fled at the earliest possible convenience.

"It isn't like you have anything to be worried about. He bolted at the first opportunity."

Caleb shakes his head before plonking back into his seat. After filling his mouth with cereal to hide the disdain in his voice, he tells me I'm an idiot before devoting his attention to the morning paper.

When he lifts the classified to get a better view of a job application, my gurgling stomach settles. The very man we're arguing about is on the front page, sliding out of the limousine we shared last night, except I'm not on his tail. He is assisting a beautiful blonde woman with a blissed twinkle in her eyes out of the car.

Although upset to see Jack with someone else so soon after he fled here, I seek out the positives instead of reacting negatively for a change. It's a hard feat, but only for as long as it takes for me to speak my next set of words. "Do you truly think anyone in our grandfather's file would choose a career that would have him constantly thrust into the limelight?"

Caleb stops chewing midchew. After staring into space long enough for me to think he didn't hear me, he locks his eyes with mine. They're throwing out an array of questions, but none leave his mouth. He merely halfheartedly shrugs, places his half-consumed bowl into the sink, presses his lips to my temple, then exits the kitchen.

I'm so desperate to unravel my confusion, I'm tempted to take off after him. The only reason I don't is that I do not want to be tardy the day after a promotion. I prefer to lead by example, which is why I apologize to Caleb for my insensitive comment in the kitchen before I have a quick shower and commence my journey to work.

Merrick greets me with his usually happy grin fifty minutes later. "Good morning, Tivy. Pleasant day."

I admire the pristine blue sky for a couple of seconds before muttering, "It sure is nice… for a change."

Merrick laughs before gesturing for me to enter the ferry before him. "Are you coming with us today?" He usually stays at the dock, preparing for the ferry's return.

"Yes." His grin competes with the blinding rays of the morning sun. "I got a promotion yesterday for exemplary service."

My mouth drops open before I throw my arms around his shoulders to hug him tightly. He's been waiting for this promotion for years. "That's wonderful, Merrick. I'm so proud of you."

The blush on his cheeks is adorable. "Thank you, Tivy. I'm quite proud of myself." He guides me deeper onto the ferry while disclosing, "We've decided to put away the extra funds each payday. In a year or five, it will go toward an Italian adventure."

"That sounds like a great idea. It's about time Adeline's wish to see Florence comes to fruition."

He looks more in love now than he ever has while discussing his wife. She truly is the love of his life. "Well, I better get a wiggle on. I don't want to be demoted the second day on the job."

Ignoring the similarities of our story, I hug him goodbye before moving to the front of the boat. The sun peeking through the buildings is warm on my arms, but the winds bouncing off the water are a little chilly.

In my hurry to leave, I forgot to snatch up the coat Jack purchased for me. It's slung over the chair in my room, right where Jack's business jacket was placed the first night he stayed over.

As the ferry chugs toward downtown, my mind wanders. I think back to the photograph of Jack in the newspaper while contemplating when it was taken. He was wearing the same suit and tie he stripped out of in the limousine, but his dress shirt was different. I can't help but wonder if that was because he had to replace the one he lost buttons from during his eagerness to undress.

Although the lady pictured with him appeared a little older than him, they did have a unique bond. I wouldn't necessarily say fire-sparking, but it's hard to tell a connection from a black and white image.

While shrugging off my unease about their relationship as a consequence of my own confusion, I exit the ferry with workers and tourists ready to enjoy their day. With an umbrella not impeding my vision, I don't catapult anyone through the turn-stile door at the front of headquarters.

I won't lie. I'm a little disappointed. I was hoping to spot Jack this morning.

Alas, rarely do my dreams become a reality.

"Good morning, Tivy," Jess beams when she spots my entrance into the office. "How was your night?" Her waggling brows freeze mid-wiggle when I sigh. "Really? You too? Ugh. I would have thought if anyone was going to get lucky last night, it would have been you."

My half grimace gives me away.

After whacking me in the arm, Jess mutters under her breath, "I knew that wasn't a new perfume. You lying little witch." She hooks her arm around mine before dragging me into the break room like our workday hasn't officially started yet. "Where did it happen? Oh... the stairwell between our apartments?" She stops, twists her lips, then breathes out with a gag. "It wasn't the rooftop hot tub, was it?"

"We have a rooftop hot tub?" When she nods, I snap out, "Since when?"

"Ah... since forever." She gags again. "Hence, no one using it. That water is as old and crusty as our landlord."

I giggle along with her this time before ending our conversation with a brief confession. "It wasn't at our building." I don't just feel a little dirty sharing intimate details while being eyeballed by people suspicious as to how I got a promotion, but Jack also mentioned that he likes to keep his work and home life separate. "But I think it was a one-time-only deal anyway."

"Sure it was," Jess mumbles with a roll of her eyes before she bumps me with her hip. "Let's see if that remains the case by the end of the day because from what I'm seeing, he looks ready to devour you alive."

My heart beats at an irregular patter when she nudges her head to Mr. Potts's old office. I don't need to peer in her direction to know who's watching. The prickling of the hairs on my arms tells me everything I need to know. Jack has arrived. You just wouldn't know it since his Mr. Carson mask is firmly slipped into place.

My eyes shift to Jess when she mutters, "Lunch?"

"Yes. That will be great."

After a quick exhale, I signal that we will catch up later before I spin on my heels and head Jack's way. His long drink-in of my body continues during the short trek.

"Good morning, Mr. Carson," I greet, my voice a seductive purr.

"Octavia," he replies, his greeting just as throaty. "I believe we have some matters to discuss this morning. Would you like to do it here or in your new office?"

I slant my head then arch a brow. "I have a new office?"

Even with his aura exuding wealth and superiority, his smile draws in spectators like a lion tamer at a circus. "Yes. Shall I show you where it is?"

I nod before my head can talk my heart out of it.

With a smile solely reserved for me, Jack advises Elaine he

will be back shortly before he places his hand on my back and guides me toward the elevators.

"Is it not on the same floor as everyone else?"

Dark strands of hair fall into Jack's mesmerizing eyes when he briskly shakes his head. After checking that the coast is clear, he leans in close, then mutters in my ear, "Seventeen floors will never be enough."

My knees pull together when a shudder of arousal shakes my thighs.

His voice couldn't be more provocative if he tried.

While snickering at my response to his tease, he guides me into the idling elevator, then pushes the button for the top level. Only the hobnobs work from the top floor, but I'm too stunned to say anything. Not only am I in a teeny tiny little space with a man who activates every one of my hot buttons by only breathing, but we're also not alone.

Roach is in the elevator with us, and although he appears to be glancing at the tablet balancing on his hand, I've spotted the occasional flick of his eyes. He's watching me as attentively as Jack.

"Ja... ah, Mr. Carson, have you met Terry Roach, Head of Advertising?"

Jack shakes his head before offering his hand to Terry. "Jack. Pleasure."

"I can say the same. I've been going over records this morning. The amount of capital you're willing to put into this sinking ship is quite commendable. That or you're a fool."

I scorn him with an evil glare, but Jack merely laughs. "Depends. If that capital isn't close to one-ten-thousandth percent of your total net wealth, I doubt you'd class it as a risk."

Jack's reply shuts Roach up quickly. He stammers over his words before he scurries out of the elevator on the next floor. It isn't the floor advertising is on, but the stuffiness in the elevator is too much for him to bear.

He should consider himself lucky to have escaped the inferno with only the slightest scald. The temperature jumps tenfold within a second of the doors snapping shut. Jack doesn't waste any time pinning me to the elevator wall with his suit-covered body and sealing his mouth over mine.

His kiss is scrumptious and confusing at the same time. You can't demand anonymity at work, then kiss me senseless in the elevator. Besides, isn't there a security officer manning the live feed?

"Jack," I mumble against his mouth when he pulls back for the quickest breather. "We shouldn't be doing this here. Someone might see us."

"They won't," he promises before he nips at my lower lip then soothes the sting of his bite with a lash of his tongue. "The elevators are programmed to go straight to the top floor, and I paid the security personnel to turn a blind eye."

His reply both excites and confuses me. Last night he pushed me away, but today, he's pulling me in like he can't breathe without me.

While returning his toe-curling embrace, I endeavor to relieve some of my confusion. "How was your meeting this morning?"

"Meeting?' He bites my neck while guiding my leg around his waist. "What meeting?"

It is hard to speak through the fire roaring in my stomach when I feel him thick and heavy beneath me, but I manage—somewhat. "The meeting you had to attend this morning. The one that wouldn't allow you to spend the night."

I don't know if he softens over my interrogation or he doesn't feel as thick because he leans back to lie directly to my face. "It was good. Nothing out of the ordinary."

"You didn't have a meeting, did you?" When another gleam of deceit darts through his eyes, I lower my leg from his waist then shove him away from me. "Don't lie to me, Jack." Needing distance, I splay my back onto the glass wall before asking, "Is that why you were photographed with another woman last night? Did you leave me to visit her?"

When he runs his fingers through his hair while cursing under his breath, I feel sick. Incredibly and undoubtedly ill.

"Who is she? Is she your wife?" I throw my hand over my mouth before mumbling through the cracks in my fingers, "Is that why you want to keep your work life and home life separate? Because I'm not a part of your private life? I'm just your work plaything?"

His eyes snap to mine. They're as dark as death. "Jesus, Octavia. No. That isn't the case."

There's nothing but honesty in his tone, but I can't help but ask, "Did you know who I was? When you helped me, did you know I worked here?"

"No." His back molars smash together when I spot his lie from a mile out. "Not entirely." He stuffs his hand into his pocket before admitting, "I had an inkling you may work here, but simply because the race was a private event. No ordinary spectators were invited."

Now the huge expense makes sense, but it doesn't settle my queasy stomach in the slightest. "Then why didn't you tell me who you were?"

When he locks his eyes with mine, nothing but unbridled truth reflects from them. "Because I like the way you look at me. That you see me. Jack. Not a media mogul or whatever the fucking ridiculous name they've been circulating through the press the past few days."

My shoulders slump a little. I like Hotshot Boss. It suits him, although I'd rather he remain solely *my hotshot boss*.

My unrequired jealousy is pushed aside for something far more emotional when Jack confesses, "And I like the way you make me feel." He removes his hand from his pocket before curling it around my jaw. "You drive me fucking crazy, but I can't seem to get enough."

He isn't the only one going mad.

Instead of repelling away from him, I fist his suit jacket and tug him closer.

"Christ, Tivy," he murmurs when a surge of electricity rockets through us. "It's only been days, but I already know I won't survive us." He kisses the edge of my mouth, my jaw, and my collarbone, and that is all it takes for my anger to evaporate and for lust to take over.

Unfortunately, it is also the time it takes for the elevator to arrive at the top floor.

"Lunch?" Jack breathes against my neck, his low tone exposing his disappointment. "I can't wait ten hours to taste your lips again. It will kill me."

"I can't," I murmur back, my voice as reserved as his. "I promised Jess we'd do lunch."

I call myself an idiot before attempting to offer for him to come with us, but before I can, he suggests, "Dinner then? I'll cook at your place, then perhaps I might have the chance to win Caleb over."

"Caleb—"

Like a tick I can't shake, Jess bounds into the elevator like a kid who had too much sugar. "Can you believe this space, Tivy? It's massive." She drags me into an area I once avoided like the plague, dropping my jaw more with each step she forces. "No more cubicles. We have walls... *actual* walls." She taps on the wall next to a door marked with my name before spinning me around and showing me her office. It is half the size of mine and minus a floor-to-ceiling window that showcases downtown Seattle in all its glory, but she acts as if it is the flashiest office she's ever seen. "I'm thinking I should place my desk here." She spreads her hands over a stretch of carpet in the middle of the space. "That way no one can sneak up on me like they did in my cubicle. I'll see them coming and have a letter opener at the ready..."

As she continues telling me her grand plans for her new space, I shift my eyes to Jack. He's discussing semantics with Elaine and a man I've yet to meet, but the instant he feels my eyes on him, they lift from the blueprints in front of him and lock with mine.

"Seven. I'll supply the wine."

He is either fluent in lipreading or knows me better than I know myself because my invitation has barely left my mouth when he dips his chin before mouthing, *"See you then."*

J ess's eyes gleam with excitement when we enter a local deli around the corner from headquarters. Despite it being late for the lunch crowd, the space is bustling with an equal number of tourists and workers.

After snagging two menus from a podium at the front, the hostess guides us into the hub of the artsy restaurant.

"I love this place. It's so hip," Jess mutters as we weave through tables filled with diners. "How did you find out about this place?"

"Jack suggested it. He said it has the best club sandwich in town." I shout so my words project over the hum of constant chatter. "He also said their chocolate mousse cake is to die for." When we reach our table, I sling my jacket over my seat, then plonk into it. The server has only just handed me a menu when I spot Jess's leering grin. "What?"

I check my reflection in the mirrored napkin dispenser to make sure I don't have anything in my teeth. I haven't eaten since breakfast, but that won't stop a massive chunk of lettuce from lodging itself between my chompers. Jess loves vegetable smoothies, and I get suckered into her diet fads a minimum of once a week.

When I fail to find anything wrong with my face, I shift my eyes back to Jess. She ignores my arched brow and questioning eyes for almost thirty seconds before she eventually gives in. "You said it was a one-time-only, *multiple* times thing." Since I'm still lost, she extends on her reply, "You and Jack. You mentioned a craving for mousse cake last night." She waves her hand around our location. "Now we're eating at a deli that specializes in that *exact* dessert. This is *not* a coincidence."

She laughs when I shove my menu in her face. "It took twelve minutes to walk here, which means we have precisely six minutes to order and eat, so stop pussyfooting around and work out what you want to eat."

After taking a moment to settle the excited patter of my heart that Jack most likely suggested this location purely so he can answer my every whim, I glance down at the menu. My stomach gurgles more in contempt than excitement when my eyes land on the prices. A turkey club sandwich may be delicious, but it is not worth thirty-eight dollars.

"Woah." Mercifully, Jess is as cheap as me. We make the same salary, but she lives alone, so there's no rent share for her. "Are there gold flecks in the cucumber? Because there better be for these prices."

Even with me wholeheartedly agreeing with her, I laugh. "How about we go halves? I'm not hungry. Your smoothie filled me up." She looks proud. She shouldn't. I'm more too queasy to eat than cheap, and the churns of my stomach are solely to blame on her vegetable concoction.

"Halves? You're on a management wage now, so why are you making me pay half?" She mockingly shakes her head. "Ms. Stingy Ass."

Although she is being playful, I can't help but respond. "There's been no mention of a pay increase."

Jess peers at me over her menu. "Then you better start asking some questions because I sure as hell wouldn't be putting in the work you have the past couple of days for peanuts. He might have a fantastic cock, but no cock is worth slave labor."

"Jess." I glare at her before slowly drifting my eyes around the patrons seated next to us. Her voice was loud enough for three blocks over to hear.

Once I'm confident we only have zealous gazes locked on us, I return my focus to Jess. "Keep your voice down. I don't want people getting the wrong idea." When confusion crosses her face, I lean in close and whisper. "I don't want them to think Jack has to pay me peanuts to ride his cock when I'd do it for free."

She hollers while waving her napkin in the air. "Thatta girl!"

Her party for one ends when the waiter arrives at our table. He looks petrified that we will stiff him a tip when we order one club sandwich with an extra side of sweet potato fries. We don't want the carbs, but it will make sharing easier if we have an extra plate.

"Is that all?"

After straying my eyes away from the chocolate mousse cake that costs as much as our sandwich, I jerk up my chin. "Yes, thank you." He stuffs our menus under his arm, dips his chin in farewell, then leaves after only the quickest glance Jess's way. "He likes you."

"What?" Jess scoffs like I'm being ridiculous, but I see her true response in her eyes. *If only Caleb felt the same way.*

I pick at my napkin, wordlessly announcing that she doesn't have to answer me if she doesn't want, before asking, "What happened between you and Caleb last weekend?"

Her huff this time around is more in pain than disbelief. "Nothing. That's the point." She fakes a sob. "I'm really beginning to wonder if he truly does only see me as a friend."

"Jess—"

"No, it's fine. Truly. I'd rather face the truth than continue like we have the past few months." She stops to consider her next set of words. "It hurts not knowing if you're good enough."

"You're more than good enough. It's just Caleb. He has..." Now it's my turn to pause for thought. "Commitment issues. But I've never seen him with anyone like he is with you. There's spark and connection. He's just scared."

"Of what, exactly?"

I shrug. "I don't know. But if anyone can find out, Jess, it is you. You just can't give up on him."

I regret my plea when the waiter returns to our table to place a napkin with a cell phone number scrawled across it between Jess and me. Jess has plenty of suitors, so is it mean of me to want her to keep fighting for my cousin, who's determined to keep her at arm's length?

I assume the waiter is putting in a silent bid for Jess but am proven wrong when he mutters, "It's from the gentleman across the room." He coughs to clear the annoyance from his throat before gesturing his head to the man in question. He's a mid to late twenties Seattleite decked out in a fancy suit. His hair is slicked back, and his jaw is rigid. He's handsome but totally up himself. "He would like to pay for your meal." He drifts his eyes to mine. "*Both* of your meals."

When the waiter remains staring at me, I gabber under my breath, "Okay," lost as to why he looks like he's waiting for me to say something.

My confusion clears when he asks, "So, is there anything else you'd like to order?"

Jess's eyes gleam with excitement, but their glint dulls when I shake my head.

"What about your cake?" Jess whispers only loud enough for the three of us to hear.

I shake my head again. If Jack suggested this restaurant because he wants me to sample the mousse cake, I don't want it to be done with the generosity of another man. Besides, I can't get angry about Jack wanting to spoil me then accept the generosity of a stranger. "And please tell the gentleman that we appreciate his offer, but we're fine paying for our own lunch."

"Okay." The waiter looks as lost as I felt earlier.

After waiting a beat, he slips the napkin off the table and attempts to hightail it to the kitchen. I say attempt as he only gets two steps away when Jess stops him. "You can leave that." After snatching the napkin out of his hand, she tucks it into her purse. "You never know when you might need a peacock in a suit." After snapping her purse closed, she locks her eyes with mine. "Surely, he'd have to ruffle a few more feathers than the barflies I tried to rile Caleb with last time."

I smile a mammoth grin. "Thatta girl!"

Twenty minutes later, Jess and I race for the exit. The club sandwich was enormous, and despite our best effort, half of it remains on our plates. Would I say it is worth its price tag? No. More because I hate wasting than anything else.

After scribbling down a generous tip to our waiter who softened a little, the longer he served us, I hand our bill wallet to a lady at the counter to ring up our sale. "Thank you for dining with us today. We hope you have a pleasant day."

I return her farewell with a smile before lopping my arm around Jess's elbow and guiding her to the closest exit. Our allotted time has run over, and I'm more than fretful of a tardy slip.

"Tivy," the waiter shouts, halting my quick steps. When I spin around to face him, he wiggles a piece of paper in the air. "You forgot something."

I check my pocket for my credit card, certain I slipped it in there after the waitress processed my payment. I realize it isn't my receipt he's waving when he snatches up two clear containers from the serving area and heads my way. My heart beats double time when I realize what he's clasping. It is two large helpings of their famous chocolate mousse cake.

"We didn't order dessert," I stammer, somewhat embarrassed I'll have to send them back if he requests payment. I was surprised the payment for our club sandwich went through without alerting that I've exceeded my limit.

Darris smiles a coy grin. "I know, but I was asked to make sure you left with these."

He shoves the cakes into my chest, leaving me no choice but to catch them or watch them topple to the floor. "By whom?" I ask once I've steadied my juggle.

Darris taps his nose, smiles farewell, then spins on his heels and saunters away.

I remain standing in the middle of the exit, shellshocked into silence. My first guess is the gentleman who tried to buy us lunch, but since he's necking it with a lady he moved onto within seconds of us rejecting his generosity, I doubt it was him, so I'm utterly clueless as to our gift giver's identity.

Two seconds later, the lightbulb inside my head finally switches on. Jess follows me when I haphazardly stumble onto the footpath, then her eyes follow the crank of my neck when I peer up at the proprietor sign above the door.

"I should have known," I murmur more in delight than anger when I spot a recently removed business name above the door. But now I'm curious if this was a recent purchase like the boutique yesterday, or did he only become a foodie after I disclosed a hankering for mousse cake?

I guess there's only one way to find out.

By the time we weave through a sea of foot commuters, dodge a slurry of lewd comments from a group of rowdy construction workers, and enter the seventeenth floor of head-quarters, my nape is dripping with sweat, and I'm breathless more from exhaustion than excitement.

"Here."

As Jess's eyes drop to the portion of cake I'm holding out for her, her tongue delves out to lick her lips. "I don't think that was for me, but I'm not going to say no." After snatching it out of my hand, she saunters to her cubicle, her steps slower than the ones we used during our race back to the office.

Once she's out of eyesight, I head for Mr. Potts's office. We won't officially move upstairs until the fit-out is complete. I have no clue how long that will take. If Jack's eagerness for long elevator rides is anything to go by, it could be finished by the end of the week.

"Oh, hi, Elaine," I push out in shock when I spot her sitting behind Jack's desk. "Is Ja… ah, Mr. Carson in?"

Sprigs of blonde curls bounce when she shakes her head. "He's upstairs finalizing the fit-out for his office. Is there anything I can help you with?"

"No. I was just wondering if he had eaten yet? Mousse cake isn't the best lunch, but it is better than nothing."

When I jiggle the container in my hand, her eyes spark with happiness. "Ah… now it makes sense." After dropping her pen onto a pile of paperwork in front of her, she folds her hands on her lap. "I'm sure he'd love something to tie him over until dinner. You're more than welcome to take it up to him."

"Oh, no, that isn't necessary. You can deliver it to him… if you want?" I'm saying no, but my heart is pleading the oppo-site. Jack said he couldn't survive ten hours without his lips on mine, and I'm enduring the exact same battle.

"I think he'd much rather you deliver it." Elaine nudges her head to the door. "Go on. I'll cover for you until you get back." Her offer makes me smile. Technically, she's my boss, so the only person I need covering for is her.

"Okay. I'll be quick."

Elaine raises a brow, mutters something under her breath, then shifts her focus back to her paperwork.

After ditching my purse and coat onto my half-packed desk, I saunter to the elevator. I won't lie. Stupid butterflies weave throughout the clumps of turkey in my stomach. I feel giddy and nervous at the same time.

"Wow," I push out with a shocked breath when the elevator dings open on the top floor. Jack's crew works fast. What was an almost gutted office space only hours ago now appears ready to be filled with workers.

"Ms. Henslee," one of the workers with piercing blue eyes greets when I walk past him.

"Hello," I reply with my customary response when I don't know someone's name. "Have you seen Mr. Carson?"

"He's in his office." When my eyes dart in all directions, the builder slants his head to hide his smile. "It's right next to yours."

"Oh..." His grin enlarges from my daft response. "Thank you."

I barely get two steps away. "While I have you..." He waits for me to spin and face him before finalizing. "My crew didn't mean any harm earlier. They just can't help but admire a pretty lady when she walks by."

My brows furrow.

I am completely lost.

"The wolf-whistling and catcalling a few minutes ago," he enlightens, the brightness on his cheeks picking up. "That was my crew. Well, they *were* my crew."

When the truth smacks into me, my mouth gapes open. "Jack fired you because your crew got a little rowdy with their flattery?" Their comments were distasteful but mainly harmless... if you like to be told how many ways you're about to be fucked.

The beat of my heart amplifies when a deep, penetrating

voice answers my question on the builder's behalf. "No. I fired him because he didn't stop them from hassling you and Jess."

I twist to face Jack standing in a doorway that butts against my new office. He's glaring at the builder, exposing that leaving him unemployed hasn't lessened his annoyance in the slightest.

"It was a bit of fun, Jack—"

Jack's glare cuts off the builder before his words. "I don't care if they had no intention to follow through with their threats." Calling their comments threats is a little bit of an exaggeration. "What they said was uncalled for and intolerable." Jack shifts his eyes between the builder and me before they eventually settle back on him. "Good afternoon, Mr. Phelps."

Mr. Phelps bows out in defeat before he marches for the elevator still idling on this floor.

I take a moment to settle the nerves that are now more based on unease than giddiness before shifting my attention back to Jack. "Jack—"

He cuts me off by veering our conversation in a completely different direction. "Why didn't you order the mousse cake for yourself? I could tell by the gleam in your eyes when you walked past the display cabinet that you wanted a piece, but you left it off your order." Since he is very much the dominant businessman you'd expect when you learn of his wealth, his cocky smirk is highly anticipated. "Your eyes weren't as bright as the hunger they displayed when you peered at me for the first time, but evident, nonetheless."

Not comfortable talking about my almost nonexistent bank balance, I shrug instead. When it doubles the groove between Jack's brows, I fib, "I'm trying to shift a couple of pounds before the gala."

His growl does wicked things to my panties. "Now, I'm even more grateful I purchased you a slice on your behalf." He walks me into his partially furnished office, plops my backside onto his mammoth desk, then snatches the container of cake out of my hand.

"I brought that up here for you," I mutter when the determination on his face makes sense. He wants to stuff me to the brim, and for once, he isn't planning to use his cock. "Well, there goes that idea," I murmur with a giggle when he pops open the container to discover it void of an eating utensil.

My insides clench when he scoops a generous helping of the cake onto his index finger before he veers it toward my mouth. "Open up," he croons a mere nanosecond before my lips part in response to his coaxing voice.

Once again, he could do anything he wants to me, and I wouldn't say no.

An unladylike moan erupts from my mouth when a mix of flavors engulfs my taste buds. The mousse is delicious, but it has nothing on the taste of Jack's skin in my mouth. I haven't sampled that since our little rendezvous in the shower Saturday.

While watching the pleat in his trousers disappear, I lick up the remnants of the mousse cake from his finger by swirling my tongue around his girthy digit. If he wasn't aware of the dangerous minefield we're tiptoeing through, he is now. Not only does the rapid growth behind his zipper disclose this, but so does his gravelly groan of my name.

"Tivy, we shouldn't. We can't. Not here."

As his eyes shoot to the partially cracked open door of his recently refurbished office, I push him back until he lands in his big leather chair with a thud before lowering onto my knees in front of him. The split in my skirt parts before slipping up my thigh to erotically expose my panties, and my chest heaves so fanatically that the buttons on my blouse are close to popping.

Any further protests preparing to leave Jack's mouth get stuffed into the back of his throat when his desk conceals me from any ruckus occurring outside. I doubt even a strand of my hair can be seen over his bulky wooden desk.

Since we need to be discreet, I don't yank Jack's pants to his knees. I don't even undo his belt. I merely slide down the zipper in his trousers, yank his cock out of his briefs, then swipe my tongue over the wide crown like I wasn't stuffed-to-the-brim only moments ago.

"Fuck..." Jack grips the armrest on his chair in a white-knuckled hold before the other one lowers to weave through my hair. "You have no idea how many times I've imagined exactly this for the past two days." He impatiently rocks his hips upward, stuffing the first inch of his cock inside my wet and inviting mouth. "But nothing I imagined came close to how good this feels."

His confession excites me so much, I hollow my cheeks before taking him to the very back of my throat with a hearty suck. His unique manly scent doubles the pulse between my legs in an instant. Everything about him is divine, and my moans echo his soft grunts when I swivel my tongue around his engorged knob.

As he encourages me to suck him off with a heap of naughty words, I drag my mouth down the underside of his cock, then swivel my tongue around his balls. When he tugs my hair hard enough for the roots to sting, I return my lips to the head of his cock, eager for more of the pre-cum I sampled earlier.

I'm turned on by his dominance, so I can only imagine it is the same for him.

I squirm uncontrollably when I'm greeted with a thick, dense droplet of pre-cum. As I pump him with my hand, more beads form on the crown of his thick cock. I lap them up, moaning when they slide down my throat before I circle his knob with my lips then lower them down his velvety shaft.

"Yes, Octavia... just like that... take me to the very back of your throat..."

Aroused by the gruffness of his voice, I hollow my cheeks more then take him as far into my mouth as I can. The groan he releases when my gag vibrates on his knob has me wanting to squeeze my knees together, but I can't. Jack's black polished shoes are wedged between them.

I should feel dirty when I grind down on his shoe, desperate for contact. However, I don't. Jack's cock thickens when it dawns on him how turned-on I am, and the amount of pre-cum leaking from his cock doubles. I drink it all in, loving how mindless we are for one another when we're the only two people in the room.

As I suck on his wide crest, I stroke and pump his veiny shaft. It is a mesmerizing few minutes that has me forgetting where we are until another voice enters the equation.

"Samuel is in agreement with me. The bathroom shouldn't be co-ed."

I attempt to yank away from Jack, but his grip on my hair doesn't weaken in the slightest. His dominant hold keeps his cock nestled between my lips while he replies to his intruder like all the blood in his body isn't pumping through his cock. "I didn't ask for Samuel's opinion. I told you what I wanted, so do it."

His authoritative tone turns me on so much, I swivel my tongue along the underside of his cock before I even realize what I'm doing.

Jack doesn't seem to mind. The groan he barely holds back vibrates through his twitchy shaft a mere second before a droplet of pre-cum beads on the crest of his magnificent cock. Right now, he is both Mr. Carson, media mogul, and Jack from Jersey. He is the most virile, formidable display of a man in complete control of his personal and business life, and I love that I get to witness both sides of his equally tempting personalities.

"If we have to close the second entry later, it will cost—"

"I. Don't. Fucking. Care. How. Much. It. May. Cost." Each one of Jack's pointed words occurs with the slightest thrust of his hips. He feeds his cock in and out of my mouth like nothing will ever come before me and my insatiable need to have him at all times of the day and night before reminding his intruder that he isn't running the show around here. Jack is. "And if I need to remind you again, you will find yourself in a line behind Mr. Phelps."

His intruder coughs before calling defeat with the slightest, "Very well."

Jack's office door only just closes when Jack mutters, "Now, Octavia. Make me come now."

The need in his voice drives me wild. I stroke and suck the velvety smooth skin stretched over the crown of his cock while jacking off his veiny, spit-covered shaft. Then, not long later, the tension in Jack's thighs soften before his head flops back with a groan.

"God, Tivy... ah..."

Semen spurts out of his cock in thick, throat-clogging streams as the most delicious rough groan rips from Jack's mouth. I struggle to swallow him down, but since I'm determined to have him as defenseless as I am when he devotes all his attention to me, I milk his cock of every drop of cum, certain the ease of his tension will far outweigh an overstuffed stomach.

I can tell the instant Jack commences coming down from the euphoria of orgasm. He loosens his grip on my hair a mere second before he strokes my aching cheeks with gentle, thankful rubs.

"Thank you. That was..." his breathlessness makes me feel invincible much less what he says next, "... phenomenal."

"I'm glad you enjoyed it." I curse my clumsiness to hell when my endeavor to gracefully stand sees my head smacking into the carved wood trim of his desk. It can't be helped. My head is super woozy since it is fogged with lust. "But I really should be getting back to work."

"What?" After tucking away his still semi-erect penis, he

shadows my wobbly steps to the door. "No. You can't leave. I didn't..." He lowers his voice when several eyes pop up to us the instant they spot us in the once-again open doorway. "Return the favor."

Although his dedication to keep things even between us excites me, I play it cool. "And exactly where can you do that, Jack?"

When his eyes follow mine to the large glass wall of his office, he curses under his breath. "I knew I should have gone with frosted glass." An inappropriate grin tugs at my lips when he murmurs, "But I didn't want you ever doubting the intent of my visitors."

"Then you might need to get a smaller desk." After spinning around to face him, I press my lips to the edge of his mouth then talk over his quirked lips. "And there will be plenty of time to return the favor tonight. You're still coming over, right?" I hate the desperation in my voice. I sound like a loser.

Mercifully, so does Jack when he replies, "I'll be there with bells on."

Our peck is as innocent as a schoolyard kiss, but you wouldn't know that from the number of eyes it awards us. The workers gawk the entirety of our three-second kiss before they follow my short trek to the elevators.

They only get back to work when my flirty wink to Jack a second before the elevator doors snap shut with me as the sole occupant inside alerts him to a missed opportunity, but he takes his anger out on them instead of the throb between my legs.

"Get back to work. I don't have to care if you work through the night. I want this office space operational by the opening of business tomorrow morning."

CHAPTER 17
JACK

"Stop fiddling. You look fine."

Marissa's eyes lift to mine, their similarities notable even with us having different fathers. "That's fine for you to say, but I've never been in this predicament before."

"You've never been on a date?"

She shoots me a wry look, doubling the chuckles rumbling in my chest. "I've been on plenty of dates. I've just never been your plus-one before." When she expresses her worries, I really wish she wouldn't. "What if I don't like her, Jack? What if I think she only wants you for your money?"

"She doesn't." My reply is direct and to the point. No one on my team would be game to directly imply such lunacy, but she's aware I value her opinion more than anyone and that I have a lot riding on this, so she's pushing the limits. "Octavia isn't like the rest of them. She understands me."

Marissa's wide eyes dart to mine. "So you told her? She knows what happened to you?"

"No," I bark out. "Don't be ridiculous."

I wasn't meant to express my last three words out loud, and regretfully, Marissa hones onto them like a missile seeking out its target. "Then you don't really know her at all, do you? If you're not being yourself, how can you be so assured she is who you think she is?"

"Because she's different, Mar. You just can't understand how different since you're not me."

When my eyes shift to the traffic streaming past our window, she curls her hand over mine. "I would if you explained it to me." When I scoff off her claims with a huff, she pushes on. "Give me a little bit of leeway, brother. You were meant to fly in and out of Seattle on the same day. Now, you're telling everyone your stay is indefinite." I almost correct her by saying 'permanent,' but I keep my mouth shut. The worry in her eyes is already tenfold. "Things were never like this for us. We've never kept secrets from each other."

She's right. I hate it, but it won't change the facts.

After a beat, I give honesty a whirl. "*Things* aren't an issue with Octavia."

Marissa bounces her eyes between mine. "Things?" When I wave my hand to my crotch, she chokes on her spit. "Oh... *things*." She sinks back into her seat and gazes at nothing for several long seconds. "Wow."

"Exactly. Wow."

Silence reigns supreme for the next four miles before Marissa eventually breaks it. "But should that be the sole basis of upending your career and starting anew across the country?" When I arch a brow, she rolls her eyes with a huff. She uprooted her life for dick, and it wasn't even a good one. "I learned my lesson as you will yours."

I shake my head in denial. "This is different. Things won't end up like that for Octavia and me."

"You can't honestly believe that, Jack. You barely know the girl. You can't possibly be considering long term already."

"You'll see. She will prove you wrong."

She folds her arms under her chest. "And if she doesn't?"

I signal the driver to pull over half a block back from Octavia's apartment when I notice an upcoming gridlock. "Then I might have to get a new sister because a new girlfriend won't be on the agenda."

"Girlfriend? Octavia is your girlfriend?" Marissa gabbers as she follows me out of the town car and onto the bustling sidewalk.

After jerking up my chin, my answer unvoiced since I'm unsure if I can refer to Octavia as my girlfriend without first asking her, I request the driver to pop the trunk so I can gather the ingredients Elaine purchased earlier today.

Marissa breathes out a girlish giggle far too immature for her forty-five years when she spots the bags of groceries. "If you had started with your wish to cook for her, I would have taken your comments more seriously." She helps me unload before locking her eyes with mine. "You only cook for people you love, and since that has only ever been Mom, Keira, and me, I'll remove the tainted glasses I'm wearing and go into this with a more open mind."

I bow my head in gratitude. "Thank you."

She bumps me with her hip before shadowing my walk to Octavia's apartment building. She grunts and moans during our three-story climb, but her gripes are forgotten when Octavia greets her with a bright grin and a friendly hug.

"I heard rumors you were in town. It is a pleasure to meet you." After freeing Marissa of the bags indenting her tiny wrists, she invites us into her home before offering us a glass of wine. "It's only been on the chill for an hour. Caleb was late home since he was called back for a second interview earlier today." When she peers at me in joy, I give her the thumbs up, aware Caleb's unemployment weighs heavily on her shoulders. "He'll join us in a minute. He's just grabbing a quick shower."

"And where is he planning to take it?"

Octavia dumps the groceries on the kitchen counter before spinning to face Marissa, her questioner. "Sorry?"

"The shower? Where is he planning to take it?" Marissa's lips twitch as she struggles not to smile. "You did say he was grabbing a shower, didn't you?"

Octavia looks a cross between laughing and cursing herself. She goes for a little giggle when I laugh at Marissa's comment like it wasn't the worst mom joke on the planet. "You will have to excuse Marissa. Her humor is as dry as the prunes she'll need to consume when I shove her into an old folk's home next week."

"You'll be there long before me." Marissa locks her eyes with Octavia. "Jack is an old soul. He's been here before."

Octavia peers at me as if I'm cute when I roll my eyes before she reoffers us a glass of wine.

I thank her with a smile before saying, "Thank you, but I'm fine."

After accepting my rejection with a shrug, she arches her brow at Marissa. "It's a good label. I picked it myself."

"All right," Marissa concedes. "But only because you twisted my arm."

As they move toward the refrigerator, I commence unpacking the groceries. The fact Octavia doesn't fuss over me or try and shoo me out of the kitchen with comments like 'it's a woman's domain' sees Marissa warming to her even faster than predicted.

Within minutes, they're discussing as many topics as Octavia and I did the day we met.

"Are you sure you're not worried?" Marissa asks Octavia a short time later while drinking in the ingredients I brought with me. Beef patties, eggs, rice, and a packet of instant gravy.

"Not really," Octavia replies, her high pitch undermining her reply. "I was leaning toward burgers until he whipped out the rice and gravy. Now I'm a little lost."

After smiling at the confused crinkle between her brow, I confess, "Loco Moco is pretty much comfort food in Hawaii. It looks disgusting, but it tastes great. It was a staple in our house growing up."

"Hawaiian, hey? That's the other part of the jigsaw puzzle I couldn't quite work out."

Since I'm striving to work out what other parts Octavia thinks she's missing, Marissa answers on my behalf. "Our mother is from Lanai, one of the smallest inhabited islands in Hawaii. She moved to the mainland when I was seven, then settled stateside a couple of years after that. Jack was born and raised in Jersey, and despite our mother's wish to drum her coastal life into his veins, he's a Jersey boy at heart."

"I'd believe that," Octavia says with a grin. "I've heard the way he says *cawfee*."

Marissa tosses a hand over her mouth to hide her smile when she laughs at Octavia's horrific imitation of my voice. Her accent is authentic, but she can't get her voice as deep as mine. "You sound just like Jack... when he hit the horrid puberty stage," Marissa spits out between bouts of laughter, her voice loud and over the top.

She's so boisterous, she startles Caleb enough he races out of the bathroom with only a towel wrapped around his hips.

Since he's Octavia's blood, I give his half-naked state leeway.

Octavia doesn't, though. "Oh my God, Caleb. We have guests. Go get dressed!"

I shoot Marissa a wry look when she mumbles under her breath. "Or not." Once Octavia ushers Caleb down the hallway, Marissa's bugged eyes finally land on me. "What?" she whispers, her eyes as bright as her flushed cheeks. "I'm single, and he's—"

"Half your age."

She *pffts* me. "Like that has ever stopped them. Guys love a woman with experience."

"Yeah, but not when their daughter is the same age as them." Keira, my niece, is not much older than Octavia. "And I've got enough obstacles to jump with Caleb as it is. I don't need you making things more complicated." I don't mention the fact Jess is also smitten with him because that isn't my story to tell.

After placing her wine glass on the kitchen counter, Marissa joins me by the sink to wash the rice. Yes, washing rice is a bad habit our family has. "What issues could Caleb possibly have with you? You're perfect, and I'm not at all biased."

Her smile slips when I reply, "Other than me testing out the durability of his furniture? Not a single thing."

Marissa looks set to gag, but instead, she nods.

"I don't know what his issue is, but his dislike is obvious."

The strainer freezes halfway out of the water when Marissa mutters, "Are you sure they're cousins?" While stepping away from me with her hands raised in the air, she murmurs, "I was just checking."

"Then go check somewhere else. Preferably in the living room since the kitchen isn't big enough for me and your gigantic insinuations."

She sways as if she's floating in the breeze of a compliment before she moseys toward the even more compact living area. Just before she exits, she calls my name, then waits for me to peer up at her before she confesses, "I like her."

Her approval makes me smile, but it won't change my game plan.

Octavia is mine, and I'll do everything in my power to keep it that way.

"Their comments were not harmless," I argue, going against Octavia's recollection of the dangerous incident that occurred during her return from lunch today. "They were crude and unrequired, hence me letting them know that."

"So, you fired them on the spot? No notice given?"

When I jerk up my chin to Caleb's question, he dumps his dirty napkin onto his almost licked-clean plate before sinking back into his chair with an impressed huff. Dinner was a raving success, and only part of it had to do with the generous helpings of Loco Moco. Conversation flowed freely, and laughter was in abundance.

Well, until it switched to business.

"Are you worried about any repercussions from the union?"

I shift my eyes to Marissa, my stickler of a sister when it comes to protocols. "For firing sexual predators?" Her eyes don't remain on me during the second half of my reply. "No. Severance packages are generally offered but not for menaces to society. They have no place in my world and will not be compensated for their foolery with my money."

Octavia curls her hand over my balled one resting on my lap before she attempts to steer the conversation back onto mutual territory. "Dessert, anyone? Jack kindly bought chocolate mousse cake from his favorite restaurant."

"Is that the one you purchased Monday... *night*." Marissa chokes on her last word when I glare at her. "Was that meant to be a secret?"

"No," Octavia answers on my behalf. "Even with the name above the door leading me away from the scent for a little bit, the paint was still wet enough to divulge his eccentricity." Her eyes dart to Caleb when confusion fetters his brows. "We will discuss this later, but until then..." she stands to her feet, then moseys to the kitchen like it is more than three steps away, "... we shall eat cake!" My cock inflates when she murmurs, "From the small taste I sampled earlier today, it is *almost* the most delicious thing I've ever tasted."

When her eyes lower to the crotch of my trousers at the same time her tongue delves out to replenish her lips, I adjust the tilt of my thigh. I already confessed to my sister that Octavia's fixed my impotency issues. I don't need her to witness the marvel in person.

Discreetness isn't on Marissa's agenda when Caleb swoops in to help Octavia serve dessert. As he moves for the bowls in the open cupboards above the range, Marissa nudges her head to the door. "Can I talk to you?" When I lift my chin, she murmurs, "Not here. Out there."

"Why?"

"Just... *because*." Her excuse is pathetic, but the pleading in her eyes can't be denied. Whatever she needs to say needs to be said now.

After standing and tucking in my chair, I say, "I will be back in a minute."

Octavia's eyes stray to mine first. "Is everything okay?"

She stops licking mousse from her index finger when I reply,

"Yes. I just forgot I had a bottle of merlot in the car that will go perfect with dessert."

She knows I'm lying, but she lets me off lightly. "Okay, but hurry back. It might not be a Jersey summer, but with so many people in a small space, the mousse might not hold out until you get back." She lowers both her smile and tone when Marissa joins me standing at the entrance of the kitchen. "Both of you."

After issuing her a smile to ensure she has nothing to worry about, I guide Marissa out of the apartment and into the hall-way. "Make this quick. She knows I'm lying, and I hate that even more than the looks you've been giving Caleb this evening." Unlike when he bolted out of the bathroom, the glances I'm referencing this time around aren't amorous. "What is your issue tonight, Mar? You said you liked Octavia, but now you're treating her differently."

"It isn't Octavia."

"Then what is it?"

Before she can answer me, the thump of someone climbing the stairs booms into my ears a second before Jess stops at the landing. She was meant to join us for dinner, but a last-minute meeting saw her taking a raincheck. "Oh, hey... Mr. Carson." Her suspicious eyes shoot to Octavia's closed door before zooming back to me. "Are you late to dinner or leaving early?"

"We're about to have dessert."

My blunt reply confuses her more, but she hides it well. "Hence, Octavia's 9-1-1 for a spatula. They're a little light on utensils."

I scoff out a breathy laugh. I learned that the hard way. Have you ever tried to flip an egg with a fork and a spoon? It isn't easy.

After waving the spatula in the air, Jess murmurs, "Well, I better get this in there before we have to eat dessert off the floor." She curls her free hand around the doorframe before angling her torso to face a frozen Marissa and me. "Are you guys coming?"

With Marissa frustratingly reserved, I reply, "We'll be there in a minute."

Jess is the quietest I've seen her as she bounces her eyes between Marissa and me before she eventually enters Octavia's apartment. I wait for her shadow to disappear beneath the door before shifting my focus back to Marissa. "Out with it, Mar."

"It's Ca—"

"Maybe they forgot there's no elevator." Octavia's giggles bound through the front door of her apartment a mere second before she pulls it open. Her happy expression slips off her face when she feels the tension radiating between Marissa and me. "You're not waiting on the elevator, are you?" When I shake my head, she grimaces before muttering. "Sorry." Her hair flicks her face when she pivots to bolt, but before she can race away, her determination to keep our relationship on an even playing field gets the better of her. She twirls around before murmuring, "If you needed a minute to talk, you could have just said that. You didn't need to lie."

"Octav—"

"It's fine, Jack. I'm just saying you don't have to wrap me in cotton wool. I'm not going to break because someone says something bad about me. We're not flawless creatures. Our faults are sometimes what makes us the great people we are."

After a smile that exposes I'm not in the shit, she nudges her head to Caleb and Jess in the living room. "Once you've finished your chat, come join us." She stops, pauses, then tries again. "*If* that's what you want. No pressure." She appears as devastated as I feel about her assumption we're hiding in the hallway, seeking an out from her company.

Marissa's high shoulders slump when Octavia locks her glistening eyes with hers and says, "Just in case, it was a pleasure meeting you." Her hand shoots out to squeeze Marissa's hand even with her eyes relaying she'd prefer to hug her goodbye. I only get one measly word. "Bye."

When the door doesn't close quickly enough for me to miss her smile dropping into a frown, I curse under my breath before devoting my focus back to Marissa. Tonight had me gathering enough brownie points to last me a good couple of months, and now my sister has gone and ruined it. Even Caleb wasn't as stiff as he was Monday night. He greeted me with a handshake and asked what I was doing for the rest of the week since it was his turn to cook this week.

After taking in my devastated expression, Marissa murmurs, "You really like her, don't you?"

"I thought we already established that." My words are rough and cut up, sliced through the frustration gripping my throat. I wasn't the only one who thought tonight was going gangbusters. Octavia did as well. "So consider anything you're going to say before saying it. I won't have anything ruin this for me, Mar. Not even you."

She swallows numerous times before she commences speaking, "It's about Caleb." Her lungs expand and release three times before she breathes out, "Why haven't you offered him a position yet? He has decades of knowledge even with him only being twenty-eight and appears extremely driven. He would be a great asset to any company."

I step back, shocked. "You want me to hire Caleb?" When she nods, I push out with a scoff, "What happened to not mixing business with pleasure?"

"One, I think it is a little too late for that, don't you? And two, I'm reasonably sure working under you will never be classed as pleasurable. In case you missed the memo, brother, you're quite the tyrant."

I would deny her scorn if it weren't true. Before Octavia entered my life, I wasn't exactly commended on my warmth.

"He would be ideal for Son Ink." When her eyes stray to the

door like Caleb is standing in the doorway, I follow her gaze. "Then perhaps once he knows the real you, he won't be so quick to judge."

She had me convinced until her last sentence. "I'm not ready for that yet." I wait for Marissa to return her eyes to me before adding, "But I'm sure there is something suitable for him under the Global Ten media chain until I am."

Just the fact I'm considering exposing my true self to Octavia and Caleb instantly softens the agitation on Marissa's face. "That sounds like a good plan..." She nudges her head to the door that's barely concealing a healthy bout of laughter. "As does that." Her eyes are once again on me. "Shall we rejoin them?"

With a dip of my chin, I gesture for her to lead the way.

The reason for the laughter is exposed when my eyes land on a blob of brown partway between the kitchen and the living room. The mousse cake didn't hold out as Octavia warned, and although her casual t-shirt caught half of the sugary goodness I'm dying to sample off her body, there is no saving the rest of it.

"I'm so sorry," she murmurs, her tone low with embarrassment. "With the dining table only having four seats and Jess finally joining us, I thought we could have dessert in the living room."

"It's fine," Marissa assures her while ignoring me staring at Octavia like the perfect dessert has been displayed on an even more flawless platter. "I really should get going anyway. It's late." She gathers her coat and purse from the kitchen counter before spinning to face me. "Will you be okay if I take the town car home?"

"I can drive him home," Caleb offers a second before I murmur, "Or I could stay the night?" I lock my eyes with Octavia. "If that's okay?"

"Umm..." She dumps what her chest saved of the mousse cake onto the dining table, snags up a dishrag then joins Marissa and me in the entryway of her apartment. "Yeah, sure. If you want." Her last two words quiver when I snatch the dishcloth out of her hand and throw it into the kitchen. I don't want it clearing away the mess I plan to clean with my tongue.

"And that right there is our cue to leave," Caleb mutters, obviously as adept to Octavia's prompts as me. Her knees barely budge an inch, but not even an audience can weaken the hue of red creeping up her neck when she deciphers my hungry stare for exactly what it is. "How does a nightcap on your balcony sound?"

Jess's cheeks inflame as brightly as Octavia's neck when Caleb holds out his hand in offering to assist her off the couch. Once he's plucked her from the springless couch, he guides her and Marissa to the door.

The tension that's been crackling between Octavia and me the past several hours amplifies when we're soon the only two people in her apartment. Although I'd give anything to ignore the small snippet of unease in the air, I can't. "Whatever you think happened out there, didn't."

"Jac—"

"No, Tivy," I cut her off like she did me earlier. "I need you to know that Marissa is as besotted by you as I—" I stop, confident it is too early in our relationship to discuss feelings, but since I'm feeding off the energy in the air, I speak freely instead. I shouldn't be shocked. I purchased a boutique and a world-renowned restaurant within hours of each other simply to impress her. "As I am. I never expected you to arrive in my life, but that doesn't mean I can't acknowledge the joy it has given me."

"Jack." This interruption is more endearing than her earlier one. "I don't know what to say. I'm speechless."

"You don't need to say anything." Lust hisses in the air when I mutter, "But you can show me... if you want."

The shy grin tugging on my lips annoys me until it changes the dynamic between Octavia and me. Her feet barely touch the ground when she bridges the gap between us, throws her arms around my neck, then seals her lips over mine.

We don't make it past the kitchen before we're tearing at each other's clothes. Buttons ping in all directions when Octavia claws at my shirt. Once she has my abs and chest exposed, she drops her focus to my belt.

With my pants huddled around my knees and Octavia stroking me through my briefs, I waddle to the dining room table before adding as many smears of mousse to the back of her shirt as there are on the front. We make out on the mess, kissing and fondling as I wish we had in that muddy, poop-riddled field Saturday afternoon.

Once my impatience gets the better of me, splatters of cake flick into Octavia's hair when I whip off her shirt before dropping my attention to her skirt. Since it's already banded around her waist, I leave it where it is, but her panties must go. They're hiding dessert from my eyes, and I've always been a man who grades presentation as highly as taste.

"Oh... God," Octavia moans when I snap her panties off her body then drag her delectable ass until it hangs off the edge of the table.

As her hands shoot up to caress her jiggling breasts, I swivel her clit with gentle circles of my thumb. It doesn't take many rotations for Octavia's moans to switch from little whimpers to full-on begs. "Please... Jack. Please. Please. *Please*." She swivels her hips, bringing her deliciously enticing cunt to within an inch of my face. "It's time to return the favor. You need to eat me."

"I thought you'd never ask." I blow a hot breath over the sensitive skin before dragging the tip of my nose down the part in the middle. When her erotic smell has pre-cum leaking into the cotton material of my briefs, I stop holding back. In a quick drop-spear-lick maneuver, I burrow my head between Octavia's legs, invade her greedy pussy with my tongue, then eat her for dessert. "Mmm," I growl against her drenched pussy lips. "The best dessert I've ever eaten."

She jerks violently when I run my tongue over her swollen clit. She's super sensitive and at the point of begging, so instead of hitting the nervy bud with back-to-back flicks of my tongue, I swivel it around the hardened point then suck it into my mouth.

Pleasure ricochets through her as she violently shakes, but it takes another two or three rotations before I get the results I'm chasing.

"Please. Jack. Oh God... please." Her fingers weave through my hair as she grinds herself against my chin. Although being restrained was something I was originally opposed to, not an ounce of worry fills me when I pin Octavia's hands above her head before using my free hand to raise her ass off the beat-up wood of her dining table.

The unrestricted access drives her wild with desire, and within seconds, she's shuddering like she's in an ice bath and moaning my name on repeat.

I slowly bring her down from the high, equally loving how quickly I can bring her to the peak of ecstasy while also knowing her first climax is merely the beginning of our exchange.

"Are you okay?" I question when the release of her wrists occurs with her rotating them like they're stiff.

"I'm great," she assures me before the ache of her wrists is compliments to her jacking me off. She drags her hand to the base of my dick then back to the top over and over again while I carry her into the bathroom to continue cleaning up the mess we made.

"Not the bathroom," she murmurs in disappointment before I fully enter the tiny space. "Caleb has a thing about getting freaky in the bathroom. It's meant to be a safe zone."

Her reply sparks a hint of worry, but her gag assures me it isn't necessary.

Perhaps Caleb's quirks are nothing close to the reason I have mine.

After dragging my eyes to her bed covered with light bedding, I drop them to Octavia whose lower half is covered with chocolate goop. "Your sheets—"

"Are due for a clean." She wiggles out of my hold before guiding me backward until my knees brace her mattress. "As are you?"

The argument is settled when she pushes me back until my ass is swamped by the bedding and her lips are circling my cock.

CHAPTER 19
OCTAVIA

My hand shoots out to my vibrating cell phone, desperate for a few more hours of sleep. You don't consider the consequences of a romp-a-thon until it's too late. I got two or three hours of sleep if lucky, and that's only because Jack succumbed to exhaustion first. We weren't even fucking when he slowly nodded off. First, it was his words separated by breathy yawns, then his head began to wobble. It only took me running my fingers through his hair for a little over a minute before the soft pants of his breath lowered to a wheeze before they eventually switched to faint snores.

I think that was a little after three, but I can't be sure. The last time I checked the time was when an alarm went off around eleven o'clock. It was an odd time for an alarm, but before I could question Jack about it, he convinced me he missed a smear of mousse.

He was lying, but I happily played along as if he didn't.

After shutting up my cell phone, I roll over to greet Jack with a good morning peck. My lips touch nothing but air when I discover the other side of my bed is empty. As I jackknife into a half-seated position, my eyes shoot around the room. Jack's pants he only removed after shuffling from the entryway to my bedroom are no longer by the door, and his watch isn't on the bedside table.

I flop back with a groan before tossing my arm over my eyes. It was presumptuous of me to think he'd sleep over two nights in a row, but he seemed so comfortable in my place yesterday. If you had only met him, you'd have no clue he's a multimillionaire.

Perhaps he took more heart to his sister's worries after having a moment to consider them. Although I can't testify that their confrontation yesterday was about me, it gave off that vibe. Marissa's eyes were full of remorse when she said goodbye to Caleb and me, but something was still off about her. I could have pressed the matter further, but come on, tell me you wouldn't have responded the same way I did after hearing a man pretty much say your entrance into his life was a gift. I was lost for words as I am now when a delicious smell wafts under my closed bedroom door.

More impatient than I am prudent, I curl the messy bedsheet around my body before exiting my room. My steps quicken when I recognize the smell. Not because I'm excited to eat Loco Moco for breakfast, but because there is only one man I know who makes that dish.

Jack.

My theory is proven accurate when I burst into the kitchen with so much spring in my step I almost barrel Caleb over. He's leaning against the refrigerator, talking to Jack while drinking orange juice out of the carton.

I snatch the carton out of his grasp before nudging my head to the glasses, then I shift on my feet to face Jack. "Good morning." Either my voice is croaky from just waking up or the number of screams I released last night. I'd say it is most likely a bit of both. "Did anyone tell you it is not customary to eat rice for breakfast?"

"Depends who you ask." He kisses my temple in a way that makes my heart melt before he gets back to frying eggs with the spatula Jess lent us last night. It is clean, along with the table we left in a horrible condition.

Grimacing, I spin back around to face Caleb before handing him the orange juice. He can drink anything he likes out of the carton if it keeps him quiet about the mess we left in our wake last night.

"Oh… no… you've gone and got yourself confused, girl," Caleb pushes out with a hearty chuckle when it dawns on him why I'm being overly accommodating. "I did *not* tidy up after you."

My brows furrow in confusion. "Then who did?"

Caleb shrugs before he shoots his eyes in Jack's direction. "He was awake when I came home this morning, so perhaps you should ask him."

I don't know what task to tackle first. Jack and his ability not to sleep or where Caleb slept last night.

"And we're also not going there anytime soon." After pressing his lips to a similar area Jack's did only moments ago, Caleb peers at Jack over my head. "Fitz, right?"

Jack dips his chin. "I'll call ahead and let him know you're coming. He will show you the ropes."

My eyes dart between Caleb and Jack, completely lost. The faintest pink hue on Jack's cheeks keeps him quiet, but mercifully, Caleb has no issues communicating with his favorite cousin. "Jack offered me a job. It's at the bottom of the totem pole, but he said I could work my way up."

My heart warms that Jack already knows Caleb well enough to know he wouldn't accept a job with the hierarchies on the top floor. He likes to start at the trenches and build his way up. It is the way he's always been. That's why he agreed to move to Seattle with me and have a fresh start. We've not exactly made it, but we're living our life the best we can.

"That's fantastic, Caleb. I'm so happy for you." I hug him before pulling back to arm's length. "But does that mean I have to share the cooking responsibilities again now?"

Caleb laughs. "From what I'm seeing, probably not." He nudges his head to Jack, who's doing a good job of pretending he isn't eavesdropping before he drops his eyes to mine. "*I like him.*"

"*You do?*" In my excitement, I almost vocalize my question instead of mouthing it.

He jerks up his chin before pulling me in close to ensure his next set of words is only for my ears. "Our grandfather ruined his victims. He left them heartless, so there's no way one of them would be in our kitchen, cooking us breakfast. You were right, it isn't him."

Since I wholeheartedly agree with him, I take in the way his heart beats faster during his last sentence before using his shirt-covered torso to remove a sneaky droplet of salt careening down my cheek. "I told you," I murmur more to myself than Caleb.

He must hear me as he gives me an extra squeeze before announcing that he's going to get washed up before starting his day. "Thanks again, Jack. I truly appreciate the opportunity."

I wait for them to slap hands then shake them before rejoining Jack by the cooktop. "Thank you for doing that. You have no idea how much he's struggled not working the past couple of months."

He slides a sunny-side-up egg onto a beef pattie before replying, "You're most welcome, although you should probably thank Mar. She suggested it."

"Marissa suggested that you employ Caleb?"

Jack nods before guiding me to the dining table for breakfast, where I remain muted in shock for a couple of seconds. Marissa seemed more than eager to get to know Caleb when he bolted out of the bathroom in only a towel, but after a handful of comments, she seemed a little wary of him. She wasn't rude, but she paid more attention to his mannerisms than what he was saying.

After shrugging off my confusion, I try Loco Moco for the second time in my life.

Surprisingly, even with the hour early, I enjoy it as much as I did last night.

I slant my head to hide my smile when Jack guides me around a light post by veering us onto the road instead of pushing us closer to the gate that is seconds away from a menacing dog charging the flimsy material and growling obscenities at us for the next couple of hundred feet.

The fact Jack knows to dodge that dog proves he's been watching me as intently as believed.

"How many men do you have on me?"

Jack peers up from a stack of newspapers dumped at the front of a shop before cranking his neck my way. We're walking to work, and although many commuters have stopped to admire Jack's pricy suit, expensive haircut, and devastatingly handsome face, his ease about this area of Seattle soon loses their attention.

Don't get me wrong. They perve long enough to spike my hackles, but since I can't blame them, I only keep my narrowed gaze reserved for the ones who whip out their cameras to photograph him instead of taking mental snapshots. "Hmm?"

"How many men do you have watching me?" I repeat, not buying his attempt to act coy.

After sidestepping some dog poo that's been bagged but not binned, he sheepishly replies, "Just one." His shy smile is back, and I love it even more than watching him clean up after cooking for me. "But he is my main man, so he is the equivalent of five."

I rib him with my elbow, appreciative of the candor in his tone even with it being tainted with a bit of worry. "Do I need a bodyguard?"

He contemplates my question for a second before shaking his head. "Not necessarily. It is more a precaution than a require-ment." Nothing but honesty projects from his eyes when he says, "Fitz won't step in without just cause, and he reports directly to me, so if you're worried about your privacy being invaded, your worry is unnecessary."

"I'm not worried." I cozy in close to his side when the crowd thickens the nearer we get to the port. "I was just wondering how many eyes I need to check for before we get freaky in public again."

"Octavia. Christ."

His crotch grab is cute, but it has nothing on the smile Merrick issues when he spots me. "Tivy."

"Good morning, Merrick. Lovely day."

"It is. Very lovely." When his eyes drift to Jack, I attempt to offer an introduction. I say attempt, as it seems as if my intro-duction is too late. "Mr. Carson. How lovely to see you again." Merrick ushers him onto the ferry like he's royalty. He even pulls out his handkerchief to clear the grub off a seat before gesturing for him to sit. "I never got the chance to thank you. My wife is so happy. First the promotion, then the trip." He looks set to melt into a puddle when he clasps his hands together and places them over his heart. His eyes have never glistened with so much happiness.

"It was nothing," Jack assures him before peering around to make sure Merrick's praise hasn't gained us too many eyes. "I simply had a word with your supervisor about your exemplary service the past couple of years." He speaks as if he's lived in Seattle as long as me.

"Yes, but the gift. Oh..." Merrick locks his gleaming eyes with me. "Did he tell you, Tivy? Do you know he's sending Adeline and me on an all-expenses-paid trip to Italy?"

"No, he didn't tell me." The warmness surging from my heart to my toes and back again is heard in my voice when I say, "But you deserve it, Merrick. I can't wait to hear all about it when you come back."

He looks prepared to tell me his itinerary now, but mercifully, his supervisor advises him it is time for the ferry to depart.

After thanking Jack again and telling me to button up my coat so I don't catch a cold from the winds whipping off the waters, Merrick skedaddles away.

"Don't," Jack murmurs when I peer at him with gaga eyes. "For one, I helped Merrick purely for me, and two, I've had the displeasure of using a ferry bathroom once before. I don't want to stand on a floor that filthy, much less kneel on it."

"Kneel?"

I know what he's referencing. I just want him to spell it out for me.

Jack shifts his eyes from the choppy waters to me before he drags his index finger down my nose. "Yes, Tivy. Kneel because the lapse in judgment that occurred yesterday in my office won't happen again. Your needs should always come before mine."

"Who said they didn't?" His eyes bounce between mine, but he remains as quiet as a church mouse. "Getting you off was extremely arousing for me, Jack. I was drenching wet and could barely sit still for the rest of the day." I don't help my cracked lips—compliments of a windy day—by dragging my teeth over my lower one, but it can't be helped. When you need to bring out the sex pot, you bring her out. "I may have also used the visual as stimulation last night before you arrived."

Jack fans out his suit jacket before scooting to the edge of his seat. His knee brushes mine when he angles himself to face me front on. "You did what?"

I wait a beat, building the suspense before purring out, "I *pleasured* myself."

"With the toys in your drawer?" His words crack out of his mouth like a whip.

Ignoring the insane pulse between my legs, I nod.

"While thinking about me?"

I nod again.

"Did you come?" When I delay in answering him, he repeats, "Did you come, Octavia?" louder this time.

He looks more relieved than disappointed when I shake my head. "The visual was enticing, but why fake it when you can get the real deal."

With the hand resting on his trouser-covered thigh, I teasingly graze my index finger near his extended crotch. I'm not close to touching the prize, but you wouldn't know that for the way Jack reacts. He leaps to his feet, snags my hand in his, then bolts for the exit.

Regretfully for us both, he's too late. The boat has already departed.

That doesn't stop Jack from trying, though. "I need the boat returned to port."

"Jack, don't be ridiculous. You can't alter the route to suit yourself."

"Like hell I can't." There's no malice in his tone. No anger. He is quite playful. "Do you have any idea who I am?"

His lips twitch when I mutter, "Only five days ago, no... I didn't."

God, it is truly shocking to think we only met five days ago. It seems like so much longer.

"And if I were to believe the rumors, my hotshot boss might be *smoking* hot, but he doesn't take kindly to tardiness." Either flattered by my compliment or unable to negate my claims he isn't usually as carefree as he is right now, Jack remains quiet. "Come on. We both know we're not playing hooky today. We'll have enough rumors to contend with, let's not add more heat to the flames."

Once I get Jack back to our seats, I try to lessen the bristling of tension that forever teems between us by steering our thoughts away from our insatiable need to fuck. "You disclosed last night that your mother is Hawaiian, but there was no mention of your father. Is he around?"

I want to settle the electricity surging between us, and my question does exactly that. In an instant, Jack's face deadpans, and his hands ball into fists. "He's around. Just not in an emotional sense."

"So financially?" I ask, reading between the lines.

He scoffs out a laugh. "If you're asking if he is who I got the capital off to start my company, you're sniffing the wrong fire hydrant, Octavia."

I remain quiet, hopeful he will continue without prompting.

Mercifully, he does a few shallow breaths later.

"Marissa and I have the same mother but different fathers. Marissa's dad was killed on duty when she was eight. My father was his lieutenant." He drags his hand over his head, making my fingers green with envy before he mutters, "Someone's title isn't always synonymous with their reputation."

His comment stabs my heart with pain, but I play it cool. "How many years after Marissa's dad's passing did you join the family?" Marissa is gorgeous and has aged well, but it is clear there is a decent age gap between her and Jack. She also mothers him too much to act as if they are siblings close in age.

"Seven years later. Supposedly, I was such a handful, I wouldn't have made it to a toddler if it weren't for Marissa. She watched me while Mom worked nightshift, then became a parent herself only a couple of years later."

Loving his openness, I ask, "Only the one niece? Or do you have an arsenal of kids you're waiting to spring on me until it's too late, and I'm already snowed under?" I curse myself to hell when the statement smacks into me. I pretty much just insinu-ated that I'm falling for him.

Noticing I look set to flee, Jack curls his hand around mine to hold me in place before he replies, "Only the one with my blood for now, although I have a handful of children I class as nieces and nephews even without them sharing my DNA. They don't have anyone else, so I stepped up to the plate for them."

The pride in his voice inches my lips higher, but regretfully, it doesn't keep him talking. We spend the rest of the trip in silence, his lips only moving again to thank Merrick for the umbrella he offers us when clouds form on the horizon.

The weather has taken a brisk turn—just like our conversation.

It could be that we're approaching headquarters, but it seems like more than that. Something Jack confessed has stirred up bad memories, but since I don't know exactly which part, I'm unsure how to smother it.

We hold hands while leaving the port, down the bustling side street, and along the sidewalk of headquarters, only releasing them when we reach the turnstile entry door at the front. Although Jack's hand hovers above the small of my back as he guides us to the elevators, it doesn't seem as intimate as handholding. I've watched him guide female employees out of his office this way, so if it were seen as sexual, I'd be fuming mad twenty-four hours a day.

We're joined in the elevator by over a dozen people. Most get off before we reach the top floor, but Roach and Elaine exit with us, which means we part ways with only the slightest dip of our chins in farewell.

It is such a letdown after an awesome sixteen hours.

Some of the unease gurgling in my gut is pushed away for excitement when my eyes take in the grandeur of our new office space. Jack's team worked a miracle, and what was once a shabby top floor filled with bulky furniture and outdated cubicles is now a million-dollar office space with even more pricy views.

"Impressive, isn't it?"

I stray my eyes to Elaine before nodding. "I can't believe they put this together so quickly."

She smiles. "Jack hates wasting time." Her grin softens to a shy smirk. "I thought you'd know that better than anyone."

I'm torn between rolling my eyes and sighing. Jack's mixed signals are exhausting, and I only had a few hours of sleep last night, so instead of contemplating what the hell happened on the ferry, I ask Elaine, "What's on the agenda for today?"

Now she looks as worrisome as me as she shadows me into my office, where the desk is full to the brim with employee contracts.

After dumping my coat on the rack by the door, I groan before getting down to business.

S everal hours later, I can no longer ignore the protests of my bladder as I have the pleading begs of my heart. If I don't use the facilities soon, the coffees Jess arrived with this morning are going to make a mess of my new leather chair.

Elaine's head pops up when I mutter, "I'll be back in a tick. Nature calls."

She smiles before continuing to sign a stack of paperwork. Her focus only returns to me when I head for the staff bathrooms in the corridor. "Where are you going?"

"To the bathroom." My tone is as pointed as my brow.

I thought everyone knew what 'nature calls' means.

She shakes her head as if she thinks my daftness is cute before asking, "Why use the staff facilities when you have your own bathroom?"

"I have my own bathroom?" I don't know whose high-pitched girly voice that was, but I'm reasonably sure it wasn't mine. When Elaine nods, the same nasally squeal screams, "Where?"

The office is decked out with gorgeous wood paneling,

molding, and cornicing, but the only door is the one I'm about to race through before my bladder bursts.

My bladder's squeals are pushed aside for curiosity when Elaine presses a button under my desk, and one of the wooden panels pops out from the wall to expose a pristine bathroom fitted with black and gold accessories.

"You need to be careful. There is also a panic button under your desk. If you hit the wrong one, you'll have twenty security officers racing in on you in the middle of..." Her grimace finalizes her reply. "It's happened before."

"To one of Jack's previous *girlfriends*?" I stumble over my last word. Can I call myself Jack's girlfriend without first discussing that with him? And do I want to know about his past loves with how radio silent he's been today? I haven't seen him since we left the elevator. It isn't necessarily that he's avoiding me, but my bruised ego is certainly taking it like that.

Ignoring my heart's brutal twist, I brush off Elaine's shocked expression as a consequence of her not wanting to break the non-disclosure agreement she signed before working with Jack before entering the bathroom.

It is even more spectacular up close. A double shower with multiple heads takes up a majority of the back wall. The vanity stretches from one wall to the next, and there is both a toilet and a bidet.

Confident the mirrored wall next to the toilet is mirrored like the one in the elevator, I slip into the bathroom—closing the door behind me—do my business, flush, then head to the vanity to wash my hands.

Even the hand soap is designer, and it smells divine when I scrub it into my skin. As I dry my hands on the washable hand towels, my eyes flick to the vanity next to mine. The products on that side of the sink are far more mannish. It still has the soap dispenser and moisturizer combination, but instead of a floral perfume being offered as a refresher, it has aftershave.

Curious, I pace toward the sliver of light announcing there are two hidden doors to this bathroom. Since I know whose office is next to mine, my steps are almost too fast for my body to keep up with. I more stumble toward the door than walk, but mercifully, the man I'm racing for is too invested in a heated conversation to notice my approach.

"I can't uninvite her, Elaine. How would that look?" Jack pauses for a second before he starts again. "That's why I need you to decline my invitation." He grips his phone so hard I wouldn't be shocked to discover he's cracked the screen. "I know it's for fucking charity."

I duck back with barely a second to spare.

Jack swivels his chair so fast, you'd swear he has eyes in the back of his head.

When he stands from his chair, I abort my mission. Tension is already radiating off him in invisible waves, so I don't want to siphon his mood even more by being busted spying on him.

I race for the other end of the bathroom so fast I burst into my office like the boogeyman is chasing me.

Even Elaine startles.

"Are you okay?"

I wonder how many Elaines Jack knows when she peers up at me with concerned eyes. Her cell phone isn't attached to her ear. It isn't even on the desk.

"Yeah… ah…" I pivot to point to the bathroom door. "I couldn't work out how to get it open. I thought I was going to be trapped in the bathroom for the rest of the day."

Elaine is either slow or she wants this conversation over as quickly as me. "There are sensors near the door. You just need to move close enough for them to detect you, then they open."

I almost breathe out, "*Yep! I just learned that the hard way,*" but I keep my mouth shut before once again getting back to work.

My head pops up when Jess bounds into my office. She has changed out of her work clothes and become the envy of every female in the vicinity in a body-hugging pair of yoga pants and an X-back crop top.

"Ready?" When I grimace, she enters my office with a groan. "How can you forget Whack 'Em Wednesday? We do it every week."

"With Jack…" With him being the sole cause of my confusion and forgetfulness of late, I cut off my excuse before veering for an easier one. "Can I get changed once we get there? I have spare clothes in my locker."

"You can do whatever you like as long as you get your booty moving." She moves around my desk then plucks me from my chair. "We're competing against Linc and Tristan today. If we beat them, we're in the finals."

"Then maybe you should pay more attention to the ball instead of Linc's racket."

Jess scoffs off my idea as if it is ludicrous before she guides me past Jack's office and loads me into a waiting elevator. It is ludicrous of me to glance toward Jack's office to make sure he knows I'm leaving when I spin to face the front of the elevator, but for some reason, I do.

I don't want to be the cause of more torment for him.

That's why I've steered clear of him today.

My heart beats faster when I spot him sitting behind his desk. He's barking orders into his cell phone, but instead of his attention being rapt on the documents in front of him, his eyes are on me, his watch as hot and fiery as ever.

"Yep. I'm definitely going to need to check you for burns," Jess mutters when the elevator doors snap shut a second before it commences its descent.

I plonk onto the bench seat outside the squash court Jess is still playing on before running a towel over my sweat-drenched head. I have no clue how Jess talked me into playing squash competitively, but I'm reasonably sure it went along the lines of, "It's great for your glutes. Your flat butt will be a thing of the past in no time, and it only costs five dollars a game."

Since it was cheaper than a gym membership, I signed up.

I won't lie. I enjoy it. Sometimes Jess and I have to compete against each other, but most of the time, we play side by side. I went down in my game against Tristan, but Jess is currently in the lead in her set.

"You were fierce out on the court. You just need to keep your head in the game instead of on personal matters." When I peer up, I spot the gentleman with burnt orange hair and an almost blond beard who works for Jack. "Fitz. It's nice to officially meet you, Octavia."

I shake the hand he's holding out in offering before peering past his shoulder to Caleb, awkwardly hanging back. "How's he doing?"

Fitz signals for Caleb to join us before replying, "Surprisingly well. Although I'm fairly sure Mr. Carson only placed him on your watch since he's related to you."

His reply soothes the knock my ego copped earlier, but I need a little more. "Does Jack have jealousy issues?"

Fitz's lips twitch. "When it comes to you, yes?"

"And before me?"

It takes him longer to answer this time around. "I can't exactly answer that."

"Because of the NDA?"

I can tell he wants to arch his brow, but he keeps his expression impassive. "No. Because I don't have any data to go off before you." Before I can grill him on his reply, he shifts his focus to Caleb. "Please ensure Ms. Henslee and Ms. Arkwright are returned home safely, then I won't need you again until the a.m. Understood?"

Caleb bobs his head. "Yes." I struggle to hold in my giggles when the arched brow I was anticipating earlier pops onto Fitz's face, forcing Caleb to add, "Sir. Yes, *sir*."

"Very well." Fitz's eyes drop to me, their sternness lessening before he advises, "Mr. Carson asked me to give you this." He hands me a folded-up piece of paper before turning on a dime and marching away. Yes, I said marching, as his walking style implies a long lineage of military assignments.

Caleb physically relaxes once Fitz is out of eyeshot.

"A bit of a stiff?" I ask, reading between the lines.

Caleb pulls on the collar of his fancy new dress shirt. "A bit? That guy couldn't be more robotic if he tried." He unknots his tie, unbuttons his suit jacket, then straddles the bench seat. "But he knows what he's doing. You didn't even know he was watching you the past two hours until he approached, did you?"

I whack him in the stomach and tell him to shut up before shifting my focus back to Jess. "She's having one hell of a game."

"Yeah… because her opponent is paying more attention to her ass than her swing."

I take a second to relish the jealousy in his tone before muttering, "Can you blame him? He's asked her out a handful of times this season, and all he's ever gotten is a maybe."

"A *maybe*? What the fuck?" Caleb looks prepped to storm onto the court and knock Linc out. "*Maybe* I should show him what happens when you can't take a hint a girl isn't interested."

"Or *maybe* you should stop treating her as if she's only a friend, and she'd give him a straight-up no."

When Jess slams home a win, she spins to include me in her victory. When she spots Caleb standing at my side with his fists balled and the vein in his forehead almost bursting, instead of shaking Linc's hand like she normally would, she swats his bottom with her racquet before instigating the hug he usually orchestrates after each match.

My heart beats in my ears as I wait for Caleb to decide how to respond. I'm hopeful he'll finally stake a claim to Jess or at the very least tell Linc to get his hands off her ass, but I'm left disappointed when he mutters, "I'll meet you out front in five," before he storms for the exit.

Jess appears as disappointed as I feel when I finally read Jack's letter. It is a brush-off 101.

> *Octavia, I have some business to take care of this evening.*
> *I will see you tomorrow.*
> *Jack C*

"What is it with the men in our lives?" Jess asks after joining me at the bench and reading Jack's message over my shoulder. "They can't see a good thing even when you wave it in front of their faces."

Since I agree with her, I remain quiet while shadowing her into the locker room to get changed.

The next morning, I wake up with a crook in my neck and an empty apartment.

Caleb left a note on the refrigerator to announce his absence.

His message is more detailed than the Dear John letter I got from Jack yesterday afternoon.

Jack had some special guests arrive last night. He needs me to show them around today. Won't be back until late, but here's my share of the pizza.

A twenty-dollar bill is tacked under his note.

After snatching his share of our pizza off the refrigerator, I trudge to the bathroom, confident the promise of greasy food and a long shower will be the only things keeping me motivated since Jack ditched me for someone else.

"I'm not comfortable with the assumptions you're making, Grant. If Jack..." I inwardly curse myself. "If Mr. Carson wants to let Slade go, it will be for a legitimate reason. It also isn't my prerogative to overturn his decisions."

"But you can. The hiring and firing of staff is *solely* your responsibility."

"That isn't true. Ja... Mr. Carson is the CEO of this company. He does not need to follow the chain of command when it comes to *his* staff. He can fire anyone he wants. Me included."

Grant tosses an employee file onto my desk. "Yeah, all to suit his own objectives." He shoves his fingers through his spiked hair, making it stand on end even more. "He bought SS to suppress us. To drown out our right of free speech." I attempt to interrupt him, but his next set of words lodge mine in my throat. "If you don't believe me, read Slade's file. He was preparing a feature on Jack when we were bought out. He doesn't know who, but Slade is reasonably sure someone tipped Jack off about the story."

When I peer at the file, my curiosity getting the best of me, I spot nothing but pages and pages of redacted files. "There's nothing in this but a handful of names."

"Exactly," Grant exclaims with his hands thrown in the air. "Since Jack now owns this company, employee confidentiality and the NDA formed under that means not a snippet of Slade's feature can be publicly aired." He settles his temper a smidge before trying another angle. "In all honesty, I don't care what skeletons Jack has in his closet, but Slade is a good journalist. He is the only decent one we have, but instead of utilizing his skills, Jack let him go." His tone is neither deceitful nor anger-filled when he mutters, "If you want to save this sinking ship, you need him to overturn his decision."

Although I want to remain stubborn for the good of Seattle Socialites, I can't. "I'll talk to Jack."

Relief fills Grant's face. "Thank you, Tivy. I truly appreciate it."

While returning his smile, I show him out of my office. Nerves are telling me to wait a beat before confronting Jack, but with my conversation with Grant in the forefront of my mind, I head for his still-closed office door instead. It's been shut all day but more because no one has been game to veer near it. Jack's fuck-off vibes are strong enough to be felt through soundproof glass.

After rapping my knuckles on the highly varnished wooden door, I peer through the glass separating Jack from his workers. I don't know if it is relief that passes through his eyes when he spots me or concern, but whatever it is, he signals for me to enter his office after exhaling a big breath.

"Hey." I hate the lowness of my voice. Absolutely loathe it. "I need to speak to you about Slade."

"His removal from Seattle Socialites is not up for discussion."

His abruptness startles me but not enough to stop me from seeking clarification. "Why?"

Jack stops scribbling his name on the bottom of some forms before peering up at me. Regret is featured in his eyes, but it isn't his strongest emotion. Protection is, which is odd. "Because I said so, and my position awards me the courtesy of not needing to disclose a reason."

"Is it because of the article he was writing about you?"

Fury isn't an emotion I've ever seen Jack wear before now. "You read that?"

"No." I toss Slade's folder onto Jack's desk with the intensity Grant did to mine. "But if you're truly worried about what he knows getting out, why let him go? Why not use the company's NDA as a way to suppress what he knows? When he leaves Seattle Socialites, you can't stop him from writing that article for another company."

"Yes, I can," Jack refutes, his tone stern.

"How? You can't control every news article in the country—"

"Yes, I can!" he repeats, louder this time. "Because this is the exact reason I got into the media conglomerate to start with, so I can choose what I share or do not share. It is not forced onto me or coerced with a handful of praises."

So that's where his anger stems? He's mad that I wanted him to open up to me yesterday.

"No one is coercing you to share anything, Jack. They merely want you to be a part of their life." By them, I mean me. "As your recruitment officer, I'm telling you this is a mistake. As your *once* girlfriend, I'm telling you you're an idiot."

He calls my name when I bolt out of his office, but he doesn't follow me.

That hurts more than his radio silence over the next seventy-three hours.

CHAPTER 21
OCTAVIA

"C ome on. Let's go. I'm not taking no for an answer."

"Go where, exactly?" I groan between Jess's shoves when she marches me down the hallway of my apartment and into my room. "I'm penniless, dateless, and…" I hold back my last word. I will not be miserable for a man who can't see what is right in front of him.

Further, Jack and I were meant to be a one-night stand.

We just got a little carried away with the number of nights involved.

My eyes snap to Jess's so fast, I mentally book an appointment with my ophthalmologist when she murmurs, "To the gala."

"We can't go to the gala. We're not invited." That stung to say as much as it did to see a tuxedo dry cleaning bag in Elaine's hand when she left work earlier than usual last night. She didn't say it was Jack's, but the peacock blue coloring of the tie gave it away. "I also don't want to go. I'm too old to play games."

"Too old? *Puh-leaze.* You're a baby. You just feel a little worn down because you've been here before, fighting the same damn battle." Jess ruffles through the minuscule selection of dresses in my closet. "And we are invited. All employees are. It is one of the perks of being umbrellaed under Global Ten Media."

When she pulls out a dress far too improper for a charity event, I snatch it out of her hand and place it back on the rack. I should then march her out of my room, but my curiosity is once again too high to discount. "How did you find out about that perk?"

What she is saying is true. It was part of the conditions drafted in all the new employee contracts, but they haven't been approved yet, so it is merely speculation.

"It was included in the employment package I was offered yesterday." I stare at her with my mouth gaped and my eyes bulged, hoping like hell that what she is hinting at is true. She's been eyeing a promotion for years. She just hasn't been lucky enough to use her journalism degree just yet. "I finally got my foot in the door. It isn't a huge position, only small editorials, but it's a start."

"Oh my God, Jess! I'm so happy for you." I hug her tight, loving the way her excitement is felt raging in her chest. "When did you find out?"

She inches back before disclosing, "Yesterday. Jack offered it to me after his meeting with Slade. He's being bumped to politics, and I'm moving to editorials."

"Slade is staying with Seattle Socialites?"

Jess nods before devoting her focus back to my closet. "If rumors about his new offer are true, he won't be going anywhere anytime soon."

I'm pleased Jack took my advice, but it doesn't ease the stabbing pain in my heart any. Excluding our exchange in his office, we haven't spoken in three days. If we had a relationship, that's almost as long as we were together.

I breathe out slowly before getting back to the task at hand. "Although I really want to celebrate your new gig, I don't think we should do that at the gala. Both Caleb and Jack will be there, and I'm not in the right frame of mind to tackle either of them right now."

Caleb has been MIA the past few days as well. I think his bed has been slept in, but that's more because of the notes he leaves on the refrigerator than actual confirmation of an unmade bed.

"He instigated Thick Thighs Thursday, then didn't even bother to show up."

Jess huffs. "Tell me about it." After taking a handful of breaths to lower the severity of her pulse, she shifts on her feet to face me. "He is one of the reasons I want to attend the gala." I bow a brow but remain quiet. Jess doesn't need prompting. She can talk underwater. "You know that special guest Jack had that he wanted Caleb to show around?" I barely lift my chin half an inch when she pushes out, "She's a girl. An attractive, mid-twenties, New York native with glossy hair and a flawless face." She breathes out slowly. "And if that isn't bad enough, he is accompanying her to the gala tonight." I try to assure her that is part of Caleb's job description, but before I can, she adds, "As her date. He isn't on the job tonight. He told me so himself."

My heart sinks to my feet instead of my stomach, where it's been the past few days. "Oh, Jess, I'm so sorry."

She takes a moment to accept the genuine remorse in my tone before saying with a big breath, "So that's why we're going to the gala, getting rip-roaring drunk, and pimping ourselves out at the fancy-schmancy auction."

She had me until the auction part. "Hold on, what?"

"The bachelorette auction Elaine organized," she murmurs like I'm in on the gossip I have no clue about. "How do you not know about this?" When I shrug, she drags me to my bed, then plops on the edge. "Any single ladies attending tonight's event can offer themselves up for auction. It is strictly PG13. Lunch dates only and under supervision, of course, but all funds raised go to Jack's charity."

"Jack's charity? Tonight's gala is for Jack's charity?"

She gives me her best 'duh' face. "I thought you knew all of this." Her shocked expression switches to mischievous. "I guess there isn't much time for chit-chat when you have fucking to do." She saunters back to my closet. "But since Mr. Cranky Pants put a stop to that, you have no reason not to throw out some feelers tonight. We're both single and ready to mingle. We just need the naughtiest dress in Seattle to make them regret their idiocy."

I won't lie. It hurts knowing Jess feels the same about Jack's brush-off as I do, but it also solidifies my backbone. Jack could have just said he didn't feel comfortable discussing his personal life. He didn't have to throw me out like trash, and the reminder of that has me switching things up.

"Dig in the back. That's where I keep all my slutty dresses."

One hour and an exorbitant cab fare later, Jess and I step out of the mildew-smelling cab at the front of the Seattle Center. The hemlines of our dresses are much smaller than the ladies surrounding us, but our hair is styled right, and our makeup is perfect.

"Are we late?" I murmur when I notice there are far more people inside the center than milling outside.

Jess fans down the hem of her dress before lifting her head. After slinging her eyes to the left and dragging them to the right, she locks them on me. "I'd say we're right on time."

The cattiness in her tone makes sense when I peer in the direction she's facing. Jack is exiting a stretch limousine a few spots up from us. He isn't alone.

"That's Caleb's date," Jess murmurs when a gorgeous blonde slips out behind Jack.

"Are you sure?" I ask, certain she isn't Caleb's type. He likes women with curves and eccentric personalities, whereas this woman looks far too prim and proper.

She screams wealth, Caleb's unfavorable type.

Hurt clouds Jess's eyes when she nods. "Yes. I came over to grab my spatula yesterday. They were in the kitchen. Caleb was shirtless." My heart pains more when a second after fixing her dress, Caleb swoops in to collect the nameless blonde from Jack. He guides her up the red carpet, stopping and posing for the paparazzi on the way. "I told you."

Although I want to assure her it could still be a part of his job, I can't speak. I'm too busy holding my breath from Jack bobbing back toward the limousine to help someone else out.

I exhale a relieved breath when Marissa gracefully slips out of the back of the stretched limousine.

My relief doesn't linger for long. Marissa has spotted me, and although she gives me an apprehensive smile, she also rats me out to Jack.

I take a cautious step back when Jack's eyes sling my way. They're narrowed with anger and look fierce enough to cut diamonds.

"Maybe we should go."

"Oh, hell no," Jess replies before tossing her clutch under her arm and hooking her other arm around my elbow. "He may not be with a date, but he doesn't get to invite you to an event then backtrack like he didn't."

Something in her tone gives her away.

"You didn't get your invitation from Elaine, did you?"

She peers at me with dazzling, mischievous-filled eyes while replying, "No, but I'll be sure to thank Caleb… *after* kicking him in the nuts."

With my name still on the list as Jack's plus one, and the invite in Jess's clutch authentic, we make it into the gala before

Jack, Marissa, Caleb, and his date. They're held up by paparazzi, which raises my annoyance even more.

Are they the cause of Jack's sudden change of heart?

Did he not want to be photographed with me?

He made it obvious in the alleyway that we couldn't be caught, but I thought that was because he didn't want to be arrested for public indecency.

Silly me.

"Good evening, ladies," Elaine greets, her smile bright. She hands us our VIP lanyards before asking, "Will you be participating in the bachelorette auction tonight? Most dates will likely not occur. It's all just a bit of fun."

Before Jess can reply with a big, hearty, "Yes," a deep voice at our side interrupts, "No. They will not be participating. They were just leaving."

Jess looks set to tear Jack a new asshole, but since he is her boss and he recently gave her a shiny new promotion, she can't.

I can, though.

"Yes, we would love to sign up. Which form do we need to sign?"

Jack's heated breaths hit the back of my neck when he growls, "Octavia."

Ignoring him, I arch a brow at Elaine, wordlessly pleading for her to point me in the direction of the right form.

She succumbs to peer pressure with only the gentlest of nudges. "It's this one."

"Elaine," Jack grumbles this time around.

I've only just scribbled my name across the form when Jack seizes my arm and drags me toward the exit. "You cannot stay. I forbid it."

"Why? Are you afraid I might embarrass you?" My words crack out of my mouth as fast as the steps I need to take to keep up with him. He is like a bull in a china shop—fast and without fear of destruction. "If that's the case, don't fret. You're already making a fool of yourself. You don't need my help."

When he spots the paparazzi watching our exchange with eager eyes and lenses, he curses under his breath before tugging me in a direction opposite the exit. Once we're hidden in an alcove, he locks his eyes with mine and says sternly, "I need you to leave. *Please.*"

The pain in his eyes halts my retaliation for all of two seconds. "And I need you to take your hands off me before I remind you harassment laws aren't solely reserved for office hours. *Please.*"

He drops his hand from my arm so fast, a cool breeze wafts over my skin, then he takes a giant step back.

"I don't know what is going on with you, Jack, and at the moment, I don't really care. But I'm not leaving this party no matter what you say, so if you can't be civilized and attend it with me, perhaps you should go."

I don't give him the chance to reply. I return to the registration table with Jess, curl my arm around her elbow like she did mine earlier, then drag her into the opulent room.

"Don't," I warn when Caleb approaches me with pleading eyes. "I have every right to be here."

"Unlike you," Jess snaps out before she snags a flute of champagne off a waiter's tray and downs the entire glass in one gulp.

When she snatches up another one, I veer her away from the man coming at us with a full tray. As much as I told Jack I'm planning to stay, I still don't want to make a scene.

Although I'd rate my effort as commendable, within an hour, Jess is rip-roaring drunk and dancing with a man in a flashy tuxedo, even with the dance space being used more as a meet-and-greet location.

With my feet aching, I hobble toward a cluster of tables and chairs at the side of the elegant space. Like a bad smell I can't shake, Fitz arrives at my table two seconds after I sit down.

"I'm not leaving, Fitz," I snap out, replying with the same response I've given when approached by him numerous times this evening. "I signed on for the auction, so I can't leave until I've done my part. It is, after all, for charity." I hate myself the instant my snarky comment leaves my mouth. Tonight's event is for charity, and from the scent of wealth in the room and the sheer volume of participants, it is an absolute success. I'm just not feeling spirited. Although his eyes have barely left mine, Jack hasn't approached my half of the room in the past hour, and it is irritating the shit out of me.

"That's what you want? You want to participate in the auction, then you'll leave?"

I reply purely on the knowledge the bachelorette auction is the final agenda item on tonight's list of events. "Yes."

"Okay," Fitz replies, shockingly giving in. He's even more stubborn than Jess when she wants something. "I'll advise Mr. Carson of your wishes." He bobs his chin in farewell before he makes a beeline for Jack.

If I thought signing up for the auction would make Jack jealous, I'm dead wrong. Not an ounce of envy crosses his face when Fitz whispers my demands in his ear. He looks more relieved than anything.

I learn why when five minutes later, the hostess announces that there's been an alteration to tonight's scheduled event. "We're going to start with the bachelorette auction. See if we can kickstart some matrimonial matches before the end of tonight." The crowd oohs and aahs. "So can all bachelorettes please make your way to the stage so we can get proceedings underway?" She tells the men honing in on the stage area to get out their checkbooks before she hands the microphone to Elaine so she can state the extremely stringent rules for any matches made.

I only catch the first half of her rules since Jess has found me in a sea of many and shoves me toward the stage like her legs are filled with alcohol. "This is the part we've been waiting for." I think that's what she says, but don't quote me on it. "How do I look?"

"You look... *drunk.*"

She swings her arm through the air and clicks before muttering, "Goodie... 'cause that is the exact look I was going for."

I'm not surprised when Jess's auction exceeds the ones before her. Drunk is a good look for her, and despite Caleb trying to act oblivious to that, the bids Fitz placed on his behalf is a sure-fire sign of this.

Regretfully for Caleb, a security detail job doesn't earn enough to go against the man Jess was dancing with before her auction. He bid thirteen hundred dollars to secure a one-hour lunch date with her.

Now, it's my turn, and I'm as nervous as hell. My knees wobble when I stop under the bright spotlight highlighting the stage, and it has nothing to do with the glare Jack is hitting me with. It's from the heated stare of a man on his left. He appears just as powerful as Jack, but he has an arrogant edge that is a little off-putting.

"Where shall we start the action?" the hostess queries. "What about one hundred? Do we have one hundred dollars for this beautiful lady in red?"

My throat dries when the gentleman I referenced earlier commences bidding. "One thousand dollars."

"One *t-thousand* dollars. Okay," the hostess stammers out as shocked as me. "Do we have eleven hundred?"

"Two thousand."

This bid comes from the right.

Regretfully, it isn't from Jack.

"Alrighty then. It looks like we have a bidding war on our hands. Do we have three thousand?"

I choke on my spit when bidder one attempts to knock the competition on their ass. "Ten thousand."

"Woah. Okay. Ahh…" The hostess's mouth is as gaped as mine. "Ten thousand dollars. Do we have any other interest?"

The room is silent, except for bidder number two. "Twenty thousand."

"Thirty thousand," bidder one immediately bounces back.

After shooting bidder one a riled look, bidder two waves his auction stick in the air before muttering, "Forty thousand."

I can't breathe.

I am in absolute shock.

Even more so when bidder one fires back, "Fifty thousand."

And so the bids continue until they reach an absolutely ridiculous amount.

"Thirty million dollars."

This bid is from Jack, and he looks as furious as the man who commenced bidding.

"Thirty… *million*… dollars," the hostess gabbers out between big breaths, her wheezing easily audible in the room's silence. "Going once. Going twice. And sold! Congratulations, Mr. Carson, you just bought yourself a lunch date with this beautiful young lady for thirty million dollars."

I'm so dazed, I don't realize I'm being ushered off the stage straight into bidder one's hand until he uses it to steady my swaying steps. "Whoa, careful, darling. We don't want you getting hurt." His Texas drawl is as thick as his mustache. "Although I didn't come away with a victory tonight, I'm still in with a chance, right?"

"Over my dead body," Jack interrupts, his voice fiercer than the cut of his tuxedo. "Octavia, come here."

I don't know what shocks me more. That the bidders of my auction are still fighting even after the hammer has been banged or Jack calling me to his side as if I'm a lap dog.

Thirty million dollars or not, he doesn't get to treat me as if I am a possession.

Too angry to think straight, much less stand, I tilt closer to the gentleman keeping my legs upright.

He reads the situation in the completely wrong manner. "It seems as if the lady doesn't want to go with you, Jack, so how about you return to liars and cheats over there and leave her in my more than capable hands?"

"Stay the fuck out of this, Silas." Against the screaming protest of my buckling knees, Jack tugs me behind him in a protective manner before getting right up in Silas's personal space. "Or I'll have you thrown out of this event like I had you removed from your companies."

Silas doesn't appear the least bit worried about his threat. He huffs out a chuckle before threatening, "You wouldn't want that, or I might have more than a word with the media on the way out. I might even give them a whole exposé on the *amazing* Jack Carson."

When Jack storms Silas until they are chest to chest, I grip his arm to try and pull him away. This type of behavior is not acceptable in any form, much less at an event to raise money for victims of abuse. "It's fine, Jack. I'll go. Just let it be."

He stares Silas down, my promise not enough to keep his feet moving. "If you so much as breathe in her direction, I will take every single penny I earned for you and use it to destroy you." Like it is even possible, he takes another step closer to him. "I am not joking, Silas. Anything you think you can do to me, I *can* do to you ten times worse. I will fucking ruin you."

With Silas speechless and every pair of eyes in the room on him, Jack's fury lessens from a boil to a simmer before he spins on his heels and makes a beeline for the closest exit.

"Get him out of here," he demands to Fitz a second before he bursts through a door hidden by a thick velvet curtain. "Out. Now."

The security officers manning a bank of security cameras leap from their seats and race for the door. The leather chair of the closest officer is still warm when Jack plonks me into it before moving for a first-aid kit on a stack of filing cabinets.

"What are you doing? Who's injured?"

My eyes stray to the bank of monitors, anticipating a victim to be seen, so you can picture my shock when Jack snags my arm and twists it to face him. There are nail indents in my skin. They're thin, and have barely pierced my skin, but Jack acts as if I've been mauled by a bear.

He cleans them with antiseptic ointment before carefully placing Band-Aids over them.

The guilt marring his handsome face clears once the marks are covered, but the pain in his voice hasn't eased in the slightest. "I didn't mean to grab you so hard. I was just desperate to get you away from him."

"Desperate enough to spend thirty million dollars to make sure our lives didn't cross paths?"

When his eyes lift to mine, the pain in them shreds me raw. Thirty million dollars is chump change compared to how much he'd spend to keep me safe.

"Is he the reason you've been pushing me away the past few days?"

Before he can answer me, one of the monitors on my right answers on his behalf. After breaking through an emergency exit door at the side of the gala, Silas pulls himself out of Fitz's hold before snagging a cigar out of the breast pocket of his tuxedo. It isn't just his movements that give him away, but also the fancy diamond-encrusted cutter he uses to chop off the top of his cigar. I've seen it before.

"He was on the ferry." I sling my eyes to Jack. "The morning

you started withdrawing. He was on the ferry. I saw him…"
When recognition flares in Jack's eyes, I mutter, "And so did
you." His silence is more answering than any words he could
speak. "Why, Jack? Why did you let him come between us?" The
hurt I've been experiencing the past few days is projected in my
low tone. "I thought I had done something wrong. That I was
pushing you for too much too quickly."

"No, Tivy. You weren't. I was the one pushing. It was just…"

"Just…" I prompt, hating that I'm pushing but incapable of
holding back.

He rakes his fingers through his hair before shifting his eyes
to the bank of monitors. I don't know what he sees, but it puts
his barriers back up faster than I can snap my fingers. "I can't
discuss this here." The droop of my shoulders from the belief
our conversation is over doesn't linger for long when Jack
mutters, "I need you to come with me."

"Where?"

The unease suffocating the air of oxygen shouldn't make his
smile so endearing but try as I may, I can't ignore how quickly it
alters the tension to excitement. "I wasn't meant to show you
this until tomorrow, but for the commission alone, I'm sure
she'll entertain the idea of a late-night exchange."

Before I can ask him what the hell he's on about, he plucks
me from my seat, guides me out of the office, then commands
for Fitz to have his limousine pulled to the front of the gala.

F lashing bulbs and the bright lights of the cameras recording our every move blinds me when Jack exits the gala via the entrance he used when we arrived. Although he weaves us through the paparazzi like Fitz and Caleb's job description needs altering, we still get flung a range of questions.

"Jack, who is your mystery date?"

"Would you care to elaborate on why you're leaving festivities early?"

"Mr. Carson, this way. Please. One shot, and we'll leave you alone."

Jack keeps moving, his steps only slowing when one deep voice asks, "Is it true you founded this charity because you have first-hand experience in what the recipients are going through?"

My heart sinks when Jack retaliates to the man's insensitive question. He grabs the snickering pap by the shirt before bringing him to within an inch of his face. I'm anticipating for him to let go of my hand so he can ram his spare into his heckler's face, so you can imagine my shock when he simply snatches the media credentials from the pap's neck, stuffs them into the pocket of his trousers, then continues until we reach the limousine behind the story-hungry group.

We're more shoved into the back seat than ushered in, and the main pusher is the man I'm confident Jack will ensure is unemployed by the end of the night.

Grant wasn't lying when he said Jack fired Slade solely so he couldn't write a story about him. The instructions Jack passes onto Elaine via his cell phone a second after the limo pulls away from the curb ensures it is no longer hearsay, let alone spotting Fitz isolating the paparazzi in question from the rest of the pack from the rear window of the limousine.

Even with my intuition warning me to tread carefully, I dump my purse on the floor of the limo before bridging the gap between Jack and me. I don't climb onto his lap like I did the first time I comforted him in the back of one of his vehicles. I merely curl my hand over his, silently advising him that I'm here if he needs me.

My heart tries to resurrect itself from the sludge in my stomach when Jack tugs my hand onto his lap before he continues with his conversation, "I am aware of the time, Elaine, but I don't care. If she wants this commission, have her meet with us within the hour…"

Jack's words are drowned out when a pamphlet flapping on the floor near my clutch gains my attention. It is for tonight's event, and since my worry is now higher than my anger, I pay more attention to the itinerary than I did previously.

Jack wasn't scheduled to speak at the event he left early, but several other notable men were. Most prominent, Memphis Tate, once world-renowned NFL player and known sexual abuse survivor.

Memphis was snatched from the front of his childhood home when he was six. He escaped nine days later. Although his perpetrators were never found, Memphis uses his high-profile gig to keep children safe. He conducts talks at schools, shopping centers, and outreach programs across the globe.

I know this because I attended one of his workshops a couple of years ago. His story is harrowing but only a small part of the brilliant man he is.

It has me wondering if the same thing could be said for the man sitting next to me.

Jack has finished his phone call, but instead of interrupting my thoughts, he watches every expression that crosses my face when I realize the charity he founded isn't solely for victims of abuse. Its main focus is rebuilding the lives of children who were sexually assaulted.

When it dawns on Jack that he has my utmost devotion, he coughs to clear his throat before saying, "Speaking out like Memphis does is not an easy thing to do. Many men don't. They bottle it inside and let their lives be led by the shame and humiliation behind it."

"Like Silas?"

He looks both relieved and worried before he dips his chin. "Yes." He licks his dry lips before adding, "Events like the one we attended tonight are meant to encourage openness by not hiding behind shame victims don't deserve to have. It is about being honest with those closest to you in a safe and understanding environment—"

I curse the late hour and lack of traffic when the driver pulls to the curb of a building on a leafy street before announcing via the PA that we've arrived at our destination. It reminds Jack that we're not alone, which mentally re-erects the wall he was only just lowering.

"Thank you," I whisper in a near sob when Jack removes his tuxedo jacket and drapes it over my shoulders to protect my chest from the cold winds before he opens his door and assists me out.

Once we enter an elaborate foyer with a doorman in a top

hat and a glistening chandelier, we're ushered to an elevator by a lady who looks tired but ready to perform the sales pitch of her life.

It dawns on me that this is the case when our arrival at the penthouse has her listing off features like we're buying the latest model Rolls Royce. "This home features four bedrooms, five bathrooms, and is sitting a little under seven thousand square feet. The building is popular amongst locals with families and entrepreneurs such as yourself." After gesturing for us to exit the elevator first, she asks, "Do you have any children? There are excellent schools nearby—"

I stop her before she can get truly started with her sales pitch. "We're not married. We barely know each other, and as lovely as I think it would be to have five bathrooms, one, I'd hate to be responsible for cleaning them, and two, isn't five a little bit of an overkill?"

My reply hits the bullseye. The grin I've missed seeing Jack wear the past three days is back stronger than ever. Regretfully, his heart-stopping smile doesn't convince the real estate agent that she's not getting a sale tonight when he asks, "Are there views like this in every room?"

Her eyes light up, no doubt from mentally calculating the commission she'll gain if she keeps Jack on her side of the fence before she nods. "There's even one in the bathroom. When you're sitting in the tub, you can see snow-capped mountains."

As she guides Jack into the master suite, I step into one of the many living areas. As much as I'm not a fancy-schmancy girl, I can admit it wouldn't take much to adapt to such regalness, although an elaborate property such as this will *never* be in my price range.

Well, not anymore.

The end table would cost more than my monthly rent, and don't get me started on the suede couches.

The queasiness making me want to fold in two eases a little

when Jack stops to stand in front of me a short time later. He brushes the back of his fingers down my cheek, highlighting its paleness before asking, "What do you think?"

His gleaming eyes expose he's already made his decision, so instead of telling him it would take me ten lifetimes to pay this off, I say with a shrug, "It's nice, I guess."

"You guess?" After spinning me to face a view so spectacular it should be priceless, he cozies up to my back, then wraps his arms around my waist. His closeness sends my senses into overdrive, but it has nothing on the frantic beat of my heart when he adds, "For sixteen million, I had hoped for something a little more enthusiastic than 'I guess.'"

My eyes bulge over the monetary amount stated, but before I can announce that he could buy my entire building for that amount, he twists his torso to face the lady hovering back enough not to impede on a personal moment but close enough to have her night made. "I'll take it. Immediate purchase. Cash sale. I'll even toss in a couple of million for the furniture. I don't have time to decorate."

"Yes, Mr. Carson. Of course. What a wonderful investment you've made this evening."

As the agent digs paperwork out of her soft leather suitcase, eager to get the sale wrapped up—and perhaps get back to bed —Jack presses his lips to the shell of my ear and murmurs, "Pick a room, any room, and it will be yours for as long as you want it."

"Are you insane? I can't live here." If he isn't deranged, he is clearly deaf because he kisses my temple before he pulls away to sign paperwork like I never said anything.

Over the next forty-five minutes, Jack, Elaine—who arrived looking as flustered as a I feel—and the real-estate agent talk a bunch of mumbo jumbo while I stand awkwardly at the side, too scared to sit on anything in case the tanning lotion I rubbed into my legs this afternoon ruins the pristine furniture.

Once forms have been notarized and Elaine shows the agent out, Jack rejoins me at the window overlooking the bay. "Did you find a room you like?" After the events that forced us together tonight, the deceit in his tone isn't shocking, merely unwanted.

When he peers at me with an arched brow, waiting for me to answer, I shake my head. He barely took his eyes off me for a second during talks, so he knows I haven't strayed from my spot. I'm just entertaining his wish for this not to be as awkward as it feels.

"Then how about we explore them together?"

His fingers entwining with mine keep my words lodged in my throat for approximately thirty seconds. "I can't stay here, Jack. We've only just met, and I like my apartment building. The neighbors are friendly and—"

"This isn't a place for you to live," he replies, interrupting me and my long-winded denial. "It is a place for you to feel comfortable in and seek shelter if you ever need it." He spins and walks backward, his hand never leaving mine. "If you need time to think, you can come here, and I won't interrupt you…" God save me. He brought out the shy smirk like I can't feel his raging heart through our cojoined hands. "No matter how urgent the need."

I sock him in the stomach, hopeful an edge of playfulness won't have my next question stinging him too harshly. "Why would I need a place to think?"

When his smile sags a little, it takes everything I have not to set it back into place with my tongue. The only reason I don't is because the Jack standing before me now is neither a media mogul nor a hotshot boss. He is Jack from Jersey. "Because I am a difficult man to deal with, Octavia." He rolls his eyes like his next statement isn't factual. "I've also been told I can be some-what demanding on people's time." He drags his thumb over a vein protruding in my hand before admitting, "I am trying to approach this differently." He gestures his free hand between us during the 'this' part of his sentence. "I want you to have space to grow in our relationship, but I also need you to know that it is a *safe* space."

"I'm safe anywhere that I am with you. You don't need to purchase a penthouse apartment for me to feel that way."

He tugs me in close, stealing any further objections from my head. I can't be so near his devastatingly handsome face and act nonchalant. "I need this, Octavia. I need to know if you want to run, you have somewhere safe to flee to and gather your thoughts." After staring at me long enough not even my head can form an objection, he adds, "I won't force this on you. I will *never* force anything on you, it isn't who I am, but I need to know you have somewhere you will feel safe and protected even while believing you're not."

"Jack…" I should say more. I need to say more. I just can't. You couldn't hear the unbridled devotion in his voice and the unvoiced promises that he will never hurt me. You couldn't see the truth in his eyes when he said he won't force anything on me, and you also couldn't feel the turmoil his words caused my stomach because there is no one else in the world right now but Jack and me.

It is just us.

After a beat, I ask, "Will you use this place too? Will you let it be your private sanctuary if things become too much for you too?" When he shakes his head, I breathe out sullenly, "Why not?"

"Because I can't hide who I am from you, Octavia. I tried tonight and look where it got me—"

"Buying a ridiculously overpriced apartment to give me an unneeded safe haven?"

Dark locks of hair fall into his eyes when he shakes his head while muttering, "Worried I'll lose you forever once you know the real me."

The shame in his voice kills me.

It is worse than a thousand bee stings.

And since it was most likely a monster like my grandfather who put it there, instead of telling him he's being outrageously showy, I balance on my tippytoes and seal my lips over his.

"Nothing you could tell me will change how I feel about you, Jack," I talk over his lips. "Nothing at all."

CHAPTER 23
JACK

Shivers cascade through our conjoined bodies as I walk Octavia through the penthouse I purchased with the hope the glitz and glamor will hide my hideously ugly insides when she learns about the real Jack Carson.

Although this isn't why I brought her here, I should shut down the intense need to have her at all hours of the day and night immediately. I wasn't lying earlier this week when I said Octavia has my head in a tailspin. I've never acted so heedlessly before, but I also wouldn't change a thing. The man I've been the past week is the man I've been trying to portray for the past twelve years. I don't want to waste another second acting like they're not the same person.

Views of the Seattle skyline stretch as far as the eye can see when we enter the main suite of the penthouse. Elaine was seeking a suitable location for me to bunk during my prolonged stopover in Seattle, but the instant I saw it, I knew it would be perfect for Octavia. It is close to her work and has enough space that no matter how suffocating my secrets become, she'll never feel claustrophobic.

"Are we allowed in here?" Octavia asks through kiss-swollen

lips when I plonk her onto the large bed in the middle of the room before moving to close the shutters.

This building is one of the tallest in Seattle, but I don't want to take any risks. The media was already sniffing out a scandal when I failed to board my private jet last week. Mercifully, they never considered searching for me in the headquarters of a magazine I was disbanding purely because of the fluff piece a journalist wrote about me late last year.

I could have ordered a retraction, but rumors I had birthed three children with two baby mommas within a month of each other overtook rumors that I was on a no-sex sabbatical, so I decided it was best to divide and conquer instead. I disbanded the glossy gossip magazine seeking any associates of mine who hadn't signed a non-disclosure agreement before meeting with me, then I shifted my focus to Seattle Socialites.

Thank God I take jabs at my private life personally or the ravishing image of Octavia splayed out before me with an erratically panting chest and slightly parted legs may not have occurred, and I'd still believe I was born with a broken appendage.

God, she is perfection. Her body is tight and compact, but her tits are so luscious, I had to constantly remind myself the past week that the purpose of my assignment at headquarters was to rid the predators from the team, not become one.

It took everything I had not to ravish Octavia on my desk at any given moment.

It is a fight I won't win this time around.

A moan rolls up my chest when Octavia grips my cock through my trousers before giving it a gentle squeeze. She looks hungry, and instead of veering her away from an activity that would usually soften my cock just on the consideration, I encourage her boldness. I don't see blowjobs as punishments anymore. I haven't since Octavia sucked me off from beneath my desk earlier this week.

"Tell me what you want to do to me, Octavia. Tell me, and I'll let you do it."

She palms my cock, doubling its hardness, before lifting her eyes to my face. "I want your cock between my lips."

"And then?" My words are practically growls. That's how unhinged she makes me. How confident.

"Then..." she shifts her position from sitting to kneeling before adding, "... you're going to eat me for dessert."

Ah... so she did notice my lack of appetite this evening.

There were appetizers as far as the eye could see, and I was famished, but my hunger just had nothing to do with food and everything to do with the indecent length of Octavia's dress.

The gleam in Octavia's eyes keeping the blood feeding my dick hot dulls a little when I murmur, "Since you've already eaten, isn't it fair that I eat first?"

The flare darting through her eyes exposes that she knows I'm deflecting, but since I've caught a glimpse of her panties through the high ride of her dress's hemline, I brush off her concern as if I'm not.

"Did you wear these for me?"

She shakes her head, but I spot her lie a mile out.

"I like them. The color suits you." I push back on her shoulder, exposing more of the lacy red number barely concealing how wet she is. "Although I much prefer the coloring of the treasure they're hiding." When the rise and fall of Octavia's chest doubles from my confession, I mutter, "Show me what they're hiding, Octavia. Give me a peek of what I deprived myself of the past three nights."

Octavia was right when she said I pushed her away because of Silas. To everyone at the function tonight, Silas was my once business partner. Only we know our ties stretch much further than that. They started back in Jersey when he was an altar boy, and I was a boy looking for the fastest route to juvie.

My hand slips down to make sure my cock is still hard since

memories of my past are surfacing. Shockingly, it is. I shouldn't be surprised. Octavia parted her legs at my request before slipping her panties to the side. I can see the mess my mouth caused her delicious-looking pussy. She's drenched through, and when she fixes the lace material of her panties back into place, it doesn't hide a single morsel of her wetness.

While stroking my hard cock through my trousers, I drop my other hand to the button at the top of the fastener of Octavia's dress. It pops open without too much force and loosens the fitted bodice of her dress enough that her lavish breasts are exposed to my hungry gaze.

"Oh..." she murmurs with a groan when I drag the back of my hand down her budded nipple.

It peaks even more, straining against the thin material of her bra. When I roll the tight pink pebble between my index finger and thumb, her head thrusts back and her shoulders meet.

The more I tweak her nipple, the further the heat on her cheeks extends to her chest and the more her seductive scent streams into my nose.

Desperate for another taste of her delicious skin, I pull down on the lacy window covering her breast, then suck the hardened bud into my mouth. I can't tear my eyes away from her flushed face when my mouth causes her to squirm beneath me. Her expression when she is on the cusp of climax is what dreams are made of.

When she comes, her eyes sparkle with so much life, I'm convinced they'll never be extinguished of happiness no matter how many sordid secrets I share with her.

As her fingers weave through my hair, I suck harder, shocked I have her on the brink of ecstasy by doing something as simple as fondling her breasts but also delighted.

"Please." She tears at my hair when I slip my hand between her legs, then locks her eyes with mine like she's aware I won't make another move without her assurance that this is what she wants. "Touch me. Please, Jack."

She watches me through mascara-coated lashes when I slip her panties to the side and slowly insert a finger inside her. When I'm greeted by slick, hot wetness, I quickly switch it to two fingers.

"Don't stop," she begs when the fit is tight.

The walls of her vagina clench around me, making it seem as if I'm forcing my way in instead of being welcomed without pain.

The thought fucks with my head more than a malfunctioning cock.

I almost retreat until the sheer pleasure in Octavia's voice convinces me she isn't in any pain. "It feels *sooo* good. I swear to you, it isn't painful." She rolls her hips so her clit grinds against my palm. "Oh... God. Oh..."

"There? Does it feel good there?" I ask after adjusting the curl of my fingertips.

Although I'm not overly experienced with certain aspects of sexual activities, pleasing a woman with my fingers and mouth has never been an issue. I got them off without a worry. It was only when they tried to repay the favor that we faced issues.

That isn't a problem with Octavia, though. I'm so fucking horny, I am seconds from blowing my load in my pants. That's how much she turns me on. I feel like a teenage boy with nothing but the next hookup on his mind.

"What now?" I need her to guide the pace, or I'm going to tug her panties to her ankles, line up with her entrance, then drive home. Although confident her face alone will keep me hard for years to come, I'm so fucking desperate to have her heat wrapped around me once more, I'm growing impatient.

"Eat me," Octavia blurts out before the quickest flash of unease darts through her eyes. "Sorry. I can be kind of crude when horny."

"No, you're not," I reply before pushing back on her shoulder with the hand not wedged between her legs. "But I should be. I bartered to eat first, yet I made you wait."

When her back becomes one with the fluffy duvet covering the mattress, I push up her dress's hem until her red, lacy thong is fully exposed. "Jesus fucking Christ. These better be for me." I stuff my finger between the elastic waistband and her feverish skin before carefully prying it away. "Just the thought of another man seeing you like this…" A rough growl finalizes my statement. "Tell me you wore them for me, Octavia. Save me going on a hunt for an invisible man when that invisible man is me."

My eyes snap from her racy number to her face when she mutters, "I wore them for you."

I want to bang my chest. I want to shout from the rooftops that I got the girl and the millions, but instead of doing either of those things, I thank her by dragging her panties down her quivering thighs, spreading her thighs the width of my shoulders, then sucking her clit into my mouth.

The first spear of my tongue between her pussy lips has my head drunk on lust. Her taste is the equivalent of a bottle of expensive whiskey. It has me giddy and legless after only the quickest sample.

I lick her pussy, tease her clit with my tongue, and have her screaming my name in no time.

Then I do it again before the high of her arousal on my tongue gets close to vanishing.

When I crawl up her spent body, kissing and licking with every inch I cover, Octavia's eyes slowly flutter open before locking with mine. Her cheeks are flushed, her hair is damp at the roots, and nothing but unbridled lust is beaming from her hooded eyes.

"What now?" I mutter against the jiggly globes of flesh on her chest before circling my tongue around her budded nipple.

Her hot breaths float across my cheek when she murmurs,

"Fuck me."

My lips raise against her goosebump-riddled skin before I give her nipple one final graze with my teeth, then I try to scoot back to the end of the bed so I can remove my clothing. I say 'try' because Octavia's impatience for skin-to-skin friction is more bursting than mine. In a quick yank, tug, and pull maneuver, she tosses my belt across the room, lowers the zipper of my trousers, pulls the rigid material over my ass, then commences ripping at my shirt with so much intensity, she pops more than a handful of buttons.

Since I am as impatient as her, her delectable backside is scooped off the mattress, and the head of my cock is knocking at the entrance of her pussy before I realize I'm not sheathed. Then I remember condoms aren't needed with Octavia.

With a tight ring of plastic not hugging the base of my cock, I widen the spread of Octavia's thighs, gather her hands together, pin them above her head, then line up with the entrance of her pussy. "Are you—"

"Yes," she interrupts before she digs her heels into my ass and nudges me forward. Her breathless grunt switches to a moan when her impatience sees the first three inches of my cock ramming into her without preparation. "That shouldn't feel as good as it does, but my God, it feels…"

The groan that finalizes her praise increases the rock of my hips. I pump in and out of her on repeat, loving how well our bodies move in sync.

When my sixth grind bottoms out at her cervix, I mumble an apology under my breath before rearranging the tilt of her hips so she can accept a little more of me without extra pain. "Is that okay?"

"It's perfect. It is great. It feels unbelievably good."

My thigh muscles clench along with her pussy when I add a flick to the end of my rolls. As I drive her to the brink, her fingers clench around my hand while her toes dig into my ass.

We move as one for the next several minutes, our pace a little slower than the other times we've slept together.

"Oh... oh... *oh*..." Octavia moans on repeat, her screams lyrical gold to my ears.

While driving into her deeper, I demand, "Look at me. Let me see how wild I make you."

Her eyes open and lock with mine as a shiver darts through her sweat-slicked body. While maintaining eye contact, I rock into her again, pinning her to the mattress with both a lusty stare and my exhausted body.

Wave after wave of pleasure rolls through her when she lets go of the tension making her body a sweaty, sticky mess. "Jack," she calls out in a hoarse whisper.

Her moan alone is enough to race cum to the crest of my cock, but I hold back, aware her needs must always come before mine.

As she slowly comes down from an obscurity I once thought was out of my reach, she wiggles beneath me, silently begging for her hands to be released. "Please," she implores when her soundless pleas don't get through to me. "I won't touch you. I just want to..." *Touch you,* her eyes speak on her behalf.

"I-I can't. I don't want to..." My words trail off when not even the disappointment crossing her face softens my cock. It grows harder and somewhat thicker. It truly seems as if she is the magic pill I've been searching for the past fifteen years.

Confident I have the perfect solution to our situation, I roll us over until Octavia is perched above me. After swiping the crown of my dick across her throbbing clit, demanding her attention back to me, I slowly push back inside her.

Her moan has me wanting to ram in like a madman, to mark and claim her like she will never be anyone else's, but the flitter of pain in her eyes stops me. I take it slow, only giving her as much as I believe she can take and not an inch more.

It is a hard feat. She feels amazing wrapped around me. This is literally the best thing I've ever experienced—her warmth, her slickness, and the way she whispers my name as her body is once again overtaken by something far more powerful than any emotion I've ever expressed.

There are no negatives right now.

No wrongs.

Just two people with enough connection to power the lights of Seattle.

"Fuck, Tivy," I murmur when she adds a little swivel to her hips. She rides me mindlessly with nothing but the thrill of her next release on her mind.

I let her guide the way, confident I'll find my own release when she unearths hers. That's how much power she has over my body. She makes previously defunct objects functional again.

"Oh… oh… *oh*…" she singsongs again, her pitch increasing with each moan she releases. "I… I… I…"

The sting of my fingers digging into her hips to still her swaying movements push her over the edge. She jerks violently, her grunts ramping up when I add to the pleasurable zap darting through her by rolling her clit with my thumb.

It takes her several long minutes to disperse her shakes, and when she does, her body is spent and relaxed, and her eyes are almost shut.

"I can't," she murmurs in a whisper before she dismounts my cock and rolls off me. "I can't move my legs. You need to take it from here, Jack. I-I can't."

With a detailed explanation not needed, I rip off my dress shirt, adjust her knee so it's bent in front of her and sitting high on the mattress, flatten my torso to her back, then enter her for the third time tonight.

It feels just as good this time around as the previous two.

As I rock into her with steady, smooth pumps, one of my hands slides up to her breasts to tease and fondle them. I tweak her nipple like the wish to come isn't pulling every muscle in my body taut, positive I can work another orgasm out of her before focusing on my release.

"Jack," she pants a short time later, her voice back to its earlier needy moan.

Octavia relaxes into the rolls of my hips before she matches them grind for grind. I have no idea how long we dance this perfect, intricate routine, but my legs soon become as exhausted as Octavia's, and my breathing just as irregular.

As if sensing my wish to come, Octavia squashes her knee deeper into the mattress, opening herself up for more before encouraging an aggressive rhythm that fills the air with mugginess.

"Oh…"

I take her harder and faster, loving that her chase intensifies with mine and that she'll cross the finish line with me.

When she comes again, I bury my face into her neck, then groan through my own release. My body shakes as every last bit of my energy is dispensed into a blinding orgasm that is as physically exhausting as it is mentally.

On the verge of collapse, I still the grinds of my hips, roll off Octavia, then toss an arm over my tired eyes.

As I struggle to catch my breath, silence reigns supreme.

It is only broken when I mumble, "I should have asked for two hours."

Octavia giggles about the breathless deliverance of my words before she rolls over to snuggle into my chest. Her exhaustive exhales tickle a handful of my chest hairs when she asks, "Was an hour not enough for you?"

After arching a brow, I stare down at my crotch—my still semi-erect crotch.

"Oh God," she pushes out with a moan, her heart rate picking up. "Do you take something to keep it that firm? Because I'm reasonably sure no guy is meant to stay hard for as long as you do."

I wish. Not even Viagra worked for me and my issues back in the day.

After rolling onto my hip to mirror Octavia's position, I confess, "This apartment was staged for sale, so valuators need to price each piece of furniture so the total can be added to the contract price before execution tomorrow morning." With a huff, I roll my eyes. "I told my valuator to give me an hour before arriving."

"In normal circumstances, an hour would be plenty of time." After kissing me in a way that has me believing a three-day marathon romp still wouldn't suffice, Octavia pulls back and mutters, "But do you not still think this is a stupidly crazy thing to do? Maybe you should use the cooling-off period to your advantage and tell them the mattress was too firm for your liking."

I take in her flushed cheeks, dilated eyes, and spent face before shaking my head. "No, I don't. Especially not for this price tag." I bite my tongue before confessing that I would have spent a lot more than sixteen million to reach this peak of satisfaction. Not even the thirty million dollars I bid for a lunch date with her comes close to what I'm willing to spend to keep her here, at my side, sexually sated and looking at me like I can do no wrong. "But since I requested an hour, and they kindly granted it to us even with it being late on a Saturday night, I guess we better get cleaned up before the calvary arrives."

Loving the absolute awe in her eyes, I tap her naked backside two times, slip out of bed, then tell her to meet me in the bathroom. I want to be in a prime position to see her expression when she spots both the massive walk-in shower and the uninterrupted view of Mount Rainier.

It is nowhere near as spectacular as her face in the midst of ecstasy, but it is still an aesthetically pleasing sight I want her to remember more than the secrets I plan to share when we leave our little bubble.

T he buzz of multiple orgasms withers when Jack flashes me a playful grin before he hotfoots it to the attached bathroom. His pace is brisk but not fast enough for my eyes to lose the opportunity to appreciate the rigid lines in his back and his glorious backside.

They're spectacular, but no matter how much my libido tries to override my head for the second time tonight, the marks slashed across Jack's back won't allow it. He's marked—badly—and no matter how much I want to deny the facts, I no longer can.

Jack isn't a random stranger's victim. My grandfather is his monster, and I just slept with him in the sixteen-million-dollar penthouse he purchased so I'd have a safe place to get away from the demons a member of my family gave him.

Oh God. This is far worse than I could have ever imagined.

Too sickened with myself to stay put and almost certain Jack won't want me here when he learns the truth, I yank my dress in all directions to cover my private parts, then scoot off the bed. Tears trickle down my cheeks when Jack's playful hum projects from the bathroom. He sounds truly happy like nothing I could tell him would steal his joy.

Since I know that isn't close to the truth, I snatch up his pants from the floor before hightailing it to the front door.

He can't chase me if he doesn't have any clothes to conceal himself with.

"Tivy," Elaine mutters in shock when I race past her so fast, I almost knock her over. She just exited the elevator with a man of a stout build and glistening eyes. "Is everything okay?" Her eyes stray between the open door of the penthouse and me when I frantically stab the close button on repeat. A million questions filter through her eyes, but only one escapes when she takes in the black pants I'm gripping for dear life. "Are those Mr. Carson's pants?"

Her question barely leaves her mouth when she is bumped for the second time. "Octavia," Jack murmurs as he pushes Elaine out of the way, striving to reach the closing doors before they slam shut. His dress shirt is buttoned wrong since it was thrown on in a hurry, and his hands are maintaining his modesty. "Wait!"

Well, they *were* maintaining his modesty before he uses one of them to bang on the now-closed elevator doors.

Mercifully, his attempt to open the doors is fruitless.

They remain tightly shut.

When I stab my finger into the button for the lobby, and the elevator jolts to life, Jack barks out, "Demand for the elevator to be returned to the penthouse!"

"I can't," I hear Elaine reply before her voice is gobbled up by the elevator's rapid descent. "We don't have those access codes yet."

I reach the lobby so fast, the security officer manning the reception area only just picks up the shrilling phone on his desk when I dump jack's pants near the reception desk, then whizz by him.

"Ma'am!" he shouts before signaling for the doorman to grab me.

Years of defensive maneuver training comes in handy when I shrug out of the doorman's hold before sprinting through the double glass doors at the front of the building.

I'm so numb and shut down, I don't have any clue on the direction I'm running until the pavement pounding under my feet for several long miles is switched for water, and the gentle sways of a ferry lull me back to reality along with the burning cuts on my feet.

I stop picking gravel out of the wounds on my feet when a familiar voice says, "Tivy, dear girl, what happened to you?" Merrick guides me to a row of seats a young couple just vacated since we're close to pulling into port. "You're drenched and bleeding. God, you could catch pneumonia."

"I'm-I'm fine. I... ah... umm..." How can you tell anyone the horrors of your family? I've never been able to. That's why Caleb and I moved to Seattle, so we wouldn't have to live with that disdain anymore. We couldn't even walk down the street without being ridiculed and gawked at with disgust. "It's nothing. I'm fine." Like always, I try to deflect matters from my fucked-up family's past to something else. "Why are you here? Your shift doesn't start for hours."

"Rosco's little girl was sick. I said I'd fill in for him." After accepting a blanket and a bottle of water from a fellow worker, he mutters, "I'm glad I did. I was clearly meant to be here for you."

"I don't deserve it. I don't deserve *any* of it," I mumble through a sob.

After pushing away the bottle of water Merrick is holding out for me, I stand to my feet. No amount of pleading will hide the grimace that crosses my face when the cuts on the bottom of my feet protest my sudden movement, so I set it free.

"Octavia—"

"I'm fine, Merrick. I just need a moment to think." I stumble for the exit when I recall Jack's reasoning for buying the penthouse.

Did he know this would be the outcome of our night?

Is he aware of who I am?

No, he couldn't because there's no way he'd look at me the way he does if he knew.

"Sorry," I mumble to a fellow passenger when I take a right off the pier instead of left. I can't go home just yet. I need to get my head in order first.

I don't know how long I stay standing on the old wooden dock at Hamilton Park, but it's long enough for my clothes to be drenched through from an unexpected downpour and for the sun to start warming my front.

It's even long enough for Caleb to find me, and he hates the ocean more than anchovies.

"Tivy... fuck." He rips off his rainproof jacket Jack's company supplies all employees when they start, pulls it over my shoulders, then grips the top of my goosebump-riddled arms. "Where the fuck have you been? Jack is going out of his mind."

"Jack?" I murmur, my mind still sloshed and precariously balancing on the cusp of sanity.

"Yes." He nods before wordlessly demanding the attention of my wandering gaze. "He organized the search party. Every member of his crew is out looking for you, but no one has seen you since you exited the ferry four hours ago."

Four hours ago?

I must have heard him wrong. I couldn't have been staring at the swell of the ocean for that long. Surely, my panic attack couldn't have lasted that long.

I realize it did when Caleb rubs my arms, endeavoring to get me warm. His watch shows it is almost seven in the morning. "Come on, let's get you home and dried before we call Jack."

His second mention of Jack's name sets off waterworks. A sob tears from my throat at the same time a barrage of words escapes my lips. "He's him. The one I told you about. The boy with the scars on his back. That's Jack. That's him. He's our grandfather's victim. The one who... who... who... It's him."

"No," Caleb denies, his voice not as sturdy as his grip on my arms. "It can't be him. His identity has never been disclosed. It was removed from everything. The files. The police reports..." His panicked eyes bounce between mine when he mutters, "From you."

"It's him!" I shout, my devastation delivered with a stream of tears. "I saw them. I saw the marks on his back. It's him, Caleb. He's the one who... who..." I can't say it. I couldn't back then, and I can't now either.

Caleb's eyes bounce between mine for several long seconds before he mutters, "Are you sure, Tivy?"

Snot dribbles out of my nose when I nod. "They're not something I'd easily forget. You saw how horrific his scars were in the evidence file, would you ever forget them?"

"No," he admits, his tone lower than his previous ones. "I'll *never* forget."

After staring out at the temperamental ocean long enough for my tears to dry, he returns his focus to me. "What do you want to do, Tiv? You didn't see Jack when Fitz and I arrived at the penthouse to collect him. He's not going to back down easily. He's under. You snowballed him. You're embedded under his skin."

"I know," I mutter through a snivel, my heart breaking all over again. "Because he's not the only one who got pulled under. I was right there with him." A devastating sob tears from my throat when I mutter, "I am still there with him."

When I drag my hand under my nose to catch the contents spilling from there, Caleb gives me a sympathetic stare. He will never admit it, but I know this is the exact reason he won't let

Jess leave the friend pedestal. He doesn't want her bright demeanor stained by our sullied history, so instead of announcing he also has feelings for her, he pretends he isn't interested in her in that way.

"Is there somewhere we can go? I need time to gather my thoughts before I tell him."

"You're going to tell him?" Caleb sounds partly shocked but mostly relieved.

"Yes." I nod, my head bob sending fresh tears trickling down my face. "He deserves to know." I choke on my last two words. "It is going to hurt, but I have to tell him."

Caleb rubs my arm, offering silent support before asking, "Can I be there when you do?"

I immediately shake my head. "No. This isn't something that should be shared with an audience. He will need time to process things." My heart whacks against my ribs when I peer up at him with glistening eyes. "Time I'm not sure he'll be willing to give me once he knows who I am."

I'm lost to a sea of tears again, my devastation too perverse to ignore for a second longer. This hurts more than it did years ago when I learned my grandfather wasn't the admired man people made him out to be. He was a monster, and the fact Jack was one of his main victims makes his crimes so much worse.

"Come on. Let's get you home and changed before you get sick." Caleb bands his arm around my back and guides me to a blacked-out sedan idling at the curb. After slotting in behind me, he signals for the driver to go before he drags Fitz's cell phone away from his ear. "You know him. Seeing her like this will only make matters worse." He doesn't nudge his head my way to announce I look like an absolute mess. I can feel how mattered my hair is against my back, and my nose and eyes haven't stopped running in hours. I'm also an ugly crier. No amount of lying will alter that. "Let's just get her home and cleaned up first, then you can call Jack and tell him anything you like. Tell him I drove her myself, that we separated to cover more ground. I don't fuckin' care if you throw me under a bus if it gives us a couple of minutes to get her in the right headspace so we can stop more harm from occurring."

Caleb appears to be getting through to Fitz, but his loyalty to Jack rings through. "Mr. Carson is not—"

"Here to give orders, Fitzgibbons," Caleb interrupts, frustrating him more by using his full name. "It's five fucking minutes, man. Will it really kill you that much to ignore his directive for five fucking minutes?"

When Caleb's fists ball, I curl my shuddering one over the closest one to me. His body temperature is so high, it makes the shakes hampering mine so much more obvious. I'm shuddering like I'm in an ice bath, and the chatter of my teeth can't be hidden in the silence of the cab.

After flicking his eyes between Caleb and me for what feels like hours but is merely seconds, Fitz taps on the privacy partition between the driver and us. "Take us to Octavia's apartment," he demands when the glass slides down, his voice uneased.

A sense of unease washes through me when the driver locks his terrified eyes with Fitz before replying, "Mr. Carson—"

With a stern look that announces his decision is not up for discussion, Fitz mutters, "Leaves all discretions to me when he isn't at Octavia's side. So, as requested, take us to her apartment. *Now.*"

The driver dips his chin before signaling to bypass the West Seattle Bridge instead of going over it. With the hour early and it being the weekend, it doesn't take long for him to pull in half a block up from my apartment building. He can't idle at the curb since people have cleaned out their attics in preparation for the annual curbside collection pickup on Monday.

"Five minutes?"

Fitz notches up his chin in silent response to Caleb's request. "But not a second more."

Caleb is quick to unload me out of the car but not quick enough for Fitz to miss his grumbled comment. "It will take him at least thirty to get here from HQ, so I doubt a couple of seconds will hurt."

He eats his words when our arrival at Jess's floor of our building has us stumbling onto a confrontation between Jack and Jess.

"You'd have to know where she'd go to seek solace. You're her friend, aren't you?"

"Yes, I'm her friend." Jess gets up in his face like her livelihood isn't in his hands. "That's why she would usually come here, but you made that impossible by placing security on every corner of the block."

"For her..."

Caleb barely spins me half an inch when Jack realizes he and Jess aren't the only two people in the corridor. The anger on his face fades in an instant when his eyes land on me.

"Octavia..."

Even if Caleb wants to stop him from approaching, Jack doesn't give him the chance. He pushes him aside as if he is the weight of a feather before he pulls me into his chest.

I don't realize we're moving until he demands the police officers, detectives, and half a dozen security personnel in my apartment to leave. The smell of our intermingled scents on his skin set off waterworks again. His unique scent reveals he hasn't showered since I left him. Nothing but finding me has been on his mind the past six-plus hours.

As Jack weaves through the dozens of men in my apartment, I can barely breathe through my sobs let alone demand to know why the police commissioner is in my kitchen.

"I'll come down to the station later to finalize the paperwork and donate enough funds for you to run for attorney general three times over if you will just get the fuck out." No amount of power or wealth can deter the devastation in Jack's voice. It is bristling with pain and almost swamped by regret. "Please, Aaron."

No one could deny the plea in his voice. Not even a man with an impenetrable shell. After dipping his chin to Jack's request, Aaron Rickman orders everyone to leave. "Leave it," he barks at a group of men manning a temporary command station on my dining room table. "We'll come back for it this afternoon."

Caleb stands at the side of the living room when a stream of plain-clothes detectives, beat cops, and the commissioner veer past him. Only once our apartment is empty does he lock his eyes with me. "*You okay?*"

He's not asking about my mental stability. He knows that is shot to hell. He is merely checking if I am okay being left alone with Jack while he goes and handles Jess, who I hear shouting in the hall.

When I nod, he appears as if he wants to bolt, but his feet remain rooted in place, his heart as torn as mine.

"It's okay," I assure him, my quivering lips undermining my effort to quell his worries. "Go to Jess."

He almost shakes his head until Jess's angry roar reverberates through our apartment. "Get your hands off me!"

He's out the door in an instant, and even quicker than that, Jack plants my backside onto the counter next to the sink.

Needing to rip the Band-Aid off before the hurt in Jack's eyes siphon my heart of even more blood, I mutter through trembling lips, "Jack—"

"Shhh," he interrupts, his voice still pained. "I've got you."

An involuntary hiss leaves my lips when he raises my feet to inspect them. They're still cut up and bleeding, but standing shoeless on a wooden dock for hours on end has added splinters to the open wounds.

"You shouldn't have run, Tivy. You should have stayed." Before I can get in a word, Jack mutters, "But I shouldn't have been so stupid either." After fishing a pair of tweezers out of the top drawer like he is intimate with the floorplan of my apartment, he returns his focus to my feet to dig out the slivers of wood. "I should have warned you about my back. I should have been honest from the start."

"Jack, no—"

He continues speaking as if I never spoke, "I just liked the way you looked at me, and I selfishly didn't want that to change."

He peers at me through long lashes when I murmur, "It wouldn't have changed. Nothing you could say would make it change."

He takes a moment to gauge the authenticity of my reply before asking, "Then why did you run?"

"Because..."

My words clog in my throat when his brows pull together tightly. He darts his eyes between my lips and chest three times before he eventually locks them with my face. "Why are you shivering?" Before I can answer him, he unearths another untruthful fact as to why I can't stop shaking. "Your hair is drenched through. Why is your hair wet?" His ragged exhale fans my cheeks when he pulls back Caleb's raincoat to expose my soaked dress. "We need to get you warm. If we don't, you're going to catch pneumonia."

"I'm fine—"

He cuts off any further argument with a rueful glare. He wants me warm, and come hell or highwater, our conversation won't recommence until my lips and the tips of my toes are no longer blue.

I anticipate he will drag in the bedding from my room or a heap of towels from the linen cabinet to wrap me in, so you can picture my shock when he toes off his shoes and lowers the zipper of his brand-new trousers.

When his hands shoot to the buttons on his dress shirt, I beg my mouth to move, to speak the words screaming through my head, but no matter what I do or how hard my head pleads for me to make this right, my words stay trapped in my throat, and Jack continues stripping.

A sob I'm not anticipating rips from my throat a few seconds later. Jack assumes it is in response to the chilly ache that zooms through my body when he commences peeling off the clothes that are so drenched, they cling to my goosebump-riddled skin, but that isn't the case. It is in response to Jack removing every article of clothing bar the plain white T-shirt he was wearing underneath his tuxedo shirt.

Instead of letting my tears soak the front of his shirt like the showerhead does the back when he enters the shower stall by walking backward, I do what I should have done when I spotted his scars for the first time. I protect him as fiercely as he is endeavoring to protect me.

Jack balks when I push back from him far enough so my hands can shoot down to the hem of his shirt. If he wants to protest about me stripping him bare, he leaves it too late. I drag it up his rock-hard stomach and over his thrusting chest before whipping it past his head and dumping it onto the tiled floor.

His heart rate mimics the speedy incline mine is undertaking when I band my arms around his waist and bury my face into his chest. My fingertips brace the scars he's ashamed of, the marks my grandfather gave him, but I hold on tight, confident nothing is more important right now than him knowing he has *nothing* to be embarrassed about.

He did *nothing* wrong.

Several long minutes pass in silence. It isn't long enough for the water to run cold, but it gives Jack plenty of time to believe the reason behind my comfort. I'm not ashamed of his scars. I'm embarrassed that I know the person who gave them to him and that it took so long for anyone to storm in and stop him.

"Jack—"

He doesn't shush me this time or render me speechless by squashing his index finger to my lips. He uses his tongue, lips, and hands to turn my objections into dust and my heartache into need.

My lungs secure their first entire breath in almost seven hours when Octavia's lips part at the lashing request of my tongue. The weight on my chest feels infinitely lighter from the groan she releases when I spear my tongue into her mouth. I drag it along the roof of her mouth, tasting a palette that is uniquely her, yet so exquisitely delicious, it should be available worldwide.

A man would never taste a finer wine.

It was stupid of me to forget the marks that kept my playboy title fictitious, heedless to show them off without warning, but I wasn't lying when I said Octavia makes the woes of my past seem nonexistent. For years, I hid behind a shame I don't deserve to have, but I also didn't want to be painted as a victim, so instead of fighting as I am now to keep alight the only thing I have worth of value, I let the monster win.

No matter how small the reward or how undeserving the recipients were, I threw myself into every project I could find. Charities, businesses, a media chain that stretches from one side of the globe to the next, I've done it all, yet not one single achievement I have amassed the past twelve years has given me greater contentment than having Octavia breathless beneath me, involuntarily shuddering through the aftermath of countless orgasms.

When she ran from me, I thought I'd lost the chance to experience that again.

I thought it was out of my reach.

I'm a fool.

My kiss alone has Octavia on the cusp of climax. Now I just need to push her over the edge.

"Jack..." She breathes into my mouth when I guide her legs around my waist before I shift on my feet so her back can brace the tiled wall. I won't drop her, but I need her back far enough I can watch how her skin heats from the tips of her toes to her neck when my cock is sunk deep inside her. "We shouldn't... we need... there's so much we need to talk about."

Her last word comes out garbled from me rocking my hips forward. I drag the crown of my cock over her aching clit before locking my eyes with her already flushed face. I won't enter her without permission. No matter how loud the silent pleas are, I will never take anything not willingly given.

"Jack..." Octavia hiccups, darts her eyes around the bathroom, then slowly returns them back to my face. She watches me as intently as I watch her before she whispers. "W-we can't." An expression pulls on my face. I can't tell you exactly what one, but Octavia could. She has a way of reading me like no one else has, and her confidence that she knows me as well as I believe she does changes the angst in her tone to need in under half a second. "Caleb has rules about no hanky-panky in the bathroom. You're meant to get clean here, not dirty."

"So, you're not saying no. You just don't want to do it here?" My voice is steady and without pitch, but I am feeling anything but calm.

The tight band around my chest loosens its firm hold when she bobs her head. It allows me to secure another breath, but my lungs aren't close to being as replenished as they were only moments ago.

"But..." When her eyes stray to the floor and her teeth catch her lower lip, I growl out her name, "Tivy." Her nickname always breaks through her barrier first, then my gentle eyes obliterate it. "Just like you, nothing you could say will change how I feel about you." Our conversation seems nowhere near as serious as it is when I push out with a chuckle, "You drive me crazy, and I'm reasonably sure my shrink is going to start billing me double, but I'm here for the long haul. I'm not going anywhere. That's why I bought the penthouse for you. Because I will *never* run from you."

The heartache her face hasn't stopped wearing since I spotted her in the hallway of Jess's apartment deepens a little when she murmurs, "Promise?"

I brush her hair out of her face so nothing interferes with her ability to see the honesty in my eyes when I reply, "I promise."

When she exhales a relieved sigh, her breath fans my cheeks. It appears set to be replaced with a string of words, but before one can fire from her tongue, the buzzer on her apartment door roars through the bathroom.

Octavia spreads her hand across my thrusting chest when it swells in response to someone being at the stoop of her apartment so early on a Sunday morning. "It's probably just Caleb checking in."

The barrier she barely dropped while holding me tight in the shower resurrects when she wiggles in my arms, wordlessly requesting to be put down.

I let her go—reluctantly—and within half a minute, she's out of the shower and curling a towel around her still somewhat chilled body.

"I'll get it," I advise, my tone announcing my command isn't a suggestion. Her towel barely covers her voluptuous curves, and although Aaron left with only the slightest incentive—I would have given more than a donation to his campaign to have five minutes alone with Octavia—I can't be guaranteed Fitz cleared out the extra personnel we brought in when I spotted Silas mockingly staring at me on the ferry.

He wanted me to spot him that day, and I played right into his hand when I took his bait for the second time in my life.

"Why wouldn't Caleb use his key?" I ask when the buzz vibrates again, longer this time.

My speed increases along with agitation when Octavia answers me with a nonchalant shrug. Caleb has three keys because I made the locksmith supply extra copies when I had the lock fixed after Monday Movie Marathon. I hated the thought of Octavia having nothing but a flimsy lock between her and many of the perps in the building surrounding hers. The records Fitz showed me had me even more determined for Octavia to eventually live fulltime at the penthouse. I just couldn't let her in on my plan until she warmed to the idea of me spending so much money on her.

My annoyance almost takes a back seat when a strong flower scent wafts into my nose following the abrupt opening of Octavia's door, but the large bouquet of flowers doesn't simply hide a nosy florist spying on his clientele. It reveals the devil's imp has been let off its leash, and he wants Octavia to be his next plaything.

"What the fuck are you doing here, Silas?" As Silas places the flowers onto the entryway table, I tug Octavia behind me, my need to protect her far outweighing running from a monster from nightmares.

Silas smiles a slick grin while running his hand across the stubble on his chin. "Lookie here, lookie here. The rumors are true. You finally found someone capable of inflating that limp dick of yours." My jaw tightens so quickly it almost cracks when he shifts his eyes to Octavia. "I wonder if he'll feel the same when I tell him who you are because you haven't told him, have you?"

"Talk to fucking me," I demand when he speaks to Octavia as if I'm not in the room. "She isn't a part of this, Silas, and you won't be any more if you don't leave right now."

My words are strained through clenched teeth. I am angry and mad, but most of all, I'm fucking petrified that he's going to share all my dirty secrets with Octavia before me.

She doesn't deserve to find out like this. No one should be told their boyfriend doesn't deserve to breathe air, much less relish the oxygen she breathed back into his veins.

"You walked away with thirty million dollars, but you won't get one penny of that if you don't keep your end of the deal. You signed an NDA—"

"For what happened to you!" Silas yells, going with the same excuse he always used. He hates that I have a majority of the vote on anything that occurs with the payout we got for an incident that occurred to us back in our teens because, in the eyes of the court, I am Priest Maskretti's only victim.

I was four the first time he showed an interest in me. I was from a broken home, and my father was an abusive alcoholic, so my mother thought he'd be a good influence, that his upstanding morals and ties to the community would stop me from spending my youth in and out of juvenile detention as my father had.

I was six the first time Priest Maskretti inappropriately touched me.

Eight when he asked me to return the favor.

I didn't know what we were doing was wrong until I was twelve and Silas was eighteen. That's how well Priest Maskretti groomed his 'little boys.' They never spoke, not even while being grilled by detectives Marissa's dad worked with before he was killed on duty.

I wouldn't have come forward at all if it hadn't been for

Marissa. She tried to get me to talk for years, but it was only when she jimmied the lock to the bathroom and saw the marks herself did she finally get me to open up.

The floodgates were only opened once, then they were jammed shut until now.

My focus returns to the present when Silas shouts, "No one cared about the rest of us! No one asked us what we wanted!"

"Because none of you would come forward. You left me out there swinging the bat by myself." I can't breathe through the anger enveloping me. I can't think straight, which means I blurt out stuff I shouldn't be saying in front of other people. "I was a fucking kid, Silas. Toward the end, you were a grown man. You should have said something."

"I tried!"

"Bull-fucking-shit. You did *nothing* but shift the focus off you by putting it on me."

"Because you couldn't please him like the rest of us. You didn't have what it takes." For the first time in almost two decades, regret fills his eyes. "I also didn't expect him to do what he did. I didn't know he'd take it that far."

"You're a liar." The fury roaring through my veins burns like hell. It scorches through me, making not only my words hot when I shout, "It was your idea for him to whip me with his thurible," but my skin as well. "You even suggested for him to put it next to the fire so not only did it bruise me, but it would burn me as well. Inside *and* out."

I remember that we're not alone when my underhanded confession I was sexually abused with instruments sees Octavia take a stumbling step backward. Since her hands are covering her mouth, no doubt struggling to hold back the vomit racing up her food pipe, she trips on the turned-up corner of the rug, landing harshly on her knees.

"What the fuck are you doing, Jackson?" Silas's roar rumbles through my chest when I bend down to assist Octavia up. "Let the bitch bleed."

When he spits at her feet, blackened fury beats through me. I rear up in an instant and shove Silas so hard, his thump into the entryway table breaks the cornice away from the drywall behind it.

"Are you fucking kidding me? You're taking her side?" Silas straightens his shirt as if he's still wearing his tuxedo before saying with a sneer, "That little bitch deserves everything I plan to do to her." He locks his eyes to mine. They're as black as death. "What was Priest M's favorite punishment for you when your dick wouldn't rise to the occasion? Rosary beads up the ass or the pointy end of his personalized thurible?" He shuffles from foot to foot while rubbing his hands together. "Maybe I should force both up her virginal hole at once. I bet she'd like that. Wouldn't you, Octavia *Maskretti*?"

My mind is spiraling, but it won't stop me from saying, "Shut your mouth, Silas." I'm not solely reeling from him sharing secrets he legally cannot share, but I'm also stunned by Octavia's lack of rebuttal to him referencing her as Priest Maskretti's family. "Shut your fucking mouth before I shut it for you."

"You don't believe me, Jackson? After everything we've been through, do you really think I'd lie to you about this?"

Everything we've been through? He's acting as if we survived an afternoon thunderstorm, not a sexual predator who had over forty victims during his priesthood at the number one orthodox church of New Jersey.

"It wouldn't be the first time you've lied, Silas."

He scoffs off my claims with a wave of his hand and a *pfft* before he drops his eyes to Octavia huddled at my feet. "Tell him… or I'll tell him how you kept the spark alive by scouring his sealed records the instant you left his bed."

"That's not what happened," Octavia breathes out, equally shocked and determined.

"Oh, that's right," Silas pushes out with a chuckle. "You left him in your bed before having a giggle about his 'issues' while he was sleeping from 'supposed' sexual exhaustion." He air quotes 'supposed.'

I don't know what shocks me more, Octavia's lack of denial again or the sheer confirmation in her voice when she snarls, "You've been watching me?"

Silas bites out a chuckle. "Not you, sweetheart. Him." He nudges his head to me during his last word. "Have been for years." My anger gets a second wind when he strays his eyes to mine. "It's what happens when you're scrooged out of two hundred million dollars."

"Money you didn't earn."

"That money is a trust for victims of Priest Maskretti!" he yells, his face reddening with anger. "You weren't the only one he fiddled with, Jack. I was swallowing his cum for years before you turned up." I almost feel sorry for him before he says, "So that money is as much mine as it is yours."

"It *was* as much yours as it was mine until you used your status to force yourself onto someone. That was my only term, Silas. You can't be like him. You broke the *only* term, and you lost because of it."

My settlement was one of the highest ever received. It was so substantial, the judge didn't feel right handing that amount of money to an angry eighteen-year-old who just endured years of court testimonies, media scrutiny, and belittlement from my peers, so he set up a trust fund instead. I could use the money to set up a business or buy a house, but I couldn't squander it away like Silas did his first few years under the trust.

For the first year, I let it sit, confident it would cause more trouble than good. But as the years rolled on and the shame deepened, I was desperate to hide the reason I had a trust fund to begin with.

I wanted the power to control what was written about me. The media seemed a good place to start. I bought the local Jersey paper the following week. I'd only been there three days when every archive about my court case was obliterated from the records, and the final files approved for print were burned. Then I shifted my focus to the towns and cities surrounding my home state.

Within four years, I was touted as the media mogul of the modern times, and everyone referred to me by a different name.

Jack from Jackson was easy, and by adding the removed letters of my given name to my previous surname, the perfect alias was formed. Jackson Car became Jack Carson.

It was almost too simple, and until this day, no one has correctly joined the pieces of the puzzle together.

Well, I didn't believe they had.

When I shift on my feet to face Octavia, she stops shooting daggers at Silas to return my stare. Regret takes hold of her features even faster than disbelief grips my heart. I wordlessly beg her to deny Silas's claims, to announce she has no clue what he's talking about, but the longer she stares at me, the closer the world falls in on me.

"No," I say on her behalf, confident she couldn't be related to *him*. She makes my dick ache—she makes it fucking work—so she can't also be related to the very thing that broke me to begin with. "You're Octavia *Henslee*. You introduced yourself as Octavia *Henslee*."

It was stupid of me not to let Fitz do a background search on her, but I thought the unusual circumstances of our meet meant I was safe.

How foolish was I?

"Octavia Henslee *Maskretti*. Daughter of Simone Henslee and Douglas Maskretti." While scrubbing at his chin to hide his broad grin, Silas chuckles under his breath. "And you accuse me of being fucked in the head. At least I'm not getting boners over the granddaughter of the man who raped me on the altar with his incense burner."

"Shut the fuck up, Silas!"

He acts as if he can't feel the fury burning me alive and that I'm not seconds from following through with my threat. "Oh, man, wait until everyone from the trust hears about this." Blackened rage singes my veins when he shifts his eyes to Octavia and asks, "Will you at least confirm he fucked you at least once? They might go easier on him if they have a reason to stop looking at him like he's a pansy. First a limp dick, then rape by association." He returns his eyes to me. They're gleaming with bitter mockery. "Who was better? Priest M or his granddaughter I pretended was on her knees in front of me instead of her wrinkly old grandfather?"

I'm blinded by rage, blackened with hate so dark before I can consider the consequences of my actions, I charge Silas.

My hand darts up to suffocate my scream when Jack rams into Silas with so much force, they land in the hallway outside my apartment with an almighty thump. Too blinded by rage to notice his towel slipped off partway during his charge, Jack straddles Silas's hips before he throws his fist into his face. He hits him over and over and over again until the redness on his face matches the blood on his knuckles, and Silas is no longer laughing.

He isn't even moving.

"Jack, stop," I beg when he continues pummeling into him, oblivious to the fact he's unconscious.

The words Silas spoke were disrespectful and in poor taste, considering he, too, is a victim of my grandfather, but I doubt they'll excuse a murder conviction. If I don't stop Jack, he'll lose more than the millions Silas is chasing.

He could lose his life.

"Jack!" I shout again, louder this time. "Enough."

When my shout does me no good, I crawl across the beaten floorboards of my entryway before throwing my arms around Jack's sweat-dotted torso and attempting to yank him back.

My insertion into the violent situation doesn't reduce the power of Jack's fists in the slightest. He gets in two solid hits before he notices me clinging to his back like a monkey, and it only sees him altering his swings so I don't catch an accidental elbow.

Several painfully long seconds later, I shoot my eyes to the stairwell when, "What the fuck?" sounds from a familiar voice. Caleb is standing at the stoop of the stairs. His eyes are wide, and his mouth is gaped.

"Help me," I beg, shocked by his lack of gall. He usually participates in bar fights he wasn't even a part of. He has aggression issues, and not all the time can it be taken out on a boxing bag.

"Why the fuck is he naked?" he asks while assisting me in pulling a belligerent Jack off Silas. Even with it being two against one, it takes everything we have to keep him off Silas. "You didn't..." he gives me a look as if to say, 'fuck him' before muttering, "... right?"

"No." It was close, but I save that snippet of stupidity for another occasion. "We showered to get warm." The heavenly reminder of our shower doesn't keep my hopes high for long. A police siren just went off. It sounds as if it was right outside.

I do the same hand and knee scuffle I did to get to Jack, but this time, I head for the window that peers down at the street. "Fuck..." I half scream, half murmur after glancing past the dusty roller blind. "There's a patrol car outside. Someone must have called in a disturbance."

My mind races a million miles an hour when I sling my eyes back to the near massacre. Silas's face is barely recognizable, and neither is Jack's. It is hardened with too much rage to represent the cool, calm, and collected businessman he usually portrays.

A glimmer of clarity shines through the carnage. "Take him to Jess's apartment."

Caleb looks up at me as if I am insane. "What?"

"Just do it, Caleb." I snag up the towel that slipped off Jack's hip and toss it to Caleb. "He can't be here when they arrive. If he is, they'll put him away."

"Maybe that's a good place for him to be right now." When I shot him a how-dare-you look, he holds his hands out in front of him. "I know I'm not one to talk. I just—" His reply is cut short by officers in the foyer demanding residents to remain in their homes.

"Hurry," I beg when their footsteps grow louder. Jess is only one floor below us. He could make it to safety if Caleb hurries.

Caleb must reach the same conclusion as me. After curling his arm around Jack's limp body, he stands to his feet, tugs him into his side, covers him the best he can with the towel, then gingerly makes his way to the stairs.

I watch them disappear onto Jess's floor before shifting my focus to Silas. He's breathing. The ripple in the blood pooling at the corner of his mouth exposes this, not to mention the slow rise and fall of his chest, but I still check him for a pulse, aware the spasm of a deceased body can be deceiving.

I swear my grandfather's thighs twitched for hours after my father cut him down from the office at the back of his church.

I've only just placed my fingers on Silas's neck when the cocking of a gun's hammer freezes both my hand and my heart. "Ma'am, I'm going to need you to step away from the gentleman."

"I was just c-checking him for a pulse," I stammer out, my voice not as strong as I'm aiming for.

A young officer with blond hair and green eyes peers at the blood splatter I mentioned earlier on Silas's bottom lip before he lowers his gun and speaks into the radio clipped to his shoulder. "Operator, we have a possible 10-52. Send medics." He waits for the operator to advise an ETA before crouching down in front of Silas and me. After checking his pulse and rolling him onto his side so he doesn't choke on his tongue, he asks, "How long ago did you find him like this?"

"Ahh..." I hate lying, but since this is one lie that may help somebody, I run with it. "Around five minutes ago. I was in the shower and heard a bang."

My story is even more believable when I remember I'm wearing nothing but a thin towel.

"Can I get changed?" I thank my lucky stars that he's a rookie officer. He takes pity on my almost undressed state instead of worrying about any evidence being destroyed before the forensic team is brought in. "I won't be a minute."

I race into my apartment before he can change his mind. It takes me a good thirty to forty seconds to work out why I can't find my cell phone. I left it at Jack's recently purchased penthouse.

After tossing open my laptop, I sign into the Facebook messenger app and veer toward Jess's name. I'm in the process of typing out a message when one pops up.

Jess: *Jack is gone.*

As my heart rages against my chest, I type a string of words.

Me: *Where? And why did Caleb let him leave?*

I begin to wonder if Jess's fingers can move at the speed of light when her reply pops up not long after mine is delivered.

Jess: *Jack didn't give him much choice. He wants to turn himself in.*

What?

Leaving Jess hanging, I race back out to the hallway. The officer peers at me in surprise when he notices I'm still in a towel, but it has nothing on the shockwaves that pelt through me when I notice Jack cautiously approaching the officer from behind. He's wearing a pair of Caleb's sweatpants and a shirt, but his face is still full of torment and his hands are bloody.

I shake my head at him, silently pleading for him to return to Jess's apartment or, at the very least, wait until he has a lawyer present before handing himself over, but my pleas come too late. The officer has noticed his approach, and with his hands and face still bloody, he draws his gun and demands for Jack to lay on the ground face-first and intertwine his fingers together.

"Retain your right of silence," I suggest to Jack when he is handcuffed and read his rights, ignoring how eerily similar my father's voice sounded when my grandfather was arrested partway through a sermon.

No one would believe he was guilty, not even when a member of their own blood came forward as a witness for the prosecution.

Time moves at a snail's pace when medics and a handful more officers flood the hallway outside my apartment. Jack is carted away by two plain-clothes officers a second after Caleb and Jess join me by a still motionless Silas.

After throwing his arm around my shoulders like my shakes are because I'm cold, Caleb asks, "Do you know where they're taking him?"

I shake my head, my shock too high for words.

"It will probably be the southwest precinct," Jess replies on my behalf. "It is the closest." Caleb locks his eyes with Jess. He doesn't speak, but Jess has no trouble understanding his request. "I'll meet you out front in five."

With a smile bigger than the sun, he tosses her a set of keys before spinning me around and directing me to my room.

"Where are we going?" I ask when he commences yanking down pants and a shirt from my closet before snagging a pair of panties from my bedside table.

Caleb tosses my clothes onto my bed before turning away so I can get dressed in private. "If you want to help Jack, you need to tell them what Silas did and said."

While tossing on sweatpants sans underwear, I say, "I can't do that. Jack doesn't want it disclosed."

"Not what he said about the past." His voice exposes he

heard Jack's shouted words today. "What he said now. How he's stalking him and shit." He quickly glances my way to make sure I'm covered before he turns around and says, "This isn't the first time Silas has broken the restraining order. He's had multiple infractions." His voice softens a little along with the unease on his face. "This is the first time Jack has reacted, though."

"Jack has a restraining order against Silas?"

Although I will happily go without underwear, my breasts are too heavy to consider not wearing a bra, so I move to the drawer to switch out my panties for a bra while Caleb nods.

After clipping my bra together underneath my oversized shirt, I twist the clasp around to the back, then shimmy it up my chest. "How do you know all of this?"

"It is part of my job. Silas is trouble. He wants to make Jack's life a living hell." He hands me a pair of shoes from my closet while disclosing, "That's why I was assigned to be Keira's date at the gala. Jack didn't trust that Silas wouldn't turn up. I was to watch Keira, and Fitz was assigned to Marissa." His eyes are neither humored nor angry when he mumbles, "No one anticipated for you to throw a wobbly." When I shoot him an angry glare, he cocks his head and smiles. "But the good thing about you being a stubborn witch is that it exposed Silas was already aware of your influence in Jack's life." His smile sags when he confesses, "I also think he might have been who stole the files from my bedroom."

"What! Someone took our files?" His head barely bobs an inch when I slap him across the chest. "You were meant to destroy them!"

"He took them before I could."

"Goddammit, Caleb. If that gets out... if the world learns what Jack went through, he will never forgive me." That shouldn't be my first concern. Getting Jack off manslaughter charges should be my first worry, but for some reason, the prospect of him never speaking to me again seems more urgent.

"Did you tell anyone that it was taken? Does Fitz know?" My chest sinks lower and lower when he shakes his head to each of my questions. "We need to fix this."

"That's why I'm taking you to the police station." When I peer at him, lost as hell, he adds, "I can't say anything. Jack's NDAs are tighter than a nun's cu—" My narrowed glare has him swallowing the remainder of his reply before he says, "Fitz and I can't say anything..." He demands the attention of my wandering eyes before adding, "But you can."

I wish what he was saying was true, but it isn't. "I signed an NDA too. To the world, I am simply Jack's employee." *Probably even less than that now to Jack.*

"Yeah, you are," Caleb agrees, digging the knife in further. "But he wouldn't sue you."

I scoff at the certainty in his tone. "Jack may have defended me before he knew who I was, but I don't see him doing that now."

Caleb waits a beat before asking, "So you're not going to help him? You're just going to let him rot in jail for teaching a leech nothing in life is free?"

"No," I reply, shaking my head. "That's not what I said. I'm more than happy to break the terms of my NDA if it will help Jack, but I need to make sure you're okay with me doing that because that nest egg we act as if it doesn't exist won't exist if I go through with this, and I get sued. We will have nothing."

Caleb doesn't ponder the worry in my voice for even a second. "And has that slowed us down once the past decade? We survived a pandemic, a housing crisis, and months of unemployment, and we're still standing. If Jack wants to take the money our grandfather left us, let him. After what he went through, I'm more than happy for him to have it."

This is one of the reasons I would love Caleb even if he weren't related to me by blood.

"Alright, then lead the way."

I'm not at all surprised when our entrance into the living room has me spotting Fitz. He's standing to the side of the kitchen, and a man I've seen before but have never officially met is at his right.

Relief crosses Fitz's face when Caleb jerks up his chin in response to his silent question.

"Morris, this is Octavia. Tivy, Morris." Our handshake is awkward, but it allows Fitz to move on to more pressing matters. "We need to make this quick. The early hour will work in our favor, but if we want to keep Jack's arrest out of the papers tomorrow, we need him released from custody within the hour." Fitz shifts on his feet to face Caleb. "Tivy will come with Morris and me. Caleb—"

"Jess is waiting for me out front," Caleb interrupts, his tone more excited than worried.

He gathers our coats from a rack near the door before leading the parade outside. My stomach gurgles when I notice how much blood is on the floor where Silas once laid. He's been removed from the site, but there are still over a dozen police officers swarming our apartment.

"Keep your head down and your mouth shut," Fitz demands a second before we merge onto the footpath. The media is already here, and they're as hungry as ever. They push and shove me before asking a range of questions. Mercifully, the ones they ask about Jack are purely regarding my association with him and if I took the 'Hotshot Boss' off the market.

After being bundled into the back of one of Jack's town cars, my disbelieving eyes shoot to Fitz. He can barely contain his cockiness when he discloses, "At my request, they took Jack out the back entrance and announced to the media that they are here concerning a break-in."

"Half a dozen patrol cars for a break-in. Sounds about right."

The relatively short trip to the police station is long and silent. It doubles the churns of my stomach. I know what needs to be said and done to help Jack, but I also know the possibility of him forgiving me for sharing his secrets is extremely low. He didn't go to the lengths he did to keep his personal life private for no reason. He doesn't want a soul to know what happened to him, and I am going to do everything in my power to keep it that way.

I'll even throw myself under the bus if I have to.

My eyes dart to Caleb so fast the wooziness begging for a couple of hours of sleep doubles. His cell phone is on silent, but in the quiet of our apartment, even its vibrations alerting to a new message sounds like a jack-hammer drilling through a concrete floor.

"It's just Jess checking in," Caleb announces, his tone as deflated as my shoulders.

We left the police station over eight hours ago. Although the DA couldn't give me a then-and-there verdict, I'm confident my recollection of the events that occurred before Jack attacked Silas will go in Jack's favor. It hurt like a thousand bee stings when recalling what occurred before Silas's assault, but some good comes with a graphic memory.

Silas didn't hide his intentions for arriving at my apartment early on a Sunday morning. He made it very clear he wanted me to suffer the consequences of my grandfather's actions, and I made sure the DA and lead detective on Jack's case were aware of that fact.

My belief that Silas arrived at my apartment with the intent to commit a crime brought a self-defense plea into play. And since I was unable to recall who threw the first punch, it may not even need to be used.

I didn't lie during my testimony. The minutes leading up to the assault are a blurred mess of confusion, and something I look forward to forgetting—*once* Jack is released from custody.

"He should have been out by now. Perhaps call Fitz again."

"I've called Fitz. Numerous times. He's not taking my calls," Caleb answers, miffed.

"Then try Morris." I sound desperate. Rightfully so. I am.

Caleb stands to his feet, then gathers our empty mugs from the coffee table. "Can't. I don't have his number. That guy is a ghost. He only whizzes in when trouble is occurring."

"That is *exactly* why you should call him! Something isn't right, Caleb. I can feel it in my bones." The tremor that arrives with my words makes me feel ill. I want to vomit, but I hold back the urge when it fills Caleb's eyes with worries.

"Tiv—"

"I'm fine. I am just..." I rub my tired eyes with the back of my hand before breathing out, "Tired. Lost. Certain he's never going to speak to me again." Once again, that shouldn't be my first concern, but I'd be a liar if I said it hasn't been playing on my mind the past couple of hours. "I asked to see him after I gave my testimony to the DA. She said she'd check." My hair falls into my face when I dishearteningly shake my head. "She never gave me an answer."

"That could mean anything—"

"It means he doesn't want to see me."

Since he can't deny the honesty of my reply, Caleb remains quiet. It adds to the tension depriving the air of oxygen.

After several painfully long seconds, Caleb nudges his head to my room. "How about you call it a night. You haven't slept since Friday, and that would have only been for a couple of hours at most." When my brows furrow, shocked he noticed my sleeping routine, he mutters, "You groan every time you roll over. I stopped counting your flips when I reached a hundred."

When he plucks me from my chair, his tug strong enough for my feet to leave the floor, I whine like a child. "I don't want to go to bed. I won't sleep. I'm too worked up."

"Even if you don't sleep, you'll be more comfortable in your bed where you can stretch out." He continues forcefully walking me until I'm under the covers and wrapped like a burrito. It was how his mother always wrapped us when we were children. She said it was our safety cocoon. I've often wondered if she knew back then that something wasn't right with our grandfather. She kept clear of him, and Caleb only ever attended one service. "You good?" When I nod, Caleb smiles before nudging his head to my open bedroom door. "I'll be just on the other side if you need me."

He waits for me to jerk up my chin again before he hesitantly leaves my room. I doubt he will get much sleep tonight. He's as worked up as me. Viewing Jack's burns and scars in the evidence file we found while cleaning out my grandfather's residence three years ago was horrific enough, but it is nothing on witnessing them firsthand.

The ridicule from locals the years following my grandfather's arrest and subsequent suicide was bad enough but knowing how much of a monster he was, was more than we could bear. That file Silas stole is the very reason we moved to Seattle.

My grandfather tortured Jack, but Silas's unhanded admittance of a crime means he isn't the only one responsible for Jack's abuse. Silas was an adult during parts of my grandfather's horrible reign, so he must take responsibility for the part he played, even more so since he continues to torment Jack about it almost two decades later.

With a sigh, I roll over to face the only window in my bedroom. While staring out at the starless sky, I ponder Jack's mental state. Many decisions Caleb and I have made over the past ten years have been based on our grandfather's actions, so I can only imagine Jack's decision process.

I have no intention of sleeping, but as the minutes slowly tick to hours, my eyelids grow weary. I fight off sleep for almost three hours before it eventually pulls me under.

When I wake, my alarm clock is hollering, and my head is thumping.

It's Monday, and I'm late for work.

I dress in a hurry and use my fingers as a brush instead of the wired one sitting on my bedside table before entering the kitchen hot on Caleb's tail.

"Tivy..." Caleb doesn't say any more. He doesn't need to. His expression is telling enough. He thinks I'm a fool for believing I have a job, much less attending it today.

"I'll do more good being there than moping around here." I grab a protein bar out of the pantry before spinning around to face him. "Jack's employee contracts are very strict, but there's no harm making sure they're upheld. It's the least I can do after what I shared yesterday."

"You said what needed to be said to help him. I'm sure he understands that."

Since I don't agree with him but don't have time to argue, I shrug instead.

While waving an invisible white flag, Caleb asks, "Can I at least give you a ride in?"

I smile before leaning into his broad chest. "It's okay. I could do with the fresh air." I get two steps away from him before I spin back around, shocked this question has only popped into my head now.

Caleb reads the question from my eyes before I can voice it. "I know he's out of lockup, but I haven't heard anything else."

It isn't exactly the response I want, but it is better than nothing. "Call me at work if you hear anything else. I'll try and locate my phone sometime today."

He grumbles out a reply, but I don't hear him since I'm racing out the door. I leap over the damp floorboards where it looks as if someone tried to scrub Silas's blood from the beat-up wood before taking the stairs two at a time.

Since my mind is on other things, my heart leaps out of my chest when I forget to veer around the light post in the middle of the footpath. I don't crash into the pole, but I lose a couple of years off my life when the menacing dog hits the fence at the speed of light. He's desperate to punish me for entering his territory, and it has me thinking back to Jack's reaction to Silas's tease.

It seems out of character for him, but when you look at the entire picture, can you imagine his response being about more than what Silas said to him yesterday? It was a catalyst for years of mental and physical abuse, and it just happened to reach boiling point yesterday morning.

I smile a greeting at Merrick, but my heart isn't really into it. He must also feel the tension because although he returns my smile, he doesn't usher me to my seat like he usually does.

The trip to Seattle is cold and damp. It is the exact temperature you'd envision when your life is being turned upside down. There are no excited tourists eager to start their day. Just dozens of office workers dreading another long and dreary Monday.

I hold my breath while waiting for the elevator to arrive at the lobby. Although I could have jumped into the one that arrived when I entered my office building, I decided to wait for the elevator Jack and I regularly rode in.

Although disappointed when the doors pop open a couple of minutes later, at least the elevator is empty, meaning no one is subjected to my glistening eyes and disappointed expression for longer than necessary.

The top floor is a bustling hive of activity, and my heart

jumps into the same frantic beat when I spot a shadow reflecting on the glass wall of Jack's office.

I race his way in an instant, sidestepping a shocked Jess partway there.

"Jack—" My relief is brutally squashed when the man who spins to face me isn't the handsome Hotshot Boss I was anticipating. "Mr. Potts. Ah… hello." I scan Jack's office, certain I'm dreaming. Why would Mr. Potts be back now? Jack fired him, didn't he?

Too shocked to speak cordially, I stammer, "What are you doing here? Where's Jack?"

Mr. Potts shoves his hands into his pockets, his look pretentious. "Jack?"

He knows who I am referencing. He's just being an ass.

"Jack Carson. The man who fired you. *That* man."

It dawns on me that he may be in Jack's office, but he will never fill his shoes when he only responds to my rile with a sneer. Before Jack, he would have fired me on the spot just for speaking down at him.

After several seconds of long silence, he eventually informs, "Mr. Carson's work here is done. Now I'm back to ensure we continue onward and upward." He nudges his head to my office, his sneer blinding. "So how about we get started. I noticed you had a pile of employee folders on your desk. Return them to HR before joining me in my office. I need to dictate a staff memo to you for release."

And just like that, my promotion is downgraded to a mere assistant again. Pity, my ego won't allow it, but it must wait since I've spotted Jess still lingering at the side of Mr. Potts's office, desperate to talk to me.

"I'll return as soon as I can."

Mr. Potts tries to argue, but I'm out of his office like my backside is on fire.

"What is it?" I ask Jess, confident I know her petrified face when I see it. It was the same look she wore when Caleb dragged her out of the gala seconds before Jack pulled me into the security office. "Have you heard from Jack?"

Disappointment flares through her eyes before she shakes her head. "No, but I'm certain we have a situation in editorials." When my brows furrow, shocked she thinks I have any say at anything that occurs in editorials, she adds, "Slade is preparing a feature on Jack. It includes his arrest amongst many other *things.*"

She doesn't need to spell out what 'things' entails. Her facial expression announces the whole horrid story.

"Where is he?"

While she guides me toward a section I had once hoped to work in, I prepare the lengthy tirade I plan to unleash on Slade. It includes many of the words Grant used when defending him, but I've flipped them on their head. They include him being sued, never working again, and how there will not only be moral ramifications to his actions but legal ones as well.

"You need to consider a new field of work. My God, Tivy. I didn't know you had it in you." Jess jabs her finger into the elevator button before spinning to face me. "Slade just got torn a new asshole, but you did it in a way he wants to thank you for the invasion." Something on my face must give me away. "Oh, shit, Tiv. I'm sorry. I didn't think before speaking." Her reply confirms that she and Caleb heard every word that Jack and Silas shouted yesterday. "It is a bad habit of mine, and I really need to learn how to control it."

The genuine remorse in her voice exposes she didn't mean

her comment with malice. "It's fine. I often get caught talking nonsense."

We ride the elevator to the top floor in silence, the quiet only interrupted when Mr. Potts spots my exit. "Let's go, Ms. Henslee. We haven't got all day."

Years of being pushed around sees my feet jumping into action before my head and heart can object. I race into my office to grab a notepad and pen, my pace slowing when I spot a handwritten message on the notepad. It isn't in my handwriting, but the location and monetary amount circled gives away who wrote it.

It is the address of the penthouse Jack purchased Saturday night.

I freeze as a surge of hope darts through me.

Could that be where Jack is?

Could he be at my safe haven?

Confident I'm on the money, I tear off the top sheet of the notepad, then bolt out of my office like a maniac.

"Octavia," Mr. Potts shouts when he spots me racing in the opposite direction of his office. When I request for the rider in the elevator to wait, he shouts, "If you leave, consider yourself fired."

I dart into the elevator without the slightest falter in my strides. There are far more important things to life than financial stability. Furthermore, I've pulled myself out of the trenches once, so I'm sure I can do it again.

As I race out of headquarters, I spot a cab coming from the other direction. I toss my hand in the air, summoning it for only a second before I remember that I don't have access to my cell phone or purse, so I can't pay the fare.

"Get in," states a male voice behind me a second after finalizing my demand for the cab to stop.

Fitz looks as tired as Caleb. However, nothing but gratitude gleams in his eyes when he opens the back door of the cab for me before handing the driver a one-hundred-dollar bill. "Take her where she needs to go, then wait out front. If she doesn't return within twenty minutes, you can leave. If she does, send the bill for wherever she needs to go next to this account." He hands the driver a glossy black business card. I'm about to thank him, but before I can, he shifts his focus back to me before warning, "This isn't going to be pleasant, Octavia, but if anyone can get through to him, it will be you."

My nose tingles as fresh tears spring in my eyes. Fitz's relationship with Jack exposes it is more than work-related, so for him to believe I have more chance of getting through to him means a lot.

"What should I prepare for, Fitz?"

He licks his lips but doesn't look at me while replying, "Decades of hurt being unleashed at once." He steals my chance to reply by shutting the cab door then tapping on the roof, silently advising the driver that there is an opening coming up.

Nerves take flight in my stomach the longer the cab rolls across the asphalt. The worry in Fitz's tone when he warned what I'm approaching won't be pretty is already off-putting, not to mention Elaine's tear-streaked face when I enter the lobby of Jack's penthouse.

"Let her in," she advises the doorman before she shifts her eyes to her feet.

She doesn't look at me when I'm guided toward the elevator by a security officer. She doesn't move until I'm ushered into the idling elevator with the pin code already punched into the digital dashboard, and I'm left alone to fend for myself.

I swallow the bile burning the back of my throat while watching the dashboard count each floor. It is a long climb but worthwhile. It gives me the chance to settle some of the nerves slicking my skin with sweat and to work out how to explain to Jack that I had planned to tell him who I was, but I wasn't given the chance.

When the elevator arrives at the penthouse floor, I breathe out the nerves making me feel ill before gingerly stepping into the elaborate space. It looks the same as it did only nights ago, but the heavy scent of alcohol makes it seem nowhere near as posh.

Someone has been drinking, and by the smell of it, in abundance.

I turn toward the bedroom on the other side of the penthouse when Jack's voice roars through the double doors. "How could you not have said something? You knew who they fucking were, but you said nothing!"

He must have his caller on speaker because I hear her reply, "I tried, Jack. But then..."

When Marissa's reply trails off, Jack demands an answer. "But then..."

Her sigh ruffles the shards of my heart. "But then I saw how you looked at her when you thought you'd upset her, so I figured it would be best to give you time to work it out yourself."

"Mar—"

"But not her, Jack. I didn't know she was involved. It was her cousin—"

I stop walking at the same time Marissa's voice stops sounding out of the speaker of Jack's cell phone. He must have placed his call on mute because not even her frantic breaths can be heard.

It feels like minutes pass before Jack eventually says, "I'll call you back."

Two seconds later, he rips open the door of one of the guest bedrooms and pins me in place with a hurt-filled glare. He's naked from the waist up. Just like yesterday morning, nothing but a tiny towel is covering him. His hair is wet like he's recently showered, and an almost empty bottle of top-shelf whiskey is clasped in his hand.

The pain in his eyes when he stares at me like I'm a mirage kills me more than anything, and so does the cruel words he spits out, "What the fuck are you doing here?" For how empty the bottle is in his hands, it shouldn't splash as much liquid onto the floor as it does when he thrusts his hand to the door and yells, "Get the fuck out!"

"No." My voice is weak and pathetic, but I'm still grateful it worked. "We need to talk."

"I don't have anything to say to you."

Tears almost roll down my face when I step closer to him. "Then you can listen."

He cuts off my steps with a roar. "No! The time to listen was *before* you played me for a fool. It was *before* you acted like you didn't know who I was and before you *fucking* knew what he did to me."

"I didn't know who you were. I swear to God, I didn't."

"*God*?" He chuckles a painfilled laugh. "Of all the words in the world for you to use, you had to use that one."

I'm not shocked he lost his faith.

I did as well when I found out what my grandfather had done.

"Nothing that happened to you was your or God's fault. It was my grandfather's—"

Jack cuts me off this time by throwing his bottle across the room. It shatters over an expensive painting before scattering the floor with shards of glass.

I realize his objective was to have me running for my life when my rooted feet see his moving at the speed of light. He races for me so fast the scent of his scrubbed-clean skin hits me long before the alcohol leeching from his pores. "Do you know what he did to me? Your *grandfather*. Do you know what *he* did to *me*?" he asks, an inch from my face.

My head bob knocks him back two steps.

I didn't realize he had wanted me to lie until the devastation on his face grew from my admittance.

"So you know everything? Every detail? Every mark? Every sordid fucking thing he did to me?" He doesn't give me the chance to answer, he weaves his fingers through my hair, his hold painful before he yanks down, forcing me onto my knees. "But I bet you didn't know this because *they* all kept it a secret since it's their shame, not mine."

I inhale a sharp breath when he snaps his towel away from his body. His cock, although heavy and thick against his thigh, isn't hard or standing to attention like it was when I kneeled before it previously. It isn't even semi-erect.

I discover why when my stomach revolts at Jack's slurred confession, "He called their cum his fountain of youth. That by them giving it to him, he'd live for eternity." He unintentionally tugs on my hair firmer when he murmurs, "But I couldn't give him that. I couldn't give it to anyone because even though he told us what we were doing was holy, I knew it wasn't." I'd give anything to wrap my arms around him and hold him tight when he whispers, "But even after it stopped, it wouldn't work with anyone. No matter what I did or how many tests I took, I couldn't get hard..." He looks like he hates himself when he mutters, "... until I saw you. A descendant of the man who abused me for years. A woman who looks exactly like him. I got fucking hard over *you*."

The way he snarls 'you' is more painful than anything I've ever experienced, but it won't stop me from forcing him to see the truth. "I am *nothing* like my grandfather." When he scoffs before pulling away from me to snatch up another bottle of whiskey from a bar in his room, I stand on a wobbly pair of legs and follow after him. "My grandfather's hair was brown, mine is blonde. He had green eyes, mine are blue. He hated you, but I love you, Jack. We are nothing alike. Not at all."

When I place my hand on his shoulder, slightly pleading for

him to put down the bottle of whiskey and look at me, he shrugs me off him. None of my words reached his ears, so there's no chance in hell they'll make it to his heart.

"You need to leave."

Tears trickle down my cheeks when I shake my head. "Jack, please—"

"You need to fucking leave!" Acting as if he isn't butt naked, he grips the top of my arm, marches me to the elevator, then dumps me inside as if there isn't a blinking black contraption in the corner of the space.

My breaths come out ragged when he leans into me for the quickest second to sniff my hair before he mutters, "I *never* want to see you again."

I try to take off after him when he exits the elevator as fast as he forced me into it, not willing to give up on us just yet, but the cruel, maiming scars on most of his back and the top half of his ass freeze me in place. I never understood why the photographic evidence of his assault had random letters scattered across the welts until now. My grandfather didn't use any old thurible to hurt him. He picked the custom one my grandmother had made for him. The one that had our family name carved out of the ancient copper material.

Although I am aware it will take a lot for Jack and me to overcome this, desperation for the chance has me speaking words I shouldn't. "You said you wouldn't run, that nothing I could say would change how you feel about me."

When Jack spins around to face me, a trickle of hope drips through my veins. He isn't as hard as he was the first time I saw him naked, standing at the foot of my bed, smiling like he had the world at his feet, but his cock is most certainly erect. It is responding to the zap that surged through my body when he touched me and to the smell of my unwashed hair. It is reacting to the crazy connection that will never fully wane between us.

He is responding to me because, despite everything, he

knows what we have is greater than what my grandfather tried to take away from him. It is true, raw, and honest.

It is love.

I beg for Jack to make true on his promise that we could overcome anything, to give me the chance to prove I don't deserve his anger, but my silent pleas are left unanswered when he mutters, "Those words were spoken to someone I thought I knew. You are not her, Octavia, and the man you *think* you love is not me." He turns his eyes to the camera recording us before he growls in an angry sneer, "If she comes back here, you are both fired."

With that, the elevator doors close with me on one side and Jack on the other.

ONE MONTH LATER...

"Thank you, Tivy. It is perfect." Merrick's wet eyes glisten in the early morning sun when he lifts them to me from the *Tourist Must Visit Spots Guidebook* I purchased for him. "I can see Adeline marking out each spot she wants to visit with her bright pink highlighter."

Although Jack withdrew every other promise he made in Seattle, including the cash purchase of the penthouse and keeping Seattle Socialites afloat, I'm pleased to say he didn't renege on his offer to send Merrick and Adeline on an all-expense-paid trip to Italy. They don't leave for another three months, but since Caleb and I are returning to New Jersey this afternoon, I gifted it to him early.

"I know you have most of your itinerary already worked out, but there are a handful of places you must see." After carefully removing the book from his hand, I flip to the pages I book-marked. "Especially this one. My mother said their pastries and coffee are to die for."

"Excellent." Merrick loves sweet treats almost as much as he does his wife. "Talking about sugary gifts, Adeline asked me to give you these." My heart melts when he digs out a batch of freshly baked cookies from his backpack. "And…" I watch him in suspense when he unzips the front pouch of his bag to dig out a tiny ornament.

"Oh, Merrick." The tears I swore I wouldn't shed again pool in the corner of my eyes when I spot several famous Seattle landmarks on the silver keychain dangling off his index finger. "It even has HQ on there."

"It does," he agrees, his smile not as large as his big, kind eyes. "And the Wheel, Space Needle, and if you look closely, you can see the Aquarium too."

I squint my eyes, falsely portraying that my eyesight isn't as good as it is, before saying, "You can too. Very cool."

"It is. But that doesn't mean you can't come see them for yourself occasionally. I've missed seeing your smiling face every day the past month. Now I have to go years on end."

"It won't be years. I'll be back. *Eventually.*" My last word is a whisper.

It should hurt more going back to Jersey than it does contemplating a return to Seattle, but for some reason, it doesn't. I lived here for three years before I met Jack, but now I can't look at a single landscape without picturing him in it.

Don't get me wrong, the memories are good, but it hurts to know they'll never be replicated.

It wasn't just Merrick's vacation Jack kept his word on. His pledge not to see me again has been stringently upheld.

"I better get going. Caleb is finishing stacking the moving truck as we speak." I rub Merrick's arm before deciding it doesn't reflect how much I appreciate him. He didn't talk when I entered the ferry with a flood of tears down my face a month ago. He just sat next to me in silence before shadowing my walk home, so he knew I made it there safely. Then Caleb took over his watch.

Fitz offered me a ride home, but since I assured him his focus needed to remain on Jack's emotional well-being, he handed me some money for transportation, then gingerly entered the elevator I'd just fled.

Merrick is shocked when I hug him, but he's quick to return my embrace. "Don't become a stranger."

"I won't. I promise."

After a hug long enough to gain a handful of suspicious glares, I step back, wave goodbye like an idiot, then commence my walk home. It is odd to be out and about at this time of the day. I've barely left my apartment in the past month, but whenever I did, it was usually at night when I wanted to see the stars.

Air whizzes out of my nose when I enter the landing at the front of our apartment. Silas's blood was cleared away a long time ago, but the confusion over what happened to him hasn't lessened any. There were no reports of his assault or Jack's arrest in the papers. It is as if their confrontation never occurred.

I guess it's easy to manipulate the media when you're a man of Jack's wealth and power. He even twisted our story to make it seem as if it were nothing more than a work association. As far as the media is concerned, I was at the gala as Jack's assistant.

Yes, that hurt, but it was better than the alternative. He could have told them why we broke up, and I'd be as hated by this side of the country as I am the other side.

"Oh my God, Caleb. I told you to wait until I got home," I mutter when my entrance into our almost empty apartment occurs with the bottom of a box falling out. It is full of paperwork we don't need but Caleb can't seem to give up. He has a bad habit of keeping things no one wants to see more than once.

Such as the black and gold invite on the top of the stack.

"I can't believe you kept this."

I twist the invitation I found in the bouquet of flowers Silas arrived with that morning a little over a month ago after I sent it flying across the room. It is for a secret club that supposedly costs millions to join but only after being endorsed by one of its members.

Since I assumed that was the club Silas was intending to make me pay for my grandfather's crimes, I tossed the invite into the bin. I had wondered where it went when I failed to notice it at the top of the rubbish when I cleaned up the mess my tantrum caused.

"You never know, you might need it one day."

After rolling my eyes at Caleb's reply, I gather the documents into a neat pile, then place them on the top of the box he's wrangling. "What's left?"

My heart is pained when he mutters, "Jess took down the last of the boxes from your room, so it's just the laundry basket full of food and you."

The thought of leaving Jess hurts me more than I can explain. Even with it being my fault that she is unemployed, she's never once blamed me.

"Are you sure you want to do this, Caleb? You can stay here if that is what you want." By 'that,' I mean Jess. "I won't hold it against you."

I don't appreciate his rush to judgment, but I'd be a liar if I said his delay didn't stab my chest with pain. "We need to do this. It will be good for everyone."

"It will be. We will make it good." The gloominess of our conversation doesn't seem anywhere near as heart-clenching when I mutter, "And I'm still open to kidnapping Jess. We only cross a dozen or so state borders so what's the worst that could happen?"

Caleb laughs. It isn't his full laugh, but it shows that he appreciates my effort to defuse the tension in the air when Jess arrives to collect the last of our things. She's putting on a brave front, but she appears seconds from bursting into tears, and I'm right there with her.

I don't have a choice. I have to leave Jack behind, but the

same doesn't have to happen for Jess and Caleb. They could be together if they want. It's just Caleb's stubborn ass ruining everything. He is as stubborn as a mule, and instead of my falling out with Jack reminding him about how precious love is, it seems to have had the opposite effect.

He's more distant from Jess now than he has ever been.

Just the way he dips his chin at her before he makes a beeline for the truck proves this, not to mention the low hang of Jess's shoulders when he darts past her.

"Men are stupid," I say, hopeful she still considers my advice solid. "But they eventually pull their head out of their asses, right?"

My hopes are dashed when Jess mutters, "Maybe." She sounds as unconvinced as me.

"Are you sure you don't want to come with us, Jess? What we're endeavoring to get off the ground is risky, but no matter what happens, we will always have a roof over our heads." I don't mention that roof is being funded by the money our grandfather left Caleb and me because I'm reasonably sure she already knows.

After banding her arm around my waist, she hugs me tight before deflating my dreams. "I appreciate the offer, but I can't." She walks me to the door before spinning me around to face my now-empty apartment. "Any final words?"

I take in the scuffed floorboards and bent roller blinds before shaking my head. This place was never my home. It was just a place I resided while striving to work out where I belong.

I don't know my place in the world yet. But I will. One day.

It just won't be with Jack.

Unfortunately.

THREE MONTHS LATER...

"Mr. Carson, there is a gentleman here wishing to speak with you." Emmelyn's nasally voice shrieks through the PA system on my desk phone a second before my office doors are pushed open, and a ghost from my past walks through them.

It isn't Octavia, the lady I've strived to forget but haven't come close to forgetting.

It is her cousin, Caleb.

He looks more well put together than the last time I saw him. I can't say the same for me. I don't know if I'll ever be the man I once was. You can't gamble with fate and lose then come out the end the same man. People thought I was grouchy before. They have no idea now. I've been through seven assistants in the past four months. Emmelyn is only holding on by a thread because she flirts with Marissa more than she does me.

"I don't mean to intrude," Caleb announces as his eyes shoot to my sister and two investors interested in a story that's set to grip the country. "But I figured if she told you my name, you'd refuse my request to speak with you."

"It's fine. Come in. We were about to finish up anyway."

The dismissal of Caleb's rudeness isn't granted by me. It came from Marissa, who has a soft spot for him that has nothing to do with his glossy magazine good looks.

After offering to take our investors for a drink at a bar around the corner from our new home base, Marissa shifts on her feet to face me. *"Play nice,"* she mouths, doubling the balling of my hands instead of loosening them. *"He wouldn't have come if it weren't important."*

What she is saying isn't neither a lie nor gospel. Four months ago, I told Octavia I didn't want to see her again. To date, she has adhered to my request. The same can't be said for Caleb. He's reached out a handful of times, but today is the first time he's shown up at my office unannounced.

I didn't tell Octavia to stay away because I blamed her for the actions of her grandfather. It is the fact she knows what he did to me that I struggle with the most. Half our connection was because of the way she looked at me, wasn't it? So wouldn't that have changed the instant she knew of the sick, horrible things I let happen to me?

I could give more definitive answers if our last exchange hadn't been while I was drunk and belligerent. I can't remember the looks she gave me in the penthouse that morning, but I'm certain they weren't close to the ones she gave me only hours earlier.

Once we're alone, I shift my eyes to a stack of papers on my desk, acting as if my heart isn't racing a million miles an hour. "You need to make this quick. I have another meeting in ten minutes." That's a lie. Don't act shocked. I've barely been honest with myself the past four months, so you can't expect me to be truthful with you.

You have no clue how hard it has been for me the past four

months. I thought endless cross-examinations by attorneys making out I was lying about what happened to me to better my 'prospects' with Priest Maskretti's money would remain the toughest months of my life, but it was nothing compared to the past few months.

I don't think I've secured a single breath the entire time.

I doubt I will again.

"This won't take ten minutes." In the corner of my eye, I spot Caleb's approach. He doesn't take a seat across from me or tower over me like he did when the rage making me see nothing but black receded enough it dawned on me what I had done to Silas. He just slips an unmarked envelope onto my desk before saying, "We heard you were looking for one of these."

"We?" I know who he's referencing. He can't say her name without his voice hiking with pride any easier than me.

Caleb waits until he secures the attention of my eyes before muttering, "Octavia and me."

My heart skips a beat at the mention of her name, but I act nonchalant. "What is it?" I'm surprised when my voice comes out confident and unwavering, even with me feeling anything but.

"Open it and find out."

Over fielding a game I don't want to play, I snatch up the envelope and tear it open. My already spiked blood pressure surges into dangerous territory when I spot what's inside. It is an invitation to Chains, an exclusive BDSM club that has proven impossible to get an invitation to. I've been seeking one for months, but even offering a blank check hasn't seen my eyes landing on one, much less my hands.

"Where did you get this?"

Caleb's mask slips for the quickest second before he forces it back into place. "Does that matter? We heard you wanted one. We had one, so we're gifting it to you."

"For how much?"

His jaw tightens so fast, his reply is minced through his teeth. "I'm not here seeking a payout. It is a gift, so accept it as one." Not speaking another word, he dips his chin before heading for the door. He grips the door handle in a firm grasp, then cranks his neck back to me. He glances at me for a second before the mask he's worn throughout our exchange perpetually slips away. "Can I ask one question before I leave?"

Considering he's given me the key to enter an industry responsible for my niece's assault three months ago, I dip my chin instead of screaming out one of the many denials in my head.

My stomach tightens in preparation for his question, but it still feels like I'm sucker-punched when he mutters, "How can you blame Octavia for what happened to you?" Even though I granted his permission to ask one question, he fires off another one. "How could you even insinuate she's anything like him? If it weren't for her, he'd probably still be doing what he did to you to God knows how many other children."

I'm shocked but not enough to seek clarification. "What do you mean? What does Octavia have to do with ending his reign? *I* took him down. *I* had him convicted!"

"After *she* whistle blew on him." His confession knocks me so hard I become one with my office chair. "Octavia knows about your scars because she walked in on him..." He can't speak the words I don't want to hear him say. "She missed the bus home from school and was told to go to the church to wait for her mother to collect her. She saw what he was doing to you, but instead of hiding it as I had for years, she spoke out. She stopped him." He angrily brushes his hand across his cheek while muttering, "And she was fucking hated for it."

He steps closer to me, his stance a cross between shamed and determined. "Her dad called her a liar. The police who came to take her statement said she must have misunderstood what she saw, and the people she grew up admiring spat at her feet when they arrived to arrest our grandfather during an afternoon sermon. She was fucking ten, Jack. *Ten!* Yet she stood up to him as I wished I had years earlier. She never once folded. Not on the stand. Not after her father begged her. She fought for you…" He stops and grinds his jaw side to side before correcting, "She fought for *us* even with her having nothing to gain from it. Yet you blame her. You act as if she abused you when if it weren't for her, he would still be abusing you now."

He angrily shakes his head, the redness on his face picking up. "You're a fool, Jack. You are an absolute fucking fool. You could have let the abuse stop, you could have ended it on that altar eighteen years ago, but you didn't. You're still letting him paint you as a victim now." He's speaking to me, but a lot of what he says resonates with himself. The shifty movements of his eyes announce this, not to mention his urgency to suddenly vacate my office. "I'm not doing it anymore," he advises while racing for the door. "I'm not being his victim anymore."

Once he regrips the door handle, he cranks his neck back to face me. "You have the chance to do the same. She'd still forgive, but I don't know how long that will last. She's stronger now than she was when she met you. She knows what she deserves. You've just got to decide if you deserve her." He stares me up and down. "As you stand before me now, I don't think you have it in you." Ignoring my ticking jaw and balled-up hands, he mutters, "But what do I know? I'm a man who ignored the love of his life for years, so I'm probably not the best man to give relationship advice."

He laughs more at himself than me before he exits my office without a backward glance.

I sit in silence for several long minutes, equally shocked and confused. I believe every word Caleb spoke. His deliverance was too indicative of a sexual abuse survivor to discredit, but how am I meant to process and use that information? You have no idea how much it fucked with my head that the only woman on the planet I found attractive was my abuser's granddaughter. Her veins carry his blood. She has his DNA.

I've called Dr. Avery a minimum of two times a day for the past four months. I've attended counseling sessions and watched multiple seminars online, but nothing has worked. I'm still fucked in the head.

I slouch even deeper in my chair when reality dawns. I've talked the talk, but I've yet to walk the walk. Dr. Avery knows about my impotency issues, but she has no clue where it stems from. Excluding Marissa and the people who handled my civil suit, I've never told anyone what happened to me. They assume it is the stress of a high-profile gig. They never considered the fact that I have more issues than the group combined.

Only two people know the truth. One is rotting away in prison for crimes years of abuse forced on him, and the other is running a halfway house for troubled teens in her hometown who shunted her integrity instead of relishing in it.

"Yes, Mr. Carson?" Emmelyn asks when I press the intercom button on my desk.

I wait a beat to assess my options before breathing out, "Patch me through to Bayside."

"Bayside..." Emmelyn murmurs, lost.

Her gulp echoes through the intercom and the wall when I reply, "State prison. I need to speak with Silas Clastone."

CHAPTER 30
OCTAVIA

ONE MONTH LATER...

L ewis, an unfortunate regular at Alexander House, *pffts* at
me before he spins on his heels and climbs the staircase
two steps at a time. He's miffed I told him he can't stay
out past curfew, but since he'd rather call me an old cow in the
privacy of his bedroom instead of a concrete cell, he sucks up
'our stupid rules' and does as asked.

Nothing he could call me would be worse than the names
adults threw my way when my grandfather was carted out of
his church in handcuffs. My testimony was meant to be confi-
dential, but the name-calling started within hours of me leaving
the police station.

I didn't know at the time the extent of my grandfather's
crimes, but I did know that striking a boy's back with a thurible
while stroking yourself wasn't a 'gospel' act. The boy wasn't
crying, but the blood weeping down his back forced tears down
my cheeks.

Mercifully, my mother believed me when I told her what I
had seen. She knew I had no reason to lie, and even when my

father threatened divorce, she held her ground and took me to the police station to issue a report. We didn't know the boy's name, so to begin with, the report was merely hearsay, but as the weeks moved on and inquiries started, another person came forward.

We never knew his name or how he was associated with my grandfather's case, but his testimony was enough to have my grandfather put away.

He killed himself after the judge ruled that the evidence was sufficient to go to trial. Part of me wants to believe he killed himself so I wasn't forced to sit across from him and tell the jury what I had seen, but then I realized a monster is a monster no matter if he shares your blood or not.

He didn't care about me. He only cared about himself, and when he killed himself, the blame for his death was forced on me.

The church congregation never forgave me, and they passed their hatred onto their children. I was taunted at school for years, and it extended to my adult life. I was ignored at my father's funeral and told I would go to hell with my mother when she died two years after him. I had nothing but a share of a house that once belonged to my grandfather and a ton of hate.

Then I watched *Sleepless in Seattle*, and the churns of change commenced.

Finding the files from my grandfather's civil court case in my father's attic was the final straw that broke the camel's back. I begged Caleb to move with me that very night, and mercifully, he agreed.

I wouldn't say things have improved since I moved back home, but since my focus is more on ensuring lost teens don't go through what I did, it doesn't bother me like it once did. I still get the occasional glares when I'm shopping for groceries, and some of the older congregation members veer to the other side of the street when they see me coming, but my life is relatively normal—if not a little boring.

"What time is curfew, Blake?"

When my eyes shoot up to Blake's cap, he pulls it off his head before dropping his chin to his chest. "Ten, ma'am."

"So what time will you be back tonight?"

I smile on the inside when his reply is delivered with only the slightest stutter. When he arrived at Alexander House, his stutter made his speech barely audible. "No later than f-five to ten."

"Because?"

He locks his eyes with mine. "Because it is better to be early t-than late."

"That's right." I snag a house key off the key rack at my side before handing it to him. His eyes widen like I handed him the pink slip for a Rolls Royce. "Don't be too noisy when you come in. Some of the guys had a big day at the soccer tournament. I doubt they'll make it to curfew." The smile I struggled to hide earlier lifts my lips when a hideously ugly pink car pulls to the front of the house I purchased with the money that was left to me from my grandfather's estate. "It looks like Lori is just as eager as you." Lori is Blake's wanna-be-girlfriend. She left Alexander House a little over three months ago. She was one of our first residents. "Well, go on. Don't leave the girl hanging."

"Y-yes, ma'am," Blake murmurs before he swoops down to plant a kiss on my cheek then races for the door.

His smile when he cranks open the door of the piece-of-poo car Lori saved up for makes long days and sleepless nights worthwhile. When we opened our doors, it was just Caleb and me manning the fort. Mercifully, a handful of volunteers signed on a couple of weeks later. Now I can take the occasional day off. I just have nowhere to go—unlike Caleb.

"Mel, I'm going to take the rubbish out." It's Lewis's turn, but since he's sulking in his room instead of on the streets where he really wants to be, I'll pick up his slack.

"All right." Mel, a sixty-year-old retired nurse, slices her hand through the air before shifting her focus back to the movie she's watching with a handful of the younger teens. Their ages range from twelve to fourteen.

Since we can only afford one collection bin, I hook the bag onto the top of the pile, then push it down with all my might. As long as it holds on for its trip from the curb to the rubbish truck, the clean-up crew will accept it.

I'm blowing a wayward strand of hair out of my eye from my brutal grunts when I spot someone approaching from my left. I assume it is one of the fifteen-year-old boys racing for the door before curfew sounds at seven, so you can picture my shock when my eyes drink in polished black dress shoes, a pricy suit, and a crotch I shouldn't stare at but can't help but gawk.

After cursing my inanity to hell, I lift and lock my eyes with Jack's face. I almost give him the line that his fly is undone, but before I can, his hand shoots down to fix his zipper into place.

The hilarity of the situation isn't lost on me, and although I shouldn't laugh, the slightest giggle topples from my lips. We probably could have saved a heap of heartache if his zipper had been undone the day we met.

"Hey." Yep, that was as awkward as you're imagining.

Jack's smile makes the moon seem unimportant. "Hey." He points to a flashy car parked a few spots up from Alexander House. "Sorry, Emmelyn was meant to call and organize a time for us to meet, but when I saw you, I thought 'what the hell.'"

My head stabs at his mention of the beautiful Latina PA Caleb mentioned when he dropped off an invitation to Chains to him four weeks ago, but I play it cool. "It might have saved the flyaway hair and food-stained shirt greeting, but as you said, what the hell." I gesture my hand to the hanging open front door of Alexander House. "Would you like to come in for a drink?" As recollection of the last time we stood across from each other filters through my tired head, I add, "Of coffee."

Jack peers at the windows of Alexander House for a couple of seconds before returning his eyes to me. "Is there somewhere else we could talk?"

"Umm... sure..." I rack my brain for almost thirty seconds before saying, "There's an all-night coffee shop a couple of blocks up. We could walk... if your security guys are okay with that?" I don't recognize the person manning the door of the sports car Jack motioned to earlier, but it is obvious he is a body-guard of some kind. His stance is a dead giveaway.

"I'm sure they're fine with it. They do what I pay them to do."

Ignoring my shocked excitement about the unexpected confidence in his tone, I advise that I'll be back in a minute before racing into Alexander House to grab my purse. Like a loser who can't get a date, I lick the pads of my fingers before using the spit to wrangle my messy locks into a half-appealing state before switching out my dinner-stained shirt for a clean one.

Once I have my purse hooked under my arm and advised Mel and Nathan that I'm popping down the street for a coffee with an old friend, I race for the door. I almost bolt through it before I realize no one wants to play chase with a woman who throws themselves at the first available suitor. Furthermore, I don't know the reason for Jack's sudden return into my life, and although I'd rather be optimistic, my pessimistic side has been rearing its head more often in the past couple of months than its less evil counterpart.

Good things come to those who wait. It is proven without doubt when Lewis asks from the top of the stairs, "What is Mr. Carson doing here? Jace said our group counseling sessions were anonymous. That we could talk about them freely but not mention any names."

"They are anonymous," I ensure before pivoting around to

face him. Lewis has been attending counseling sessions for sexual abuse survivors for the past three weeks. The sessions are meant to teach survivors that there is no shame behind their abuse and that by speaking out and being honest about what happened to them, they could encourage others to do the same. "Mr. Carson isn't here for you, Lewis. I met him a long time ago. He is a friend of mine."

As he clambers down the stairs, his blond brows furrow together. He only looks confused for a couple of seconds before his face lights up in surprise. "You're the girl who saved him. The one who spoke up."

"Sorry?" I'm torn between bursting into tears and racing out to grill Jack. The only reason I don't is because I know as well as anyone that forcing victims to talk isn't the right thing to do. They need a safe environment to do that. A place that feels like home.

"He told us last week in counseling about a girl who saved him by speaking out and that he had no idea she'd do it again several years later. You're her, aren't you?"

Too choked up to deny his claims that Jack knows how I learned of his scars, I instead remind Lewis of the pledge he made not to speak about other people's confessions without their permission.

"I have his permission. He said if his story would help us speak up, we could share it."

My heart rate soars as pride floods me.

I shift my eyes back to Lewis when he admits, "It hurt to hear what happened to him, but it was also good." He licks his lips before murmuring, "He's a brave man to overcome what he did and achieve what he has."

"He is," I agree, still on the verge of crying. "As are you, Lewis. You are *very* brave."

My eyes shoot to Mel when Lewis unexpectedly slings his arms around my waist and buries his head into my neck. He's not normally affectionate. He usually bullies the other kids to get his way. I hope this is the start of him trying something new.

After returning Lewis's embrace long enough for him to push me off him with a groan about me ruining his street cred, he asks me to say hello to Jack on his behalf before he enters the living room to join the rest of the kids his age watching the movie.

I take a couple of minutes to compose myself before joining Jack on the footpath. The deafening patter of my heart in my ears is heard in my tone when I announce, "The coffee shop is this way."

"I know," Jack confesses before he knocks me on my ass with more honesty. "I've visited it a handful of times the past few weeks while building the courage to talk to you."

I hate that his confidence slips around me, but not enough to ask, "What changed your mind today?"

His nervous chuckle does stupid things to my insides. "Do you want the truth?"

I bob my head. "Please."

His smile makes it seem as if his confession is nowhere as shocking as it is. "Talking to you is the only way I can get Elaine back as my PA. She… ah.. quit when I…" He doesn't finalize his reply. The shame on his face does it for him.

My worry that he's only here to secure Elaine back on his payroll flies out the window when he mutters a handful of strides later, "I also couldn't resist for a second longer. With winter arriving early, you've started closing the drapes before sundown to keep in the heat. Traffic is a bitch from New York. If I didn't leave before lunch the past two weeks, I missed seeing you."

"You've been watching me?" That was delivered entirely different than the screechy deliverance of my question when I shouted the same thing at Silas many months ago. It was brimming with excitement, most likely fueled by the electricity zipping around us.

I thought the spark that forever fired between us would have died at the penthouse.

I was wrong. It is as strong as ever, and I'm not the only one noticing it. Jack sucks in a sharp breath after only the briefest collision of our pinkies, but he plays it cool.

"Yeah," he confesses before glancing up from his shoes. "And it's been a lot longer than the four weeks you probably think I've been watching you." He guides me past the culvert in the footpath my heel got stuck in almost two months ago before muttering with a grin. "Sorry."

His eyes shoot to mine, and they gleam with cockiness when I mutter, "No, you're not. You weren't back in Seattle, and you're certainly not now. Stalking is very much your forte." His teeth rake his bottom lip, but he doesn't deny my claims. "The only thing I can't understand is why. I get Seattle, your protectiveness was as endearing as your presumptions we weren't strangers, but why now? Why after learning who I am?"

We walk in silence for almost half a block, the intensity almost too much for me to bear, before he eventually mutters, "Because although some things Caleb said last month were shocking, others weren't." His eyes return to my face. They're still uneased but nowhere near as pained as they were months ago when he told me he never wanted to see me again. "Most particularly the part where I was a fool for blaming you for what happened to me and letting you go." Shame fills his face, but because it is in response to his actions rather than the wrongful ones others did to him, I let it slide. "I knew I was being stupid. I just couldn't stop it. I was lost and hurting, and since you were the easiest person to take it out on, I unleashed my anger and confusion on you."

"And Silas."

It kills him, but he agrees with me. Silas isn't a good man, but after further research, it was unearthed that he was my grandfather's first and youngest victim. He was only four when his 'grooming' turned sinister.

"I'm making amends with Silas." Jack purposely brushes his pinkie past mine this time, sending a scattering of goosebumps to the surface of my skin before he murmurs, "Now I'm trying to do the same with you."

Ignoring the intense zap his briefest touch caused my body, I try to look at his return to my life with a rational head. Forgiveness is a part of any recovery process, but I strongly believe his efforts should remain on himself. If he can't forgive himself and understand that he didn't do anything wrong, he will never fully recover from the horrible things he's faced.

"You don't need to make amends with me, Jack. You didn't do anything wrong."

"And neither did you, Octavia, but I still wrongly blamed you."

Although I appreciate his honesty, I truly don't believe he owes me anything. He said hurtful things but not anything that wasn't true. The woman he made the pledge not to run from isn't the same woman standing in front of him now. She was a coward who ran away when things got tough. This Octavia can admit her mistakes and stand her ground to prove not all mistakes end badly.

Also, Jack needed to hit rock bottom. If he hadn't, he'd still be hiding who he is and standing in a shadow of shame he doesn't deserve.

He's not doing that now.

The cloak has been removed, and he's finally being honest with himself.

Now it's time for me to do the same.

"There's something I need to tell you." I talk fast, ripping the Band-Aid off in one fell swoop. "Alexander is the name they placed down for you on the court transcripts. Each child, even those who didn't come forward, was given an alias from A to Z. Since you were claimant one, you were called Alexander. I named my charity after you. I know you don't want people to know your secret and that I could get sued for it, but I needed you to know why I started Alexander House."

I stop rambling when Jack curls his hand around my wrists to stop my jittery movements. When considering a name for our organization, I wanted to name it after Jack, but I didn't want a ripple effect to reach him, so I went with his court alias instead.

"It's fine, Octavia. I've known the reason behind it from day one." His smile reassures me that his growth has been mammoth over the last five months. "You do realize it takes more than signing a slip of paper to get a charity organization off the ground, right?" I'd smack him in the stomach about the mirth in his tone if he didn't have a hold of my wrists. "It usually takes months of legal jargon and a substantial backing to get the doors open within twelve months." His confident grin makes my insides as electrified as the buzz his meekest touch darts up my arm. "Unless you know the right people. They can get it done in weeks."

"You backed Alexander House?"

I know his answer, but I want him to spell it out for me.

He does that two seconds later. "Yes, I did."

"Why?" My shocked question bellows down the almost isolated street.

His eyes follow the bounce routine mine are doing before he eventually replies, "Because I understood what you were hoping to achieve and the importance behind it." He steps closer to me, making me equally giddy as I am shocked. "I just didn't think I needed the same help as the boys and girls you take in. But I was wrong. I probably need it more because even with the signs flashing in front of me in big red neon letters, I still try to ignore them." He steps even closer. "I tried to ignore you. And look where it got me?"

"Standing on a cracked sidewalk outside a rundown *cawfee* shop in Jersey?"

"No." The waft of his recently shampooed hair streams into my nose when he shakes his head. "It has me wanting to apologize for something I will *never* be sorry about." His breath tickles my lips when he murmurs, "I'll never be sorry about meeting you, Octavia. I will *never* regret your arrival in my life. But I will always regret—"

"Not kissing me sooner?" I interrupt before stealing the words out of his mouth by leaning forward and sealing my lips over his.

His lips remain frozen for barely half a second before they part at the lashing request of my tongue. Then, ever so slowly, he frees my wrists from his hold before his hands shoot up to entangle in my hair.

After kissing the living hell out of me, he murmurs something against my lips before burrowing his nose into my hair to take a long, undignified sniff. The tip of his nose is barely touching me, but my skin is on fire. I am blistering hot all over.

"Jack…" I murmur, my voice as remorseful as the clutch slowly releasing the cruel hold it's had on my heart for the past five months.

"Shh," Jack whispers before he cups my jaw so he can wipe away my tears with his thumbs. "I've got you," he promises, his voice the most confident it's been tonight. "And I will *never* let you go again. I promise you that."

EPILOGUE

JACK

ONE AND A HALF YEARS LATER...

I stare out at the crowd circling me. It is a mix of rich socialites, numerous members of the media conglomerate I used to rule with an iron fist, and a group of kids who just want a fair go.

Then there is her, the woman I tried to forget but couldn't.

My mentor.

My other half.

My wife.

Octavia is everything I've ever wanted and the reason I can talk so freely about who I am and what happened to me. She is the voice of reason when my demons try to hold me under and the sole purpose I wake every day. She keeps me sane, and although I'm sure I've made her doubt her sanity on a handful of occasions, I know I am her rock too.

Her blood hurt me, but her morals saved me. And by her teaching me that the shame I once lived doesn't belong to me, I can do the same for others.

It only takes one voice to speak up and one voice to listen to change a series of events that could stretch for decades. It isn't always up to the victims to speak out. Society has a part to play as well. Sexual abuse of minors will never end if we don't learn that.

If one child can look at me and think I am brave for sharing my story, then perhaps that will encourage them to do the same. That is why I speak at every charity event Octavia and I host. I want them to see that their abuser didn't break them. That with the right commitment and discipline, they can be anyone they want to be.

Priest Maskretti is a part of my story, but he is not who I am.

I am Jackson Car. Self-made billionaire, media mogul, and Octavia Car's husband.

And soon—very soon—a father who will teach his children that their moral obligations will forever rank higher than the affluence of their blood.

My family is not a consequence of what happened to me.

It is a reward for what I chose to be.

I chose to be me no matter how hard some days can be.

And I chose to do it with her.

My wife.

My lover.

And my savior.

Octavia.

The end!

The next book in the One Night Only Series is Caleb. It will come out sometime in October.

If you are experiencing anything Jack or Caleb has experienced, please reach out for help.

ACKNOWLEDGMENTS

This book was a crazy, emotional ride for me. But I believe every single word spoken, especially those last few from Jack. Sexual abuse, especially those directed at a minor, needs to stop. We need to work together to ensure this inhumane act has dire repercussions to the monsters who do it.

The children of the future don't need to face this.

We can stop it from happening.

But like every book I write, it needs to be a joint effort. We all must do our part to stop the predators in our community getting away with such heinous acts.

Although this was the work of fiction, the underlining message in this story is very close to my heart. If it is for you as well, please reach out and talk to someone. You don't have to share every detail or a single secret. You don't have to say anything. You simply need to know that there are people willing to listen when you're ready.

My inbox is also always open.

Now that is over, onto the thanks. I want to send a big, HUGE thank you to Chevi for the wonderful job she did proofing Hotshot Boss. I feel better knowing it's had her strict, shrewd gaze cast over it before hitting publishing.

To my husband, Chris, and Lauren, my now official team member, thank you for listening to me ramble when I convinced Jack and Octavia wouldn't get their happily ever after.

And then that leaves me with Jack, Octavia, and Caleb.

It takes courage to stand up.

It takes gut and unbridled determination to then do something with those words.

You all have those traits and many more wonderful attributes, and we can only hope victims will learn to do what you did.

It takes one voice to move a mountain, so if you can only do one thing in life, make sure it is something memorable.

Cheers, and happy reading.

Shandi xx

ALSO BY SHANDI BOYES

Lady In Waiting (Regan & Alex #1)

Man in Queue (Regan & Alex #2)

Couple on Hold(Regan & Alex #3)

Enigma: The Wedding (Isaac and Isabelle)

Silent Vigilante (Brandon and Melody #1)

Hushed Guardian (Brandon & Melody #2)

Quiet Protector (Brandon & Melody #3)

Twisted Lies (Jae & CJ)

Enigma: An Isaac Retelling

Bound Series

Chains (Marcus & Cleo #1)

Links(Marcus & Cleo #2)

Bound(Marcus & Cleo #3)

Restrain(Marcus & Cleo #4)

The Misfits (Dexter & Megan).

Russian Mob Chronicles

Nikolai: A Mafia Prince Romance (Nikolai & Justine #1)

Nikolai: Taking Back What's Mine (Nikolai & Justine #2)

Nikolai: What's Left of Me(Nikolai & Justine #3)

Nikolai: Mine to Protect(Nikolai & Justine #4)

Asher: My Russian Revenge (Asher & Zariah)

Nikolai: Through the Devil's Eyes(Nikolai & Justine #5)

Trey (Trey & K)

The Italian Cartel

Dimitri

Roxanne

Reign

Mafia Ties (Novella)

Maddox

Demi

Rocco

Clover

Smith

RomCom Standalones

Just Playin' (Elvis & Willow)

Ain't Happenin' (Lorenzo & Skylar)

The Drop Zone (Colby & Jamie)

Very Unlikely (Brand New Couple)

One Night Only

Hotshot Boss (Mr. Carson & Octavia)

Hotshot Neighbor (Caleb & Jess)

Short Stories

Christmas Trio (Wesley, Andrew & Mallory -- short story)

Falling For A Stranger (Short Story)

Made in the USA
Middletown, DE
20 October 2023